sun-kissed

Also by Melissa de la Cruz

NOVELS

Cat's Meow

The Au Pairs

The Au Pairs: Skinny-dipping

Fresh Off the Boat

Blue Bloods

NONFICTION

How to Become Famous in Two Weeks or Less

The Fashionista Files: Adventures in Four-Inch Heels and Faux Pas

the au pairs

sun-kissed

A NOVEL BY

melissa de la cruz

SIMON & SCHUSTER
New York   London   Toronto   Sydney

SIMON & SCHUSTER
An imprint of Simon & Schuster Children's Publishing Division
1230 Avenue of the Americas, New York, New York 10020

 Produced by Alloy Entertainment
151 West 26th Street, New York, NY 10001

Book design by Christopher Grassi
The text for this book is set in Adobe Garamond.
Manufactured in the United States of America
2 4 6 8 10 9 7 5 3 1
CIP data for this book is available from the Library of Congress.
ISBN-13: 978-1-4169-1746-5
ISBN-10: 1-4169-1746-2

For all the wonderful girls who e-mailed, IM'd, texted, blogged, and posted reviews—thank you for your unflagging support, cheerful enthusiasm, and many interesting questions! This one is for you. And yes, there is a lot about Mara and Ryan in this book. And to new readers—welcome to the Hamptons! Now go home. Just kidding.

Take care of the luxuries and the necessities
will take care of themselves.

—Dorothy Parker

All the riches baby, won't mean anything,
All the riches baby, won't bring what your love can bring.

—Gwen Stefani, "Rich Girl"

in seat 12A, mara hopes that all good things come to those who wait

AS THE PILOT CIRCLED LAGUARDIA AIRPORT, MARA WATERS switched off her iPod mini and put away the Dartmouth College catalog she'd been reading. She looked out of the tiny airplane window down at the Manhattan skyline—a luminous vision of steel and glass obscured by a late-afternoon haze. She'd made the forty-minute shuttle trip from Boston to New York several times now and was familiar with the commute. It was a pleasant enough journey that included stacks of complimentary magazines at the terminal and the company of crisp-looking professionals in worsted wool suits or crumpled corporate khakis, twinkling Bluetooth headsets discreetly curled behind their ears.

It was the first week of June, and barely forty-eight hours ago, she had officially graduated from high school. The ceremony itself had been a relatively straightforward affair, with a dull speech from the myopic valedictorian and the halfhearted singing of the class song (Kelly Clarkson's "Breakaway"—chosen by the administration after the class's real choice, Green Day's "American

1

Idiot," was banned). The only excitement had come when a member of the marching band flashed the stage, showing he was wearing nothing underneath his gown as he accepted his diploma. (His brightly uniformed colleagues quickly struck up a sassy bump-and-grind version of "The Strip.")

Mara had won the English prize, along with a two-thousand-dollar college scholarship. Her mother cried and her father took way too many pictures with his new digital camera while her sisters cheered from the stands. To the hearty beat of "Pomp and Circumstance," she'd joined the three hundred other Fighting Tigers in tossing their cardboard hats into the air. Afterward, over watery punch and stale Mint Milano cookies at the gym, she'd watched as her classmates exchanged new college e-mail addresses and promised to visit each other the next fall.

If only she had been able to do the same.

Mara frowned at the Dartmouth catalog, feeling envious of the cable-knit-clad coeds photographed studying on the lawn. *Wait-listed.* That was what the one-page letter inside the slim white envelope had said. Not "yes" or "no", but "maybe".

She could find out she'd been accepted in a week or even a few days before school started. Or she could never be accepted at all. Luckily, she'd been offered a place at Columbia with a generous financial aid package, and she'd put down a deposit to hold her place just in case Dartmouth didn't come through.

So now her whole summer stretched out in front of her, filled with anxiety and dread, since she didn't know where she would be in the fall. It was just so unfair. Dartmouth was her first choice, her *only* choice—as far as she was concerned. Ryan, after all, was going to be a junior there.

Ryan. When she thought of his name, she couldn't help but smile. Ryan Perry. Her *boyfriend.* It had finally happened—the two of them together at last. They'd met two years ago when Mara was working as an au pair for his younger siblings, and they had immediately hit it off. But other things and other people quickly got in the way. That first summer, Mara still had been with Jim Mizekowski, her high school steady. Mara finally gave Jim the boot the week before she was leaving, and she and Ryan had spent a blissful week together in the Hamptons. But later that winter, Mara broke up with Ryan after feeling totally insecure about the whole background-incompatibility thing—Ryan being one of those boys born to everything, while Mara was a girl who had to work hard for everything in her life.

So they'd spent the second summer apart as well. Mara had found solace in the arms of Garrett Reynolds, the rich, tomcatting heir-next-door, while Ryan sought comfort even closer to home— hooking up with Eliza, one of Mara's best friends. But that was all in the past now. Garrett was forgotten and Eliza forgiven. Over the past year Mara had often visited Ryan in New York and New Hampshire, and Ryan had finally made the trek to Sturbridge.

All her fears about what he would think—that her house was too shabby, her parents too weird, her sisters too loud—had been immediately dismissed once Ryan arrived. He'd bonded with her dad over football and polished off a record four helpings of her mother's chicken-fried steak. Megan pumped him for celebrity tidbits from New York ("Your friend did a body shot off Lindsay Lohan? Are you serious?") while Maureen declared Ryan was a great name for a boy as she patted her pregnant belly. And he hadn't said a word about the unfinished bathroom with the piece of cloth nailed to the window that substituted as a curtain or the fact that her parents kept the house at a chilly fifty-eight degrees in the middle of winter to save on heating bills.

This summer was going to be the best one yet—she didn't have to au pair anymore since she'd gotten a job as an intern at *Hamptons* magazine through a connection of Anna Perry's. It was a standard entry-level post—fetching, faxing, and answering phone calls for the editor in chief, but it tantalizingly promised a few— underline *few*—writing opportunities. "We need someone to caption all the party pictures," her boss had told her. Mara got the impression the job required the ability to accurately distinguish one Fekkai-blond socialite from the other rather than real writing talent, but at least it was a first step on the journalism ladder.

It didn't pay as much as the nannying gig (irony of ironies), and she would miss the kids and the girls—Jacqui was the only one left working for the Perrys, since Eliza had something else planned, as usual. But the best part of the job was that she would be free to live with Ryan on his dad's yacht. They were going to live together, like a real couple. It was going to be the most romantic summer *ever*.

Mara sighed, dreaming of sailing on the bay, Ryan at the helm while she lounged on the deck, suntanning. The two of them kissing while the sun set behind them.

The plane glided into the gate, and Mara turned on her phone, which immediately buzzed with Ryan's signature callback ring tone: John Carpenter's *Halloween* theme. *Doo-do-do-do doo-do-do-do . . .*

She smiled as she flipped open her phone. So what if she was wait-listed? She was still spending her third summer in the Hamptons with the boy she loved, who was waiting outside the terminal for her arrival.

And no one could take that away from her.

in soho, eliza is stuck in the fashion trenches

"EH-LIE-ZUH!"

"Eh-lie-zuh!"

"Are you listening to me?"

Snap.

Eliza blinked. Someone was talking to her. More specifically, someone was *talking down* to her. She put aside her chopsticks and tried not to look too irritated. Couldn't she even eat dinner in peace?

It was half-past midnight. She had been at the showroom since nine o'clock that morning and couldn't wait to get home for a shower. She was, for the first time in her perennially Fracas-perfumed life, seriously "funky." She took a discreet sniff of each armpit and grimaced.

"Eh-lie-zuh. Hello. Earth to Eh-lie-zuh!"

Eliza rubbed her eyes and finally focused on the person who owned that voice. Paige McGinley. Otherwise known as a Paige-in-the-ass. Her so-called boss and slave driver for Sydney Minx—famous fashion designer and all-around diva, owner of the showroom and the reason she'd had barely half an hour of sleep in the past forty-eight hours.

Sydney Minkowitz was a gay Jewish dress designer from the Bronx who'd changed his last name to the more intriguing and less ethnic "Minx." Early in his career, he'd befriended a coterie of New York socialites through vigorous ass kissing and with their support had launched a line of chic, casual, yet expensive sportswear that had grown to include licenses for accessories, perfume, housewares, candles, and linens. If you dressed, dined, or dreamed, you could bet there was a Sydney Minx product that catered to it.

The histrionic designer was opening his first boutique in the Hamptons in two days, and the whole office was buzzing with frantic activity to get all the details for the grand-opening party and fashion show completed. Like everyone in New York, Eliza had been a devotee of Sydney's early work—the waffle-knit "poor boy" cashmere sweaters that came with enormous price tags, the sexy drain-pipe trousers, the artfully graffitied logo handbags. But the designer had been slipping of late. The latest collections had veered wildly from sex-bomb attire one season to starchy, covered-up pretension the next as the label tried to connect with an ever-more-fickle audience of high-fashion buyers. You could only have so many bad collections before you were considered fashion roadkill, and with this opening, Sydney had a lot at stake.

The place was so tense that if the notoriously difficult-to-please Sydney summoned the group to yet another meeting in which he called all of his design associates, production assistants, runway models, and office interns an untalented bunch of idiots, someone was going to burst into tears. Already, one of the pattern makers had left her sewing machine in a huff after Sydney had called the dress sample she was making "a two-dollar *schmatte*, an eyesore of epic proportions, an insult to the name of couture!"

"Can I help you?" Eliza asked belligerently as she wiped her mouth with a paper napkin.

"Why aren't all the T-shirts folded yet?" Paige demanded. She was a dark-haired, sharp-featured twenty-two-year-old, a recent F.I.T. graduate who had ascended quickly from being Sydney's personal assistant to being de facto creative director of the label. "I told you, all the shirts need to go in boxes so the messengers can take them to the stores tomorrow morning!" The T-shirts, silk-screened with the designer's Photoshopped and markedly slimmer-than-life silhouette, would be given away for free in the overstuffed goodie bags to the VIP guests at the East Hampton party and sold for seventy-five dollars apiece at Sydney's boutiques around the country to the hoi polloi.

"Because I'm spray-painting all the fabric gold like Sydney asked for the 'Anna' coat," Eliza replied, pushing away the Chinese food containers. She showed Paige the metallic swatches that would be sewn onto a military trench Sydney hoped would catch the eye of the *Vogue* editor. Half of them were still unpainted.

Eliza wiped her hands on the backs of her So Low sweatpants, then crossed her arms defensively. Packing the T-shirts was, like, menial grunge work! She was Eliza Thompson. Once named in

New York magazine as the most popular girl on the prep school circuit! She'd only taken the job because she liked fashion and thought it would be a cakewalk to hang around a designer's showroom for the summer.

"Those swatches aren't done yet? Sydney needed those *hours* ago," Paige said, aghast.

Eliza tried not to look too guilty. She had taken her sweet time spray-painting the fabric just so no one would ask her to do anything else. She'd noticed that if she looked busy enough, she could avoid doing the more-boring chores.

"Anyway, forget this for now. Go help Vidalia. She can't seem to get her dress on correctly for the run-through. Then I need those T-shirts."

"All right," Eliza grunted.

"And what *is* that smell?"

Eliza froze, pressing her armpits next to her torso.

"Ew! Who ordered Chinese food?" Paige demanded, holding up the half-empty container of beef chow fun that Eliza had been munching from.

"Um, we all did?" Eliza reminded. The whole staff had sent for takeout since it was hours after dinner and they were all starving. She had been ravenously devouring the noodles when Paige had interrupted her meal.

"Well, get it out of here. If Sydney comes back and finds his clothes smelling like Chinatown, he is going to have a fucking meltdown."

Eliza shoved in a few more mouthfuls of the tangy dish before reluctantly tossing it in the trash chute across the hall from the office. She walked back into Sydney Minx's ten-thousand-square-foot loft. It was on the third floor of a former factory building in SoHo. The designer had bought it in the seventies when the building had still been an art collective. Sydney had sworn he would never leave the neighborhood but once business had taken off had quickly repaired to a swanky Upper East Side address, and the loft had been turned into the headquarters for his line.

Just the week before, Eliza had been beside herself when she'd learned her mother had talked Sydney Minx into hiring her as an intern. She'd even skipped her own high school graduation to be here tonight. Not that it mattered—after a year at Spence in New York and two years at Herbert Hoover High in Buffalo, she'd spent her last year of high school at boarding school, where she'd essentially phoned in her senior year, breezing through a host of AP classes. Wear a black gown and a cardboard hat just to receive a piece of paper? Nuh-uh. She'd asked the school to mail it to her instead. Besides, everyone knew a graduation cap made your hair flat.

The Thompsons were back on top, and for Eliza, all was right in the world. The scandal that had bankrupted her parents and doomed them to social oblivion (aka Buffalo) was ancient history. With the help of some well-connected friends, her father had made some key ground-floor investments in an abandoned warehouse property on the west side of Manhattan, which was now being developed into the hottest real estate in the city. Voila: the Thompsons were back in business. After repurchasing their old Park Avenue co-op and re-upping their Knickerbocker Club memberships, their reputation had been reinstated along with their credit cards.

It looked like all of Eliza's dreams were finally coming true—she'd been accepted early to Princeton, her dream college—but then, that never had been in doubt, what with her perfect SAT score and legacy-kid status. Plus, this summer she wasn't going to be taking care of the Perry kids, nor was she going to have to prostrate herself working at a nightclub catering to bratty celebrities. The internship with Sydney Minx was icing on the cake—allowing her to make some industry contacts (she could use a few good discounts to stretch her shopping dollars—she'd heard the sample sales were amazing!) and have a fun way to pass the time. Not that the job was any fun at the moment, but it could be, if only they would let her do something more interesting than paint fabric, steam clothes, and pack boxes.

No matter; tomorrow she would be in the Hamptons with Jeremy and her friends—Mara was supposed to be there by now, and Jacqui would be flying in with the Perrys soon enough. The three of them hadn't been together since spring break, when they'd managed to meet up for a few sun-soaked days in Cabo San Lucas. She couldn't wait to tell them all about her new gig. Of course, stapling the fashion show programs wouldn't sound too glamorous, so she probably wouldn't describe it in any detail.

She passed a full-length mirror and quickly checked her reflection. Horror of horrors—there were saddlebags under her eyes from lack of sleep, and her usually lustrous blond hair fell flat against her shoulders. Her blue eyes were red-rimmed and watery. But somehow, even while looking her absolute worst, Eliza was still the best-looking girl in the room. She'd tied her loose white oxford shirt around her waist in lieu of buttoning it, displaying a sliver of flat, tanned stomach above her baggy sweats. And even though she was wearing a comfy pair of slides, they sported a discreet Chanel logo on each side. She gathered up her hair in a loose but elegant bun, securing it with a pair of clean chopsticks.

Jeremy liked it when she put her hair up, she thought fondly. He was already in Montauk and couldn't wait for her to arrive. She had seen him just a few weeks ago at his college graduation in Binghamton, and she'd been so proud of him. Jeremy was one of the few guys who made wearing that stupid cardboard hat look sexy—his dark curls peeked out from under the cloth cap.

Dating long distance sucked, but they'd made it work, and they were going to celebrate their one-year anniversary soon. Not that it even felt like a year—whenever they were together, it was like they'd just met, and honestly, she felt like she was more in love with him than ever. She couldn't wait to see him. Jeremy was the only guy she'd ever met who saw the "real" her, who loved her because she sometimes snorted milk out of her nose when she laughed. The only guy she ever felt comfortable enough with to drop the whole princess-diva act. So many guys just expected her to be this perfectly poised mannequin. Jeremy told her he thought she was beautiful when she had a pimple on her chin.

They were planning to spend the night together as soon as she arrived in town—and Eliza knew, even if Jeremy didn't, that for the first time, it would mean *truly* spending the night together—no making out PG-13 style, the way they had been. After a year of seriously dating, she was ready to hand over her V card and make him her first. He was her one true love and had waited for so long for her to feel comfortable doing it. She was eighteen—for her, it was time. She took a deep breath and looked at herself in the mirror again.

If all went according to plan, by tomorrow evening, she would no longer be a virgin. She wondered if she would look different. Older? More mature? More experienced? And would anyone be able to tell? She'd find out soon enough.

on the upper east side, jacqui finds that packing for the hamptons doesn't help a hangover

THE DOORBELL RANG, AND THE SOUND OF BELL CHIMES reverberated loudly in the studio, but Jacqui Velasco ignored it. She was hurriedly throwing clothes, shoes, and straw tote bags into two open suitcases in the bedroom. It was just half an hour since she'd walked onto the stage with the rest of the St. Grace Academy class to collect her diploma, and she was still wearing the pretty floral Blumarine dress and round-toe Gucci heels she'd chosen for the event.

Her grandmother had already left for the airport to catch her flight back to São Paulo. It had been great to see her *avó*, who had been positively bursting with pride in her lace mantilla. After all, Jacqui had graduated with a solid B-plus average and honors in Spanish (being fluent in Portuguese certainly helped). She'd kissed her grandmother good-bye outside the auditorium and had scrambled to return home to pack for the Hamptons as soon as she could. The Perrys kept to a tight schedule and expected everyone to adhere to it.

Why, oh why, had she put packing off for so long? Jacqui wondered, even if she knew the answer only too well. Senior Week. Instead of spending time getting ready for the Perrys' annual pilgrimage to East Hampton, Jacqui had chosen to celebrate with her friends. The last forty-eight hours had been a whirlwind—there'd been a boozy bash at the Maritime Hotel, mini-golf at the Chelsea Piers, and an overnight retreat to the Catskills (campfire hookups and roasted marshmallows). Between the festivities and schlepping the Perry kids to their after-school activities, there just hadn't been any time to pack.

Her head hurt from a massive hangover, thanks to last night's tequila-soaked grad party. She opened drawers haphazardly, throwing and discarding items at random. Pucci scarf. Yes. Cashmere cardigan. No. (Too hot.) Duro Olowu caftan. Yes. Juicy cover-up. Too last year. Havaianas. Yes. White Levi's. Definitely.

She ran a hand through her thick black hair—the short, spiky fauxhawk she'd weathered for a fashion show last summer just a memory. The pixie cut had been cute, but she felt more like herself with her long dark tresses.

Her first year in New York had been nothing short of magical. The Perrys had installed her in a studio apartment formerly occupied by their ex-nanny. Jacqui had gasped when she saw the six-hundred-square-foot space—a charming, cozy room with floor-to-ceiling windows, a pretty alcove bedroom, a full kitchen, and a working fireplace. Only a block away from the Perrys' massive town house, the apartment was close enough that Jacqui could come over and watch the kids easily but far enough that she had her privacy.

Jacqui had enrolled for her senior year at St. Grace—a small, all-girls' parochial school on the west side that had accepted her after Stuyvesant, one of the most competitive public schools in the country, did not. The Perrys had covered her tuition as part of her compensation, and Jacqui's classmates quickly idolized the brash, beautiful Brazilian in their midst. Jacqui had studied hard through the year but had still managed to become very popular. After all, she was the only one at school with her own apartment, and she'd hosted a lot of parties. She found an empty beer bottle underneath the bed and chucked it in the garbage can.

The doorbell chimed again, and this time Jacqui could definitely make out Anna and Kevin Perry's quarreling voices behind the door.

"I'm talking to you—don't answer your phone when I'm talking to you!"

"Anna, this is work. It's important. Give me a sec, all right?"

"You never listen to me. Work always comes first!"

"Babe, please shut up. I need to take this."

"Oh, just go ahead, then! Where is she? Jacqui! Jacqui!"

"Coming!" Jacqui yelled. She ran over and opened the door.

Anna Perry, a vision in sparkling Chanel tennis whites, tapped her French manicure impatiently in the doorway. "The limo's here. We need to get to the Thirty-fourth Street helipad pronto or we'll lose our departure time," she ordered briskly. Kevin Perry, who looked tense and rumpled in a gray wool suit, gave Jacqui a curt nod as he put a cell phone to his ear.

"Yes, yes, sorry—just—give me a minute." Jacqui nodded, closing the door in front of Anna's face. The Perrys might pay for the apartment, but it was still her own. Besides, she totally had to hide the keg that was standing in the middle of the living room.

mara achieves
golden-girl status

MARA STRODE CONFIDENTLY THROUGH THE AIRPORT, TAKING a little-known shortcut to the baggage claim area. She was so focused she didn't notice the many admiring stares in her direction. She cut a sharp figure in her tight white Michael Stars T-shirt, pink-and-green Lilly Pulitzer clam diggers, and Tory Burch for TRB wedge sandals—recent purchases thanks to congratulatory checks from her grandparents. Her thick chestnut hair was expertly colored and styled, falling sexily just below her shoulders, and she was tan from spending a weekend on Block Island as part of graduation festivities.

She retrieved the rest of her luggage, piled it on a cart, and walked out of the sliding glass doors to look for Ryan. She found him leaning against a flat red Ferrari Enzo illegally parked by the curb.

He ran over toward her, taking long loping strides. "Hey, gorgeous," he said, plucking a garment bag from the top of the pile.

"Hey, yourself," Mara replied, her heart skipping a beat—it always did whenever she saw his handsome face. She smiled at him over her matching butter-leather Coach suitcases—graduation

18

booty from her sister Megan, who had quit the beauty shop for a gig as a sales rep, meriting a deep discount.

Ryan was wearing his hair longer, in a shaggy, college-boy cut, but otherwise he looked the same, the same burnished tan, the same slightly disheveled clothing—a worn Aboveground Records T-shirt over a pair of holey Rogan jeans, his usual rubber flip-flops, vintage Ray-Ban aviators perched on top of his forehead. Mara set the cart by the sidewalk and walked over to him, putting an arm around his waist as he fed the bag into his trunk.

"New wheels?" she asked, admiring the Italian sports car.

"Yeah." He shrugged apologetically. "My dad. I think it's some kind of guilt present. He forgot my birthday this year."

In Mara's family, guilt presents meant homemade brownies and a trip to the mall, not to the Ferrari dealership. "What happened to your old car?"

"Sugar's driving it around L.A."

Mara thanked whatever gods were responsible that the twins, Ryan's eighteen-year-old hellion sisters, were going to be absent from the Hamptons scene this year. Sugar and Poppy had "gone Hollywood," and both were actively auditioning for movie roles. So far, they had made a total of one direct-to-video horror film but had managed to attend every red-carpet premiere in town. Sugar was currently recording an album (*Melted Sugar*), while Poppy was broadening her empire from a line of perfume—"Sniffers," by Poppy Perry—to include handbags ("Stuffers") and home fragrance ("Stinkers"). They were both famous for appearing inebriated and half naked in public and, needless to say, had become very popular in Los Angeles.

Mara shook her head at the memory of the twins' exploits— she had almost forgiven them for their hand in what had happened last summer, but not quite.

"Missed you," Ryan said, leaning down to give her a kiss. His lips pressed against hers, and Mara closed her eyes, opening her mouth to his. She felt him press against her body, and she tightened her embrace; soon the two of them were totally necking in front of the terminal. Ryan buried his face in Mara's neck, and she breathed in his familiar scent—Ivory soap underneath salt water and suntan lotion. Yummy.

Several cars beeped in annoyance since Ryan's car was blocking traffic, and they reluctantly pulled away from each other.

"Mmm," Ryan said, holding her arms to her sides and squeezing her shoulders. "I think we should go."

"You think?" Mara winked, still feeling happy and dazed from his hello kiss.

Ryan raised an eyebrow at the sight of all the luggage. "I don't think it's all going to fit in the trunk." He shook his head.

"I kind of over-packed."

"I can see that." He nodded, attempting to stuff a particularly large suitcase into the Ferrari's tiny trunk. "If I'd known, I would have brought the Rover."

"Sorry," Mara said sheepishly.

Ryan cursed half seriously as the suitcase wheels became stuck in the doorjamb. Mara stood back, not wanting to get in the way. "What's SGH?" she asked, noticing a small oval sticker on the left side of the convertible's bumper.

"Sag Harbor, where we're spending the summer," Ryan explained, blushing a bit. "Anna got them for all the cars—theirs say, 'EH', for East Hampton. I couldn't stop her from sticking one on mine. It's kind of cheesy, I know."

Mara smirked. A sticker proclaiming their summer destination—trust Anna Perry, Ryan's status-conscious stepmother, never to pass up a chance to flaunt their wealth. In the end, Ryan was able to cram most of the luggage in the trunk and squish the rest in the sports car's tiny backseat. Mara balanced her brand-new Mulberry handbag on her lap and stuffed the matching tote bag underneath her feet. She felt slightly embarrassed to have packed so much—but as an intern at the Hamptons' most high-profile magazine, she was determined to look the part of a glamorous journalist, even if she would just be running to the Starbucks. She'd been in the Hamptons long enough to understand the meaning of "fake it till you make it."

Ryan climbed into the driver's seat, and the Ferrari roared out to the lane. Mara beamed as her handsome boyfriend zoomed ahead of all the cars on the highway.

Anyone who saw Mara would think she had always been one half of a golden couple. That she took for granted the kind of life most people only dreamed about. That she had been born beautiful, rich, blessed, and confident—but anyone who thought that couldn't have been more wrong.

eliza blings it on

"HEY, VIDALIA," ELIZA SAID, WALKING OVER TO A RAIL-THIN, six-foot-tall model who was half in and half out of her Sydney Minx original. "Paige said you needed help?"

"I can't seem to get this to work," the model complained in the flat, nasal tones of her native Cincinnati.

Eliza wondered if Vidalia (one name only) had changed her name to project a more exotic image and in doing so had unwittingly styled herself after a very common onion.

"Let's see, I think that's the armhole that you've got on your head, and this actually goes over here, and this one buttons to that part, and then this is loose," Eliza said, helping Vidalia out of the dress, then gliding it back over her shoulders and deftly snapping buttons and pulling the intricately shredded chiffon frock to its rightful position.

Vidalia and Eliza stared at Vidalia's reflection.

"That's it?" Vidalia asked skeptically.

Eliza nodded, but she understood why the model looked doubtful. The dress, on its own, was supposed to be a showstopper, but it still looked a little plain. It needed something. . . .

Eliza spied several gold chain belts lying on a cutting table.

"Here," she said, draping the gold chains around the model's neck. "Put these on." Eliza layered gold-link necklace after gold-link necklace. Then she switched Vidalia's strappy sandals for a pair of brown crocodile leather thigh-high boots. It was supposed to be a spring/summer collection, but everyone was going to want a pair of boots this summer—cowboy boots, motorcycle boots, why not skyscraper croc? Sandals were so over. Feeling inspired, Eliza also spray-painted the edges of the dress for a dramatic finish.

The model grinned at her reflection. It was sexy, street, and luxe at the same time, hitting just the right note of savvy and super-expensive. It was the way everyone wanted to look right now, and somehow Eliza had articulated the desire with just the right accessories.

"Better, no?" Eliza asked.

"Perfecto," Vidalia agreed, now sounding for all the world like a European heiress.

They hugged each other, feeling an adrenaline high from a job well done, an outfit well planned. Eliza smiled, dropping to her knees to pin up the skirt hem to the right length.

But when her high faded, Eliza felt nervous. It was a risky move, styling the dress and switching the sandals for boots. Only the head stylists—seasoned Seventh Avenue veterans with years of magazine experience and fashion show production under their braided Marni belts—were supposed to style the clothes for presentation.

Who knew how Sydney would react once he saw how Vidalia was wearing the dress? He might hate it. He might throw Eliza out of the studio for what she'd done. Eliza had seen it happen— she'd been backstage at a fashion show last summer when the designer had thrown a glass of champagne at a makeup artist who'd had the audacity to lend a model his wraparound sunglasses for the show. The sunglasses hadn't been on the style sheet for that particular outfit. The designer had ripped the sunglasses off the model's head so violently, he'd pulled off her hair weave. The model had had to walk the runway bald as a newborn.

Eliza panicked. "You know, Vidalia, maybe we should have you take off these chains," she suggested. "Sydney might not like it."

But Vidalia only swatted Eliza's hand away. "It's great. Don't worry."

In any case, it was too late, since all the models were being called for a final run-through. Eliza took a deep breath and walked to the middle of room, hoping her first day at Sydney's studio wouldn't be her last.

jacqui babysits a
thirty-three-year-old

BEHIND THE CLOSED DOOR, JACQUI COULD HEAR ANNA AND
Kevin continue to quarrel about his inability to listen to his wife
and her inability to let him do his job. She knew Anna and Kevin
weren't mad at her. They were just using her tardiness as an
excuse to yell at each other—something they did much too often
these days. Jacqui knew that some of it stemmed from Anna's
growing insecurity about growing older—she'd almost shot her
hairstylist when he pointed out a few gray strands of hair at her
last appointment.

Jacqui didn't know how two people could drive each other so
crazy. Anna nagged Kevin about everything from his table man-
ners to his golf drive. Kevin squabbled with Anna over the credit
card bills and the maid's housekeeping. Anna had a penchant for
hurling the closest object at hand, and so far, several of her prized
Lladro animal figurines had shattered in the heat of battle.

Last week before a dinner party they were hosting in their
apartment, Kevin had broken Anna's treasured Mason Pearson
hairbrush in two in a fit of temper. "That's a six-hundred-dollar
hairbrush!" Anna had wailed in agony, and in retaliation had

25

flicked his ear so hard during the ensuing battle that she'd broken cartilage. Enraged, Kevin had called Anna "abusive" and threatened to call 911. Things only calmed down when their guests arrived, wondering why Kevin's head was in a bandage.

Jacqui had quickly learned to usher the children away from witnessing the battles of World War III. She was an even-tempered, sunny-side-of-the-street kind of girl. She liked things to be amicable. Even her breakup with Kit Ashleigh couldn't have been more civil.

The two of them had dated soon after Jacqui had moved to New York. At first, things were great, but it soon became evident that they didn't work as a couple—Kit lost his cool every time another guy even *looked* at Jacqui (which was often) and Jacqui got tired of having to assure him 24/7 of her love. The last straw was when Kit didn't even want to take her to the newest club he was promoting because if they stayed home, then she was safe from the competition. Part of the reason she was drawn to him was because Kit always had a lot of fun. But somehow the two of them together only stressed him out. She could tell he'd almost been relieved when she broke it off—almost as if he'd been expecting it. Still, she was grateful they had been able to part as friends.

After Kit, she had dated a few boys—no one special, no one who made her breath catch in her throat and her skin tingle just at the sight of him. But Jacqui was an optimistic person. She would be open to love, and she would listen when it came knocking. After all, she had time to wait.

Like the way she could wait for NYU. They'd sent her an e-mail explaining that their decision hinged on one tiny, minuscule, nagging little detail. A problem with translating credits from her school back in Brazil. Some bureaucratic mess. Once it was cleared up, she would be sharing notes with some underage supermodel and a lone Olsen twin before she knew it.

Nothing really bothered Jacqui. After all, when you're five-ten, built like Gisele Bündchen, with a smile as blinding as the sun, what was there to worry about? Plus, she was looking forward to another summer in the Hamptons—hanging out with Mara and Eliza again—and she wouldn't have any more pesky SAT classes to keep her from partying up a storm. It was going to rock! She deserved a break after working so hard all year.

Jacqui went back to her packing, took one last look at the closet—sundresses? Espadrilles? Thongs? Check, check, check—and zipped up both suitcases. She lugged them out to the door, where now only Anna was waiting.

"Where's Kevin?" Jacqui asked. Over the year, her relationship with her famously demanding employer had become almost sisterly. Anna wasn't as terrifying or insane once you got to know her better, and they had become so friendly that Anna had even begun to confide in Jacqui.

"He's not coming. He got called for a meeting. So now I don't have a date for the East Hampton Day-Care benefit tonight. Men!"

Jacqui followed Anna into the elevator. "It's probably important."

"What's more important than spending time with his family? I swear, one of these days, I'm going to call Raoul Felder, just watch me!" Anna said, naming a notorious divorce attorney who handled high-profile marital disintegrations. "Maybe that will make him pay attention! He hardly even looks at me anymore." "Shhh—you shouldn't say that!" Jacqui said, crossing herself. Jacqui was superstitious and didn't believe in tempting bad karma. As far as she could tell, divorce was the last thing that would solve Anna's marital mess. That was the problem these days—everything was considered disposable—clothes, cell phones, relationships. Jacqui knew that once she fell in love— really fell in love—it would be forever. There would be no divorce in her future if she could help it. Her grandparents had been together for fifty-three years, until Papi died, and her parents had weathered twenty years so far.

"Why not? It's true. He takes me for granted! If I divorce him, he'll finally realize how much I do around here," Anna pouted. She'd told Jacqui that when they first met, Kevin couldn't keep his hands off her, and the two of them would jet to Barbados or Capri at a moment's notice. But years of marriage and its grueling domestic routine had left little time for such pleasures.

Sometimes, Jacqui thought eight-year-old Zoë was more mature than Anna. Jacqui hadn't realized it then, but she knew now that part of her job as an au pair was to take care of Anna as well. As if on cue, Anna rested her head on Jacqui's shoulder.

"He couldn't do a thing without you," Jacqui said soothingly as they walked out of the building and into the black stretch limousine parked in front of the awning.

"Tell that to him," Anna said bitterly. She shook her head. "Anyway, how was graduation? Everything went well?"

It was nice of Anna to remember. Jacqui climbed into the limo and told Anna a little bit about the ceremony. The class had even been able to snag Tina Fey as a speaker since her housekeeper's daughter went to the school. She wasn't their first choice—Hillary Clinton was. But the senator had canceled due to a last-minute scheduling conflict. Such was life in the city.

The car pulled away and began winding its way down and across town toward the helicopter landing. As they turned left on Park Avenue, Jacqui suddenly realized she'd forgotten to pack the most crucial item for a summer in the Hamptons.

Her favorite Rosa Chá seashell-trimmed bikini. Three pieces of tiny fabric attached by a string. She'd shown her girlfriends back in Brazil the bathing suits Americans considered sexy. They had all laughed at the size of the bikini bottoms. They looked gigantic compared to the tiny tangas they were used to wearing.

If only she'd remembered to grab it. Oh, well. It just meant she'd have fun buying a new one, even if she'd have to "Brazilianize" it a bit if she wanted to feel like herself.

somewhere, chris martin is singing his heart out

THEY ARRIVED AT THE SAG HARBOR YACHT CLUB—TINY WHITE lights illuminated the crisp sails against a dark sky. The forty-seven-foot-long Perry yacht was docked in a choice location—the first off the pier, nearest to the water. Ryan pulled up alongside the other cars parked across from their owners' boats.

"Your castle, milady," he joked, but it wasn't that far from the truth. The sleek sailboat was a twin-engine Catalina with a spacious and elegant master stateroom, guest V-berths, three bathrooms, a galley kitchen, a living room, and satellite TV. "It sleeps ten, so it should be big enough for the two of us."

Mara gasped. It was even larger and more beautiful than she'd remembered, with its hand-polished teak decks, sleek fiberglass finish, and moniker *The Malpractice* (so named after the lawsuits that had paid for the yacht) painted in platinum leaf on the transom. Three triangular flags flew at the top of the mast: the Stars and Stripes, the yacht club logo, and the Perrys' own family coat of arms. She walked to the end of the dock, removed her shoes, and carefully stepped barefoot onto the deck of the boat, where she found a trail of rose petals leading to the downstairs cabins.

"What's this?" she asked, looking at him wonderingly.

Ryan followed her down, half hidden underneath all of her luggage. "You'll see."

She followed the trail of red rose petals and found that it led to the front deck, where a table and two chairs were set for a formal dinner.

"Oh!" Mara said, clasping her hands.

The starched white tablecloth held two dinner settings, Royal Copenhagen porcelain plates in a fleur jouy pattern. In the middle of the table stood silver chafing dishes warmed by a small gaslight. The smell of roasted chicken, herbed vegetables, and other succulent treats wafted up from the table. A silver bucket by the side of the rails held a magnum of Veuve Clicquot champagne.

Ryan dumped the bags on the floor and walked up to Mara, embracing her from behind and whispering in her ear, "Welcome home."

Mara felt her eyes well up with tears. It was the most romantic thing she'd ever seen—and not at all cheesy and contrived, like an episode of *The Bachelor*. This was the real thing. And it was all for her.

A waiter in a white dinner jacket came out of the shadows and bowed. "Is it all to your satisfaction, Mr. Perry?" he asked with a slight French accent.

"Yes, thank you, George." Ryan nodded. "We'll clean this up ourselves. No need to wait on us. Have yourself a nice evening."

"Very good, sir," the Frenchman said, disappearing into the night.

"I got Jean-Luc to do the dinner—they don't usually cater and they don't deliver. But the owner's a good friend of my dad's," he explained. "C'mon, let's sit down." He pulled out Mara's chair.

Mara sat down, still overwhelmed by the entire spectacle. The night air was balmy and sweet—a fresh breeze blew through her hair, and she remembered how much she loved the Hamptons.

They opened the silver dishes eagerly. The four-hour drive had left them famished.

"Heard from Dartmouth yet?" Ryan asked between bites.

Dartmouth. Shit. Mara shook her head. For a moment, the magic faltered. Being on the wait list was the only thing that was keeping her life from being perfect, perfect, perfect. "No, unfortunately."

"They'll take you. They *have* to," Ryan insisted, cutting into the chicken. He was stubbornly optimistic that everything would work out.

"I hope so." She sighed. "Though I really can't do anything about it at this point."

"You know, I could always ask my dad . . ." Ryan said, reaching over to squeeze her hand. "He knows the university president really well."

Mara shook her head. It was sweet of Ryan to offer, but she really didn't feel comfortable asking his father to pull strings on her behalf. Part of her felt like it was an unfair practice, and she was already feeling guilty about getting the gig at *Hamptons* magazine so easily. Besides, she wanted to get into Dartmouth on her own merit.

They continued eating, and after dessert, Ryan pulled out a box from under the table and pushed it toward Mara. It was robin's-egg blue and tied with a familiar white ribbon. Mara's heart skipped, but its dimensions were too large for the contents to be jewelry.

"What's this?"

Ryan shrugged, feigning innocence, but there was a gleam in his eye.

Mara untied the ribbon and opened the box. Nestled inside the tissue paper were three-by-five note cards. Each had a tiny drawing of the sailboat in the center. Underneath, it read *Mara Waters, Sag Harbor.*

Her new address. On Tiffany stationery, no less.

"Ryan—you didn't have to . . ." she said, her eyes shining.

"Oh, it was nothing. I thought you might like it for your new job, you know? I think magazine people get off on things like this."

"Magazine people," Mara murmured, lovingly stroking the stationery. "What's that mean?" she asked.

"You know, glossy girls . . ."

She beamed. She was a "glossy girl."

Ryan stood up and took the champagne bottle from the bucket, spilling fat droplets of water on the floor. He took a napkin, placed it around the bottle's neck, and popped the cork. Faint lines of cold air whispered out of the open bottle. He quickly filled two flutes with the bubbly and handed her one.

"To our summer," he proposed.

"To us," Mara agreed, clinking her glass against his.

They sipped from their glasses in silence and walked to the edge of the boat by the railings. Mara found she couldn't keep the smile from her face.

When the bubbly had been drained, he took her champagne glass and set it on the table next to his. And in one smooth motion, he scooped her up in his arms.

She buried her face in his neck. They didn't need to say anything to each other; everything they meant to say they said with the closeness of their beating hearts. She felt so light, so airy and feminine and loved in his strong arms—as he walked down the length of the boat toward the captain's quarters.

"Oops!" he said, sliding on a few rose petals, but he regained his balance and carried her over the threshold.

Cue the Coldplay, Mara thought. *This is the definition of* romance.

Ryan maneuvered the door open and laid Mara gently on the king-size bed. She stared up at him hungrily and reached over to help him take off his T-shirt while he pulled up her blouse.

They were kissing again, his tongue deep in her mouth, when they suddenly noticed an incessant, shrill beeping.

"What the hell is that?" Ryan asked, looking wildly around the room.

"I don't know," Mara said, propping herself up on her elbows. She was down to her Cosabella thong and Ryan was in his boxers.

She spied a white, purple, and orange cardboard box vibrating in the corner. "I think it's coming from there."

Ryan hauled himself off the bed and walked over to the box. He held it up. It was a FedEx package. He looked down at the address label.

"It's for you," he said blankly, handing it to Mara.

is this what they call ghetto fabulous?

THE MURMURING IN THE STUDIO WAS INTERRUPTED BY A fearful hush and the sound of one man bitching.

Sydney Minx had arrived for the run-through.

The designer was a short, squat man with a long white pony-tail who never went anywhere without his oversized blind-as-a-bat sunglasses. He looked like a smaller, fatter version of Karl Lagerfeld, and the tribute didn't end there—Sydney was waving a small Japanese fan around madly.

All the models were arranged in a row for a final rehearsal before the show at the Hamptons boutique tomorrow.

"What is this? *Qu'est-ce que c'est?* This is terrible! *Horeeeb!*" he exclaimed in an affected French accent, pointing to a model wearing an ostrich-feather-trimmed tunic and matching silk pants. "That outfit is three thousand dollars retail, but somehow it looks like it's nineteen ninety-nine at the mall!

"And will you look at this! Someone please tell me what she is supposed to be!" he cried, slapping a model on her bottom with his fan. The girl was wearing an abbreviated cotton biker jacket over a leopard-print dress. "This is Donatella Versace committed

36

suicide! This is not Sydney Minx at all! This is not my vision! Paige! Paige!"

Eliza smiled. This was the only time the rant was worth it. In Sydney's presence, Paige was reduced to a simpering yes-woman, a sniveling, wimpy Smithers to an apocalyptic Mr. Burns.

"It's Aspen East?" Paige said weakly, referring to Sydney's "vision" of the collection, which blended ski-bunny coquettishness with Hamptons-style aristocratic summer hauteur.

"This is *not* Aspen East! It's more like Ghetto West!"

The models cowered, the seamstresses frowned, and one of the assistants began taking the dress off the nearest model with an almost violent rage. Back to the drawing board.

"You!" Sydney suddenly exclaimed, his eyes resting on Vidalia. "Come here!"

Vidalia tentatively walked out to the center and in front of Sydney. The numerous gold chains clinked softly against her skin.

"Turn around!" he directed.

She did, taking a few steps.

"Paige! Did you do this? This isn't how the dress is supposed to be presented!" Sydney's fan was shaking in agitation.

Paige shook her head adamantly. "I asked one of the interns to dress her, not restyle her!" she barked.

Eliza paled. This was it. She knew she had totally overstepped her boundaries—her job was to help zip up the dress, certainly not do anything so important as *accessorize* it.

Sydney scanned the room intensely. "Who is the intern responsible for this?"

Eliza gulped and slowly raised her hand.

"What's your name?" he asked, taking off his sunglasses and giving her a critical once-over.

"Eliza Thompson, sir."

He puckered his lips. "Billie Thompson's daughter. *N'est-ce pas?*"

"Yes, sir—I mean, Sydney."

Sydney sniffed as if he smelled something bad. He closed his eyes. The whole room was quivering with tension, half of them feeling sorry for Eliza, the other half thankful it wasn't them in the hot seat.

The prickly designer finally opened his eyes. He looked at Vidalia again. "Well, Eliza, I have to say, this is simply fabulous!"

Eliza, and the rest of the room, exhaled.

"But the rest is dog shit." His fan fluttered again.

"Er, thank you, I think," Eliza said, bowing her head. She snuck a peek at the front of the room and suppressed a grin. Paige wore a scowl on her face.

Sydney whispered to Paige behind his fan, and soon he had left the room again. Paige wearily clapped to attract everyone's attention. "All right, people. We obviously have a lot of work to do, so let's get started," she said, and the group disbanded to resume their tasks.

Eliza went back to the T-shirt pile, her face glowing. Sydney had loved the outfit—he'd even said she was *good*—no, he'd said she was *simply fabulous*. It was like a lightning bolt through the clouds. She'd loved helping style the dress. Working on the look was the first time she'd ever felt passionate about her work—really, the first time she'd felt excited about anything other than shopping.

A shadow suddenly enveloped Eliza. She looked up to find Paige looming over her. Insta–buzz kill.

"Sydney would like you to take a look at the rest of his line." Each word seemed painful for Paige to speak. "I'll take over folding the T-shirts."

Eliza leaped to attention and handed over the folding board. Even though her feet were sore and her joints ached, a sweet feeling of satisfaction seeped into her bones and made her oblivious to the pain.

Suddenly, the job wasn't so boring after all.

you can't always get what you want. . . .

THE LIMOUSINE INCHED FORWARD FOR SEVERAL BLOCKS, stuck in Midtown gridlock. All around them the streets were jammed with harried commuters trying to get out of the city early on a Friday afternoon, a veritable *Escape from New York*. Sometimes it took longer to get out of the city than it took to drive to the Hamptons.

Jacqui stretched her legs in the back of the limousine, dozing as the kids flipped channels on the built-in DVD player and Anna made phone calls. Her Sidekick vibrated, and she checked the screen. The new-message icon was flashing. She clicked on it idly but caught her breath once she saw the sender's e-mail address: admissions@nyu.edu. It could only mean one thing. The school had finally come to a decision. After a deep breath, she scrolled down to read it.

To: jacarei_velasco@stgraceacademy.edu
From: admissions@nyu.edu
Dear Jacarei Velasco,
We regret to inform you that we are unable to

offer you a position in next year's freshman class. Unfortunately, subsequent investigation of your high school transcript from São Paulo reveals that you have taken only two years of science and mathematics. New York University requires that all its incoming students complete a minimum of three years of study in these subjects. We suggest taking a fifth year of college preparatory courses to bolster your application if you choose to apply for admission next year.

Thank you for your interest in New York University, and best of luck in the future.

Sincerely,

The New York University Admissions Committee

How could this be? She'd been waiting for so long—she'd worked so hard—between schooling and the au pair gig, she'd barely even had time to hang out when Eliza was home from boarding school. Plus, she'd taken the SAT no fewer than *seven* times, and she'd even passed her AP English exam—a real achievement! Then she'd put in all that time at the dialysis center as part of her community service to beef up her application— which had been a difficult squeeze with all her responsibilities at the Perry house. She'd done everything possible—she'd rewritten her essay so many times even she herself was sick of her life story and "the most influential person in her life" (her grandmother). By rights, she was a perfect candidate—well rounded, solid GPA, likable background, killer head shot. (All the schools were asking for them now.) What could have gone wrong?

"Are you okay?" Anna asked, raising an eyebrow. She'd noticed Jacqui staring at the screen with uncharacteristic intensity.

"I got an e-mail from NYU," Jacqui said flatly. She choked out the bad news.

"I'm sorry," Anna said, her voice warm. "I went to NYU. I know it's terribly hard to get in these days. I'm sure you'll do just as well at another university."

Jacqui took Anna's words of comfort in the spirit they were offered; she knew her employer meant well. But Jacqui didn't have a plan B. She'd refused to apply to any other college as the counselor had suggested. The University of Michigan? She didn't even know where Michigan *was*. Wellesley? An all-girls' school? Forget it! So instead of college, her only remaining option was to take a *fifth* year—of high school! The humiliation!

Jacqui had heard about the dreaded "five-year plan." A few seniors from last year's class at St. Grace had returned to the school for the same program. It was usually offered to dumb rich kids who had marginal brains but oodles of money. Jacqui couldn't believe she would be one of those people. First off, she wasn't rich. Who was going to pay for another year of her tuition?

Of course, she could work for the Perrys again. She was sure Anna wasn't looking forward to breaking in a new au pair. But Jacqui had talked about NYU so much—she and Eliza were already planning on meeting up in October for Halloween, and she'd had Mara promise that wherever she ended up, they would spend Thanksgiving together. She even had a roommate lined up—a friend from St. Grace who had been granted early admission to Tisch.

Traffic finally let up, and the car deposited them in front of the barbed-wire gates in front of the Thirty-fourth Street tarmac. Anna and the rest of the family clambered out of the limousine, leaving Jacqui alone inside.

With no one to notice, Jacqui brushed away a few tears. Madison Perry, twelve years old and even skinnier than last summer, stuck her head inside the car. "Jacqui? We need to go." She saw the look on Jacqui's face. "Is something wrong? Are you okay?"

Jacqui smiled bravely. She wiped her face. "I just realized I'm wearing the wrong outfit for the helicopter. My skirt is going to be in my face from all that wind."

Madison chuckled hesitantly.

"You know, like Marilyn Monroe—poof!" Jacqui joked. She slid out of the car. This time Madison laughed in earnest.

Jacqui forced a laugh too, holding down her skirt as they ran past the scissoring helicopter blades. But her smile faded as soon as Madison turned away.

The girl from sunny São Paulo felt as cloudy as the New York sky.

when duty calls . . .
blackberries vibrate

RYAN TOSSED OVER THE CARDBOARD FEDEX BOX, AND MARA tore it open.

"What the—?" she asked as out tumbled a vibrating BlackBerry.

She tried to answer it. "Hello? Hello? Hello?" she yelled, twiddling the little knobs on the side.

"I don't think it's ringing," Ryan said helpfully. "I think it means you have a message."

"Right," Mara said, scrolling down the page and finding a blinking envelope icon on the screen. She tapped it open.

"Oh no!"

"What's wrong?" Ryan asked, climbing back into bed and kicking the FedEx box to the side. He knelt above Mara and nuzzled her neck. "Whatever it is, it can't be that important."

"Shit! I'm so dead!" she gasped as she scrolled down the screen. She looked at her watch and cursed again. "It's eleven-thirty!"

"Why? What's going on?"

"Ryan—can you please—" Mara said, brushing away his hand and turning her head from his kisses. "It's my boss!" she wailed.

"She's the only one who knows the boat address. Anyway, there's a big benefit party at Cain tonight for some day-care center, and their society columnist is stuck at some royal wedding in Saint-Tropez." Mara swallowed hard. "She wants me to be there . . . and write a whole column about it!"

Ryan sighed loudly against Mara's shoulder. "So?" he asked. "What's the big deal? You're supposed to write for them, aren't you?"

Mara blew out her bangs. "Not really. She said there was a chance I could do some writing—but mostly captions. Not a real article. You don't understand—I've never written anything like this before! The biggest event I've ever written about was the musical production of *Mary Poppins* at our high school! And she wants a column—with quotes from celebrities. How do I even do that?" Mara was terrified at the thought of actually sticking a tape recorder under a famous person's chin. Did she even own a tape recorder?

"Easy. You just go up and ask a question," Ryan replied. "It's not a big deal. I see reporters do it all the time. Besides, you've been to, like, a million parties in the Hamptons. It's all the same thing every year."

Mara freed herself from his arms. She wrapped her body in a bedsheet and ran out to the deck to fetch her luggage.

"You're leaving?" he asked incredulously. "But we just got here!"

"I have to," she pleaded, returning to the cabin with a suitcase and a garment bag. "The party started at ten! I'm already so late! Lucky was supposed to meet me there an hour ago!" She unzipped the bag and began rooting in it for something to wear.

"Relax. Nothing ever happens before midnight," he said.

He remained silent as she fastened her push-up bra back on and wiggled into a tight-fitting Hollywould dress with a sexy cutout front studded with turquoise beads.

"Zip me up?"

Ryan sighed and propped himself up on his knees. Mara turned her back to him and he carefully zipped up the dress.

She turned around to smooth out the front panels. "Do I look okay?"

"You looked better before." He smirked and switched on the sixty-inch flat-screen television.

"Why don't you come with me?" Mara asked, her face lighting up with the idea. She felt so bad to be leaving him in the middle of the night. She sat on the side of the bed to put on a pair of patent leather Pierre Hardy slingbacks, sneaking a glance in his direction. "It'll be fun," she wheedled.

"Nah," Ryan said, falling against the pillows. "I'm beat—I had to drive down from New Hampshire and then drive out here. You go. Seriously. I don't mind."

"C'mon, we'll dance a little, drink a few margaritas . . ." she said seductively, hooking the straps around her heels.

"Hypnotic margaritas?" he asked, cocking an eyebrow.

"Your favorite."

"Mmm . . ." He looked like he was about to leave the bed and put on some clothes but at the last second fell back against the pillows again. "I'm so beat, I don't think I can move. I really need to crash tonight."

"I just want us to be together for our first night," Mara pouted.

"I know, babe," Ryan said, leaning forward and putting an arm around her neck so that he pulled her back on the bed. He slipped a hand up her skirt and pulled teasingly down on her underwear. "We can be."

For a moment, she relaxed against his grip, closing her eyes. She could feel him gently kissing the back of her neck, and it would be so easy to just surrender—to give in—to let them be together. But she put a hand on his hand and eased it out from under her skirt. Reluctantly.

"I should really go. I don't want to, but I have to."

"All right." Ryan sighed again. "I understand."

She turned around to look at him in the eye. "Are you sure?"

"I'm sure." He nodded, but his eyes were bereft of their usual spark.

She still looked uncertain, and part of her just wanted to stay in the bed and be with him forever—but another part was also extremely worried about her first magazine story. A bona fide assignment! She'd just have to overcome her natural shyness and get a few quotes from the celebrities in attendance. Ask them what they were wearing and who they were dating . . . and . . .

what? She had to fill a column—eight hundred words! She hoped she could pull it off.

"I'm sorry," she repeated.

"Don't be," he said. "We've got the whole summer ahead of us."

Mara smiled. He was such a great guy. And what was one missed night? He was right—they had three glorious months ahead to do everything together.

She held up his Ferrari keys. "Okay if I drive it to Cain?"

black hawk down!

"WHAT DO YOU MEAN, OUR CHOPPER ISN'T HERE?" ANNA demanded, jabbing a finger at the chest of the beleaguered air traffic controller. "We're always slotted first for departure."

"Sorry, ma'am, but you'll have to wait till they leave," the nervous technician explained, thumbing behind him. "Then your pilot can land and you can board."

Anna looked over to where he had pointed and gasped. "What the hell is that? And what is it doing in our space!"

In the Perrys' usual spot was a magnificent army-issue Black Hawk helicopter revamped with custom detailing and luxury finishes, boasting a veritable *Pimp My Ride* makeover, from the cushy leather bucket seats to the retractable step platform. It could withstand Iraqi gunfire but was currently used to ferry its owners from Manhattan to the Hamptons in under an hour.

A boxy, behemoth, bright yellow Hummer barged into the terminal and pulled up next to the Black Hawk with a loud screech. The side door opened and three very cute young indie-rock-looking guys jumped out. One was tall and light-haired with a pleasant face and a quick, friendly grin. He was wearing a purple Atari T-shirt and baggy jeans. The second had neat dark hair and black plastic square-rimmed glasses. A hipster nerd, good-looking in that bookish way. The third was lanky and laid-back, with messy brown hair and a fine set of sideburns. He wore a yellow polyester shirt with a seventies-style spread collar that spanned the length of his shoulders and a pair of loud checkered trousers. They looked like college freshmen lost on their way to orientation.

Jacqui stood by the chain-link fence next to the Perry kids, holding Zoë's backpack and Cody's hand. She barely noticed the three guys. Cody was screaming that he had to go potty, and Jacqui had to tell him to wait until they got to the Hamptons because there was no bathroom at the helipad. He'd finally been toilet-trained at the grand old age of five, but the poor kid still had the occasional accident. Jacqui prayed he wouldn't have one now—or perhaps she could just let him go by the side of the road. He was just a little boy, after all, and it seemed cruel to let him suffer like that.

While she debated on how to handle the toilet situation, her mind searched for an easy answer to her problems. She needed to think, and it was hard to concentrate with the sound of the helicopter engines and the Hummer stereo blasting and Anna's incessant complaining.

The trio from the Hummer sauntered toward the Black Hawk.

"Sorry we're late," the tall blond one said to the air traffic controller with a wicked grin. "Ben here had a little appointment with Madame Cinq Doigt," he said, holding up five fingers and smirking.

"Duffy, man, you know she's my best customer," said Ben, the one with the glasses. He shrugged easily and laughed.

"Check it out!" the handsome one with the sideburns exclaimed. "Fucking A." He whistled, stalking over to the side of the chopper with smooth, catlike grace.

Painted on the side of the helicopter was a cartoon hand holding up its index and third fingers in a crooked *V*. Underneath was emblazoned the words *The Shocker!*

"Oh, man, Grant." Duffy suddenly raised his arms to the back of his head and looked pained. "Totally forgot I have to pick up my parents from the Vineyard in that thing tomorrow!"

"Maybe they won't notice," Ben soothed, taking off his glasses and wiping them on the edge of his shirt. "You can always tell them it's a peace sign."

"Yeah, right," Duffy said glumly as Grant punched him on the shoulder, trying not to laugh too hard.

The three of them climbed up the steps into the helicopter, completely ignoring the Perry clan.

Until they spotted Jacqui crouching on her knees, trying to calm Cody.

"You can just go here, Cody. No one will see," she said as she helped the kid with his pants buttons.

"Ten o'clock," Duffy said, alerting his friends to the direction where Jacqui was kneeling. "Hottie central."

Ben put his glasses back on his nose for a closer look. "Girls sure don't look like that at Harvard," he lamented.

Grant nodded. "No wonder Latin American women always win Miss Universe."

His friends looked askance at him. "How do you know that shit?" they ribbed.

"It's called having sisters," Grant huffed. He straightened his winged collar and slicked back his dark hair.

Jacqui didn't even notice the three boys staring at her with an intensity bordering on reverence. In the afternoon sun, violet highlights shone in her black hair, and her deep bronze tan glowed. The sweetheart neckline on her dress displayed her ample cleavage, and her slim, toned legs were taut from squatting to Cody's height. "There you go; that's a good boy," she said, relieved that the kid had been able to urinate. She brushed her hair out of her eyes, lifting and stretching her bountiful chest, which elicited a chorus of strangled cries from two of the Black Hawk's occupants.

"Yo!" Duffy said, opting for a direct approach.

"Excuse me!" Ben yelled, trying for a polite angle.

Grant merely slumped back in his seat and regarded Jacqui thoughtfully. Girls usually came up to him, and he didn't see the need to make a fool of himself. Especially as the sounds of his friends' desperate mating calls were obscured by the din of the engine roaring into first gear.

"Who do you think she is?" Ben wondered aloud as the heli-copter lifted them high up in the air and out of earshot.

"A goddess," Duffy opined.

"Relax, guys, we're going to the Hamptons. And believe me, they all look like that there," Grant assured them. But his two friends looked at him doubtfully. As far as they could see, there was only one Jacqui.

the first rule of party reporting: fabricate fun!

IN THE HAMPTONS, EVEN A DAY-CARE-CENTER FUND-RAISER merited boldface names and a swishy crowd. The first person Mara saw on entering Cain was none other than Mitzi Goober—the toxic publicist from last summer who had styled herself Mara's best friend and plied her with gifts, only to turn on her after a misunderstanding over a pair of misplaced quarter-million-dollar earrings that were supposed to be worn by J.Lo at the MTV Awards. But what was a lost PR opportunity among friends? To Mara's surprise, Mitzi greeted her with a shrill hello and immediately drew her in for a fierce embrace. It was like hugging a skeleton, Mara thought.

Mitzi was tanner and blonder than ever. But while her arms were toned and muscular, she had a basketball-sized stomach owing to the fact that she was six months pregnant. She sported a tight tank top that blared LIVING THE AMERICAN DREAM over a proud baby bump—the ne plus ultra of accessories that summer. "Yummy Mommies" were all the rage—fertility was very fashionable at the moment. Of course, once the children were born, they were quickly ushered offstage by a crew of nannies. The glamorous crowd cooed over a chic pregnancy but beat a hasty retreat when faced with the reality of actually raising a child.

"Dollink!" Mitzi cooed as she sipped on a thin red straw poking out of a blue-and-silver Red Bull can. Caffeine intake concerns? Not this mother-to-be.

"Hi, Mitzi," Mara said, relieved to see someone she recognized. Where was Lucky? She hoped she would run into him soon so she could find out what exactly she was supposed to do at the party.

"How *are* you? What's *new*?" Mitzi jabbered in her singsong voice. "I heard you're on staff at *Hamptons* this summer—that's beyond! We need to get you to meet our clients—we have some awesome things coming up this season. We're doing Sydney's opening—I see six-page spread!"

"Um . . ." Mara didn't know what to say. The idea that she would be making decisions on anything as important as a multi-page feature was absurd. She was a lowly intern.

"We'll talk, okay? I'll send you samples. Bye-yee!" Mitzi gushed, assaulting Mara with a brush of her lips on each cheek.

The minute Mitzi released her, several people whom Mara had met during the last two summers made their way to her side. They all knew she was working for *Hamptons* magazine. The same crowd who had shunned her at the end of last summer were now angling to get back in her good graces, reminding her of how they knew each other. Part of Mara was disgusted by their hypocrisy, but another part admired their tenacity. Some would call it fair-weather friendship, but such was life in the Hamptons. In their own way, they were paying Mara a compliment. It was obvious from all the attention they were lavishing on her that they considered Mara a real player. Even Alan Whitman and Kartik, the co-owners of Seventh Circle, last year's hot spot, came over to pay their respects.

Eliza's former bosses told Mara they were just back from Las Vegas, where they had opened Seventh Circle in the Desert, with an opening party that had included topless dancers re-creating the seminal dance scene from *Showgirls*.

"But I'm telling you." Alan nodded. "You've got to check out our new place, Volcano. We've got real lava coming out of the fountain. It's *intense*."

"Come over for dinner, on us," Kartik added, giving Mara a bear hug. "Mitzi'll call you. Hook us up!"

Mara smiled in a noncommittal fashion. "Hook us up!" was the rousing chorus of the evening, with everyone from desperate socialites and their scheming publicists to coat-check girls and valet attendants pitching Mara items for the magazine.

She spotted Anna Perry in the corner of the club, looking woefully overdressed and awkwardly out of place in a floor-length ball gown. While the benefit dinner had been attended by the A-list social crowd, the dessert-and-dancing after-hours catered to the younger set. Usually Anna left early with the other society wives, but there she was, perched on a tufted ottoman, balancing a drink on her knee.

Mara noticed that she was accompanied by one of the more famous Hamptons "walkers"—gay men who acted as escorts to married women who couldn't persuade their husbands to join them in the social whirl. Where was Kevin? She stopped by to say hello, and Anna greeted her warmly. "Did you see all the pictures of the kids? Aren't they so cute?" her former employer asked wistfully. "Cody's gotten so big! I miss having a baby around the house."

"There you are!"

For the first time at the party, Mara felt genuine happiness at spotting someone. Lucky Yap, the tart-tongued party photographer, was making his way toward her.

"Excuse me, Anna," Mara said, taking her leave and turning to her friend.

Lucky was wearing a voluminous velvet frock coat over a T-shirt that read FASHION VICTIM! (Edwardian irony was in, and last year's African muumuus were out this summer), with his trusty digital Nikon around his neck. He was scanning the crowd with a raised eyebrow.

"It's just exes, siblings, and stepkids tonight," he lamented, meaning the crowd was made up of those with tenuous connections to the famous rather than real celebrities themselves.

"What should I do?" Mara asked eagerly.

"What we always do: lie, lie, lie! All these parties are so motha-effing boring, but no one has to know that or we'll be out of work."

Mara laughed. She knew Lucky was joking. Or at least, she hoped he was. She gave him a rundown of what she'd observed. She thought she'd spotted a famous socialite—one of the Bush nieces—but she wasn't sure. And she had caught a glimpse of a married polo player kissing a newlywed television starlet near the coat check.

"Do you think that's enough for the column?"

"Honey, of course it is. You can put the canoodling adulterers in the "blind item" category. But I'll run the starlet's photo above it so everyone will know it was him," Lucky said wickedly.

"Oh, good," Mara said, relieved.

"Miss Mara Waters," a sexy yet familiar voice growled behind her.

She turned around. "Mister Garrett Reynolds," she cooed back, folding her arms under her chest.

Garrett brushed a saucy flop of dark hair out of his eye. He was tan and wearing a white linen shirt and cream-colored trousers. He kissed her on the cheek and acted like they were old friends and like nothing had ever happened between them—as though he hadn't dumped her unceremoniously once she'd been the victim of bad press.

"Working hard?"

She shrugged.

"Good luck with it," he said, shaking his whiskey glass. "It's my last night here."

"Oh? You're not staying in the Hamptons this summer?"

Garrett laughed as if it were the funniest thing he'd ever heard. "Oh no, *of course* not. The Hamptons are so over. We're renting out the house. I'll be in Cape Town, where the real action is." He smirked. "But you have fun—I know you'll find some way to get into trouble."

His condescending and dismissive attitude did little to dampen Mara's spirits. Garrett was an ass, and she was glad to see the back of him. She wondered how on earth she'd ever found him attractive.

She suddenly missed Ryan, who was sure to be asleep with the TV turned to *Aqua Teen Hunger Force*. She thought about heading home and crawling into bed next to him, but Lucky Yap called her over to introduce her to Jill Klompenhower, the only real A-list celeb in the joint—an Oscar-winning actress who was rumored to have recently annulled her two-week marriage to a Christian rocker. Suddenly Mara was too busy trying to remember every detail of Jill's story to pine for her sleeping boyfriend.

as heidi klum would say, eliza is "in" and paige is "out"

ELIZA HELPED ANOTHER MODEL WITH HER OUTFIT, TWEAKING it so that the girl wore the newsboy cap at a rakish angle and the lacy camisole over the dress instead of vice versa. Then she moved on to the next one and the next, making little adjustments, adding earrings here, a pair of fishnet stockings there—and before she knew it, she'd changed the entire look and feel of the collection.

There! Eliza thought. *Now, that's more like it.* The clothes all displayed an overall theme, with a sexy, beachy, jet-set vibe. More like the Sydney Minx collection of old. She had to say so herself—she was a genius!

"What do you think you're doing?" Paige demanded. She had walked out of Sydney's office and only just noticed that almost all of the models were wearing their outfits ever-so-slightly differently.

"Oh, Paige!" Eliza pouted. "You scared me."

"Sydney, look what she's done!" Paige called out ominously. "Everything is different!"

The designer emerged from his office. He frowned and cupped his chin in the palm of his hand. "Let me see."

Eliza froze. She held her breath. All her bravado momentarily left her. It was easy to feel confident and inspired when the models cooed and aahed over her changes, but they were just models—what did they know? Most of them couldn't even spell their own fake names.

"Good, good," Sydney said. "Continue," he told Eliza. "And Paige, give her a hand."

It was a moment of triumph Eliza found bittersweet. Because while she took it upon herself to feverishly spray-paint, shred, and accessorize each outfit, Paige stood to the side, bored, unhelpful, and seething with barely controlled passive-aggressive rage.

"Can I get a glue gun, please?" Eliza called to her as she pulled on a model's skirt and began pinching the fabric in a ruched pattern.

"Here," Paige said, throwing it down.

The clatter made Eliza jump, causing her to cut into the fabric with her scissors.

"Jesus!" the model yelped.

"Oh, fuck!" Eliza said, noticing the hole. She looked over at Paige, who looked the picture of innocence. She knew Paige had done it on purpose, but there was nothing Eliza could do about it.

Eliza had a thought. "Hold still," she told the model, cutting another hole in the skirt and another and another, creating a sexy peekaboo design.

A few minutes later, there was a ruckus in the back of the room. "It's too small!" the model complained. The coffee-colored leather dress she was wearing was so short it barely covered her bottom.

"What's happened now? I warn you girls, I *cannot* have another crisis! I'm already out of Xanax!" Sydney shouted, storming over to assess the situation.

"Eliza told me to put it in the dryer—and look," Paige said smugly. "The outfit's ruined. It'll never be ready for the show."

"I was going for a distressed leather thing," Eliza explained, examining the destroyed fabric with a critical eye. She had asked Paige to set the machine on delicate, but obviously the malicious assistant had made sure the machine was set on high.

The leather was nubby and indeed shrunken.

"Here," Eliza, decided, handing the model a pair of denim cutoffs. She pulled the dress higher on the waist. "It's a top!"

"Naturally," Sydney agreed, fanning away.

"Naturally," Eliza repeated, beaming her million-dollar smile Paige's way. No matter how badly Paige tried to sabotage her efforts, Eliza could do no wrong.

if only all nerf football games ended this way

JACQUI ARRIVED IN THE HAMPTONS AT SUNSET. THE PERRY estate, Creek Head Manor, was just as immaculate and photo-shoot-ready as ever, as if waiting for its close-up in *Metropolitan Home*. Laurie, Anna's jovial assistant, had arrived a week earlier to make the proper preparations, and there were long-stemmed white calla lilies blooming in all the vases and fresh Italian linens on each bed. Anna had ordered yet another renovation over the winter, and the house now boasted a solarium and a fully equipped wet bar in the master closet. The master bath also housed Jackie Onassis's for-mer bidet (purchased at an exorbitant price at auction) to match the existing Marie Antoinette bath tiles.

Jacqui made the kids dinner and gave the little ones baths, and after she'd tucked them into bed, reminding William and Madison not to stay up too late, she was finally free to unpack and set up her own room. She trudged up the rickety steps to the highest floor and opened the door, tearing through a cobweb.

After living in high style in the city for a year, going back to the au pair cottage was a bit of letdown for Jacqui. The room was dark and musty and smelled like mildew. Jacqui threw open the

63

windows and immediately wished she were back in her apart-ment's central-air-conditioned comfort. She found wrinkled per-cale sheets in the drawers and halfheartedly tossed them on the stained and lumpy mattress on the single bed. It just wasn't the same without Eliza whining about the tiny bathroom or Mara admonishing everyone to prepare for work the next day.

She sat moodily at the edge of the bed and lit a cigarette, toss-ing the ashes haphazardly into the nearby planter that contained a dry ficus tree.

Jacqui scratched her cheek and took a long puff. Eliza was still in the city, and Mara was on the boat with Ryan—best to let them alone on their first night back. In the middle of unpacking, she spotted the lights from the pool illuminating the garden pathway. Now, there was an idea. She grabbed a towel from the bathroom and walked quickly out of the cottage.

Just what she needed—a little skinny-dip to make her feel bet-ter. Anna was out at the benefit, and it was past midnight, so the kids were asleep. . . . It wasn't like there was anyone else in the house. . . . The water was warm and refreshing—the Perrys had it especially irrigated with the finest fresh water pumped in from a stream in the North Fork. She did a couple of lazy strokes, then floated on her back for a while. She swam to the side of the pool, where an icy tumbler was waiting. Thankfully, she knew where the keys to the liquor cabinet were kept.

After a few minutes, she decided she'd had enough and swam to the opposite edge nearer the path back to the cottage. She emerged from the water, dripping and naked, just as the bushes that lined the perimeter of the pool exploded with a crash.

Jacqui screamed.

Three boys wrestling over a foam football tumbled through the hedge that separated the Perrys' home from the Reynolds property.

"Twelve—twelve—twelve o'clock!" Duffy choked, still holding on to the Nerf. "It's *her*!"

"Sweet Mother of Mercy," Ben exclaimed, craning his neck. "Swear to God, I'm never going back to Harvard."

"Señorita, please excuse my stupid friends," Grant said in his slow southern drawl, which would have been charming had he not been lying on the ground, his face smashed up in the grass.

They stared round-eyed at Jacqui in all her naked glory, wearing nothing but her Brazilian—bikini wax, that is.

"*Merda!*" she cursed, wrapping a towel around herself and running back to the au pair cottage, leaving three very love-struck boys in her wake.

mara has king-size doubts about her new position

A LITTLE AFTER TWO IN THE MORNING, MARA CREPT BACK onboard the Catalina. She slowly unlocked the cabin door and softly tiptoed inside the dark stateroom. Moonlight spilled through the porthole, and Mara could see Ryan's long form huddled underneath the white goose-down comforter.

She eased out of her heels, pulling down the straps, and massaged the balls of her feet. Jill had invited them over to her Bridgehampton rental, and after a couple of vodka shots and a drunken game of "Celebrity" (the star herself winning on her Nicole Richie impersonation alone), they'd finally called it an evening.

Mara filed the story of Jill's annulment and all the details of the day-care benefit party from her BlackBerry, hoping against hope that the story would make it into the magazine's next issue. Lucky had assured her the piece was fine, but she wasn't so sure. What if her boss didn't like any of the jokes about the Walkers? Or the remark about how in the current celebrity math, two assistants of the famous now equaled one C-list star? For example, CaCee Cobb (Jessica Simpson's personal assistant and best friend) + Trace Ayala (Justin Timberlake's personal assistant and best friend) = Brooke Burke.

Her feet made a squishy noise on the thick carpet, and she locked herself in the bathroom to wash her face, shower, and change. She slipped into one of Ryan's old T-shirts, feeling the softness of the cotton against her skin.

She slid underneath the covers and quietly snuggled into his chest, angling her body so that her arms ducked underneath his armpits and held him close while her legs curved under his legs.

"Mmmmppf," Ryan murmured, patting her arm absentmind-edly. He sighed.

"Ry, are you awake? Ryan?" she whispered. "I think they made a big mistake sending me to cover the party. I don't know any-thing about writing a society column. I'm not even in society."

She was hopped up from the vodka and anxious about her story. If only he would wake up so she could talk to him about it. She could really use his support right now.

"Mmmppff . . . huh?" Ryan said sleepily. "Don't worry about it. Everything'll be fine," he mumbled.

Mara wrung her hands. What if her boss totally hated her copy? She'd be stuck with penning nothing but photo captions all summer. *L-R, Ketchup Heir, Trophy Wife, Prominent Plastic Surgeon* . . .

"Ryan, are you listening? Honey, I'm so nervous," she said.

Ryan snored loudly in response. He turned over to his other side and hugged his pillow, leaving Mara feeling abandoned on the other side of the king-size bed.

Oh, well . . . so much for that. Standing in heels for three hours was an exercise in torture anyway, so she could use the rest. She gave Ryan one final kiss on the cheek and turned away from him to face the wall, hugging the covers to her chest.

They slept like that, back to back, their bodies scarcely touching. The bed rocked softly as the boat bobbed up and down in the water, and when Mara closed her eyes, she dreamed she was floating alone through space.

there's nothing like a job well done to make a girl feel good

THAT WAS THE LAST OF IT. ELIZA HELD THE BOX FLAPS together while the other intern taped them shut. It was officially six o'clock in the morning, and the entire staff had been working all through the night. Eliza felt slightly delirious, but she was exultant. The final choices for the show turned out incredibly— she'd placed over-the-top jewelry on all the models, played with different textures and patterns, and succeeded in creating a super-glamorous spectacle. Sydney couldn't have been more pleased nor Paige more annoyed.

Eliza was on cloud nine. She'd never worked so hard and felt so good in her life! The collection was amazing—even Paige had grudgingly remarked on how gorgeous everything looked. She was so proud of herself. This was even better than scoring a 5 on all of her AP tests.

They'd packed each outfit in acid-free tissue and hung them inside plastic bags in a portable closet that was going in the truck to the Hamptons. The messengers were arriving in an hour, and the clothes would be in the store by the next morning—the day of the party.

Eliza planned to catch a few hours' sleep and then drive out to the Hamptons later that afternoon. She nodded good-bye to the rest of the team and went home for a well-deserved shower.

In an uncharacteristic fit of generosity, Sydney had allowed everyone to take the company car service home, and a fleet of black Lincoln town cars were parked in front of the building. Eliza directed hers up to Park Avenue.

It was wonderful to be home—truly home. The doorman tipped his hat and held the door open for her, and she felt an immeasurable amount of pleasure as she walked into the marble lobby, decorated with rococo-style pastel murals of nymphs and cherubs. She took the carpeted, mirrored elevator to the twenty-first floor. The Thompsons' homestead had been in Eliza's mother's family since the early part of the twentieth century. It was a "classic six," but a "luxury twelve" was more like it, since it was double the usual square footage, with a soaring, three-story entry space and a balcony that overlooked Central Park.

Her parents were already in the Hamptons, back in their Amagansett "cottage" (their ten-bedroom country house could only be called rustic according to the standards of a Ralph Lauren ad), and Cheka, their maid, answered the door sleepily in her nightgown. Eliza was shocked to realize she'd probably been working harder than Cheka all evening and most likely getting paid less for it. It was strange—Eliza would never have thought of herself as someone who enjoyed working, but a day in Sydney's studio had suddenly changed that.

All of her friends from Spence did nothing more than make hair appointments, shop for clothes, and talk about boys. Sure, there were those brilliant girls who went to Williamsburg for the summer for acting camp or interned at magazines or the White House, but Eliza had never been interested in being one of them.

She never thought a hard night of work would actually make her feel more energized, not less. But having the opportunity to express herself creatively and using her innate talents to make something beautiful brought a level of satisfaction she'd never experienced before. Eliza felt inspired, and she was glad she'd taken the internship at Sydney's company. She couldn't wait until the show itself.

A few hours later, refreshed from a nap and a much-needed shower, Eliza packed the last of her monogrammed Goyard bags and called downstairs for a taxi. She took the taxi to their garage across town, which housed her new ride—a sporty new Land Rover LR3, an upgrade from last summer's leased Jetta. Her parents had bought her the car as a prize for getting into Princeton, her father's alma mater. The SUV was polished to a shine, and Eliza threw her stuff in the back and hopped inside the driver's seat.

A clipped British voice greeted her as soon as she gunned the engine. "Good morning, Eliza. Where would you like to go today?"

"Good morning, car!" Eliza chirped back. It always cracked her up to have a conversation with her automobile. Eliza punched their address in Amagansett into the automated GPS system.

The car began giving her directions, and Eliza drove it out of the lot and pulled out into traffic. "Telephone," the car informed her as a flashing symbol on the dashboard lit up.

"Answer," Eliza said.

"Answering telephone. You are connected."

Eliza heard the sound of waves in the background and Jeremy fumbling with his cell phone. "Hello? Hello?" he called. "Liza, are you there?"

"Hi, baby."

"Hey." He had a voice that melted her heart. A deep rumble. Eliza felt a twinge of pity for any girl who didn't have a guy with a voice as sexy as Jeremy's. She remembered how Charlie Borshok, her former paramour, had a voice like a hyena and tended to laugh in a high-pitched giggle.

"I just left the garage, and I'm about to go into the tunnel. I should be there in a few hours." Her conversational voice was quickly replaced by schoolgirl cooing. "Did you miss me?"

"Not one bit," he joked.

She steered the car into the cavernous Midtown Tunnel, and the signal started to fade. "Jer, I'm going to lose you. I'll call when I'm on 27, okay? Love you!"

There was no answer. The symbol on the dashboard was dull. She'd lost the connection. No matter. She'd call him again once she got past the tunnel. She felt a thrill thinking of the special custom-made lingerie set in her luggage. The palest pink silk, with satin ribbons. Jeremy didn't know it yet, but tonight her V card would expire. Hopefully the world wouldn't end before then because Eliza had absolutely no intention of dying a virgin.

the devil wears louboutin

THE FIRST GIVEAWAY THAT THIS WASN'T GOING TO BE A normal job was the sight of her boss's heels perched on top of her desk. Mara admired them from the corner of her eye. They were hot-pink patent-leather Louboutins with fire-engine-red soles—the status-conveying detail that communicated each pair's five-hundred-dollar price tag to observant and shoe-savvy females everywhere.

For a decade Sam Davis had ruled the New York media world. She had single-handedly transformed several sluggish, out-of-touch magazines into cash-cow bonanzas, starting with *American Teen* and working her way up the "pink ghetto" of women's magazines, from *Sophisticated* to the Spanish import *Anna Claudia* to the mainstream *Glitter* to her most famous reinvention yet—*Them*—a notorious weekly celebrity tabloid that fed the public desire for knowledge about the intimate private lives of nubile reality television stars. Sam Davis was the reason pop starlet Chauncey Raven, newly married to her former backup singer Daryl Wolf and mother to four-month-old Liam Spenser Raven Wolf, had already totaled two Mercedes-Benz convertibles in high-speed paparazzi car chases through Malibu.

Sam Davis bent the media landscape to her will, and her

trajectory had seemed to go higher and higher. For years, it seemed she was unstoppable. Thinking she could conquer all, she set her sights on reinventing the intellectual-mag market. She proposed a magazine that was equal part *Harper's* and *InStyle* that would make "smart people sexy." She did this by putting Nobel Prize winners in skimpy outfits and having actresses review the latest literary tomes. The high point had come when a reality show host summed up a Pulitzer Prize–winning book on famine in Africa as "making her hungry for more." The magazine folded after three issues, her multi-year contract was canceled, and as quickly as she had been the toast of the town, she was a laughingstock.

Hence the exile to the Hamptons. She swore it was to get back in touch with her family (she worked sixteen-hour days, her staff reported, even while her five-year-old son was in the hospital with a brain tumor) and to enjoy the slower pace of Hamptons reporting (garden shows, horse shows, show-offs). But New York knew the truth—she was over.

But not out. Sam Davis was eager to put her personal stamp on *Hamptons* and shake things up once again.

Mara waited eagerly while Sam was on the phone harassing her assistant about her coffee. "Haven't I told you a thousand times? A dry cappuccino has *no foam!*"

She still couldn't believe she'd landed such a sought-after gig. The speed of it still made Mara's head dizzy. All her life, she'd been told getting ahead was the result of hard work and discipline, but how could she believe that when with one simple phone call—one connection—she'd landed the job of her dreams? It didn't seem quite fair. What about all the other girls who had applied for the position but weren't lucky enough to have once worked for Sam Davis's college roommate?

But thoughts like that were "lame" according to Eliza. The world operated on the Rolodex system. It was all about whom you knew— the more important and worth knowing, the better. At seventeen, Mara was surprised to find she knew quite a lot of those people.

"Yes?" Sam asked, finally acknowledging Mara's presence. She was a solidly built woman of thirty-six with a hard, lined face. Her jet-black hair was meant to look punk, as was the dog collar around her neck, but somehow, stuffed into a too-tight Vivienne Westwood sweater and thigh-hugging bootleg Shagg jeans, Sam Davis still managed to looked like any other suburban mother of three but one who was desperately—and vainly—trying to hold on to her rebellious youth.

"I'm Mara Waters. Your new intern. I filed the story on the benefit at Cain last night."

"The what?" Sam asked. She whipped her feet back onto the floor, her pink shoes disappearing in a lurid flash. "Oh. Right. Got your copy. We cut it."

"Oh," Mara said, stung and disappointed. All that work, leaving Ryan, and the piece hadn't even run. Plus, it proved her worst fear—she wasn't a writer. She couldn't even make a society gossip column exciting. This was seriously depressing.

That morning, Mara had woken up in bed alone. Ryan had

left a note saying he'd gone off to surf. He had a habit of waking up at dawn to catch the waves. She'd felt a little sad—last night they'd been too tired to hook up, and then they hadn't even been able to spend the morning together. She'd planned on making them a romantic breakfast in the galley kitchen but had had to settle for a cold bagel alone by the television.

"I thought about running it next week, but by then it'll be old news. And we don't do old news at *Hamptons*," Sam Davis declared pompously.

"Of course." Mara nodded. She began to put her notebook back in her bag. It was obvious she was about to get relegated to the keeper of the office supplies. Her shoulders slumped.

But to her surprise, Sam gestured for her to take the seat across the desk, and, after Mara removed the piles of manuscripts, magazines, envelopes, and FedEx boxes lying on top of it, she did.

"Listen, it's not a big deal. Happens all the time," Sam said, rolling her eyes. "It was a little heavy on the puns—but otherwise not a bad read. A little wordy. You buried the lead by putting the polo player hooking up with the NBC star in the fourth 'graf. But you'll learn."

Mara perked up. "Really?"

Sam shuffled through some papers on her desk and found a hard copy of Mara's story. She skimmed it quickly. "There are some nice things here—'celebrity math'—that's funny. I like that. We need more of that."

Mara glowed. She'd thought that was a cute turn of phrase.

"Tell you what, the managing ed hired another intern, some favor to the publisher's sister-in-law or something. So it turns out, we don't need you to intern," Sam said.

But before Mara's face could crumple, Sam finished her sentence. "But I do need someone to fill in the Social Diary column regularly. Courtney von Wilding called. She's spending the summer sailing the Mediterranean on some Greek prince's boat and won't be back in New York till the fall." Sam sighed. "That's what I get for hiring some junior socialite to write the Diary column. It's almost impossible to get those girls near a keyboard. Ruins the manicure."

She pulled out a few old issues of the magazine and threw them across the desk in Mara's direction. "You're going to cover fashion shows, the polo, benefits, dinner parties, who's in, who's out, what they're wearing, who they're sleeping with, who got snubbed at the fireworks this year. Let's shake it up a little! Give them something to read between all the Cartier ads."

Mara nodded, scribbling furiously. *Who in/out, read btw Cartier ads.*

"Sydney Minx is opening his new boutique tomorrow. I want you there; make sure you get an interview with him. Let's do a full profile. More of that outsider-turned-insider stuff you do. Maybe we'll do it as a cover. See what the old bitch has got up his sleeve. I want three thousand words by Monday."

Three thousand words! Practically a novel! And had Sam Davis said "cover"? This was her big chance!

"But before I forget, there is one thing I desperately need," Sam Davis said. "Socks."

"Socks?"

Sam pointed to her feet. "Socks. For my tennis game. I need some. Get Sydney to send some over. Tell them we're shooting for a fashion page."

"Sorry—call in some socks?"

"Are you deaf? Yes. Here's the number," she said, throwing a card at Mara. "I'm late for my lunch at Nick and Toni's."

And with that, Sam Davis departed.

Mara stared at the scrap of paper in front of her. Did her boss actually expect her to ask a designer to messenger over some socks? Why couldn't Sam just pop down to the store and buy a pair? Or go home and pick up her own?

She dialed the number.

"Goober Public Relations," said a silky female voice she recognized as Mitzi's assistant's.

Mara immediately hung up the phone. She just couldn't bring herself to ask someone to send over some socks, especially not Mitzi. Not even with the crazy excuse of needing them for a fashion photo shoot. They were just white socks—they sold them at a drugstore for $1.99. Maybe she should just run down there and buy some. But what if Sam noticed they weren't Sydney Minx socks? Was there something special about Sydney Minx socks?

Luckily, she had another idea. She quickly dialed Eliza's cell.

"Liza?"

"Mar! Holla!" In Cabo, they'd played Gwen Stefani's album on Mara's iPod speakers until their ears bled.

"Holla back, girl! Where are you?" Mara asked, feeling a flush of happiness at hearing Eliza's throaty voice. This summer, the three of them would be together again—and who knew what kind of mischief they would find themselves in?

"Stuck in traffic on 27, as always. I should be there in an hour, though."

"Listen, I need some socks. For my boss. Sam Davis. Do you think you guys can send some over?"

"Socks?"

Mara quickly explained.

"Oh yeah. Don't worry. I heard she does that all the time, calls in for every little thing. No one even lends her any clothes anymore since she always lies and says it's for a shoot and then they see it on her at some premiere party. But she and Sydney go way back, I heard. I'll get one of the girls in the shop to send over a pair. What's her size?"

Mara surreptitiously kicked the Louboutin shoe box under the desk so that she could see the label. "Ten and a half. Literally Bigfoot." She snickered.

Eliza beeped off the line and then beeped back on. "They'll be there by noon."

"You're a lifesaver."

"More like a socksaver." Eliza giggled.

"Guess what? I'm writing a cover story on Sydney Minx!"

Mara said, her voice rising with excitement. She doodled on her notepad, writing, *By Mara Waters,* and, *Social Diary by Mara Waters,* and tried out a few byline bios: *Mara Waters lives in Sag Harbor with her boyfriend. This is her first piece for the magazine.*

"Shut up!" Eliza gasped.

"Seriously. They're making me the Social Diary columnist. Isn't that crazy?"

"Insane," Eliza enthused. "Oh my God, you're, like, going to be so important!"

"You shut up!" Mara laughed. Eliza tended to exaggerate, but it was still nice to hear. She put her feet up on the desk just as she'd seen Sam Davis do. There was no one around who would be able to see her anyway.

"Will you put me in the story? I styled the whole collection."

"I'll see what I can do," Mara replied in a professional tone.

"Oh," Eliza said, disappointed.

"Loser, I'm only kidding. Of course you'll be in it," Mara promised.

"Phew. For a minute there, I thought I might have to bring you my super-duper-big-head-shrinking machine," Eliza teased.

"See you at the Perry house?"

"If I don't see you first!" Eliza threatened.

Mara smiled as she hung up the phone. She couldn't wait to see her friends.

jacqui tunes out prelude-to-divorce radio

THE KIDS TRIED TO PRETEND THEY DIDN'T HEAR THEM, BUT the house reverberated with the sound of poison and bile. Kevin and Anna were fighting over the intercom. Again.

Jacqui looked at the white box by the toaster and wished she could shut off the speakers, but their Hamptons intercom was different from the New York system. In New York, when you beeped for a certain room, you got a private line. But in the Hamptons, which had older technology, when you pressed a button, your voice carried to the fifteen other intercom speakers in the house.

"Goddammit, where the hell are my golf clubs? How come I can never find anything in this house?" Kevin bellowed.

"Don't blame me—I wasn't the one who sent them out to get varnished!" Anna screeched.

"It's not like you do anything around here! All you do is spend money! And by the way, that little stunt you pulled on my ear is serious. The doctor said it's become infected!"

"So what? I don't care! I'm so sick of the way you treat me. I'm your wife, not your assistant anymore!" Anna screamed.

"Yeah, I know. My assistant does more work than you do!" Kevin retorted.

"Screw you! I want a divorce!"

"Fine! You've got one!" Kevin yelled back. "You probably just want to be with someone younger! It's not like you ever want to do anything that I want to do!"

"Earth to Kevin. Your friends are *bo-ring*!"

"Well, you won't have to hang around them anymore, will you?"

"I mean it this time!" Anna threatened. "I want a divorce!"

"Go ahead! Call your lawyer!"

"He's on speed dial! Just watch me!"

"They don't mean it," Jacqui said as she ladled out organic, steel-cut Irish oatmeal into the children's cereal bowls. The idle threat of divorce was thrown out so often, it lacked any punch. "Seriously."

Madison rolled her eyes. She pretended to be indifferent to her father and her stepmother's quarrels, but since Anna was the only mother they had—their real mother, Brigitte, had absconded to a Sri Lankan ashram and had hardly laid eyes on any of them in years—it was evident the fights spooked her. When a long shriek of Anna's voice screeched over the intercom, Madison accidentally upset her glass of orange juice on the table.

"Don't worry about it," Jacqui said, helping her wipe up the spill with a wad of paper napkins.

Eleven-year-old William didn't take his eyes off the adventure novel he was reading. The hyperactive little boy had calmed down, surprisingly without the help of any medications, and a miraculous transformation had taken place. Whereas it had been so hard to shut him up before, now you could hardly get him to talk. He had grown tall and lanky and was looking more like Ryan every day. The two older children tried not to show their anxiety, but the noise was clearly bothering Zoë and the baby, which was what they all still called Cody.

Zoë's lower lip trembled and it looked like she might cry, and Cody, the only one who was Anna's biologically, was pressing his hands against his ears and screaming.

Her fuse already dangerously short, Jacqui walked over and pulled the plug out of the white box, which immediately stopped squawking. They could still hear the rest of the house echo with the elder Perrys' quarrel, but now it was muffled and distant.

"C'mon, eat your fruit," she coaxed, handing around a bowl full of raisins and prunes.

"Anyone home?" a cheerful voice called from outside the screen door.

Jacqui looked up. Mara walked in, bearing a large basket filled with warm, fresh-baked muffins from Barefoot Contessa. Their cinnamon-and-nutmeg smell filled the kitchen. And for the first time since she'd gotten the bad NYU news, Jacqui actually felt like smiling.

"Hello, hello!" Mara said.

"Holla!"

Mara came over and hugged Jacqui. "You look so great!"

Jacqui twirled. She was wearing a blousy eyelet Derek Lam

halter top and slim gray plaid Bermudas. "So do you. Is that a Tory tunic? *J'adore!*"

Mara nodded and pulled out a seat from the counter, while the kids immediately dropped their oatmeal spoons and raided the muffins.

"My God, William, you've grown like a weed!" Mara said. "And Madison, you look so pretty in that shirt."

"It's Bill now. He doesn't like to be called William anymore," Jacqui said fondly. "And we found that shirt on sale at Jeffrey last week, didn't we, Mad?"

William gave Mara a shy smile and went back to his seat. Mara raised her eyebrows at Jacqui, who merely shrugged. For two summers, the boy had terrorized them with his hyperactive tantrums—it was hard to reconcile the Super Soaker–wielding brat with the quiet boy reading a book.

Mara ruffled Cody's hair and kissed Zoë.

"So, how was your first night on the 'love boat'?" Jacqui teased, making air quotes with her fingers as she collected the untouched bowls around the table.

Mara blushed and looked meaningfully at Ryan's younger siblings.

Jacqui nodded and quietly explained that as soon as their grandparents arrived, she and Mara could have some privacy. Kevin's parents were taking the kids to their estate on the far end of the island, where they would spend the day fishing in the pond and riding horses. The no-nonsense Perry elders didn't approve of nannies, and so Jacqui basically had the day off.

When the kids had left, Mara told Jacqui about the amazingly romantic dinner that Ryan had prepared, only to have it interrupted by a work assignment. "I had to leave him—I didn't really have a choice," Mara defended herself.

"Tough," Jacqui said.

"Yeah, but it's okay. We'll have three months together." Then she told Jacqui all about her new job and her crazy boss.

"That's fantastic, Mar. You're, like, a real reporter," Jacqui marveled. "I'm so proud of you, *chica*."

Mara beamed. Jacqui always knew the right thing to say.

They compared their respective graduation ceremonies, and the subject soon landed on their college choices.

"I'm still on the wait list at Dartmouth; can you believe?" Mara groaned. "I'm sooo bummed. How about you—did you hear from NYU yet?"

In an instant, her stomach sank. Jacqui couldn't think of a reply—she didn't want to own up to her rejection, especially after having given Mara the impression that she was a shoo-in. Plus, it hurt too much to admit it out loud. She had never felt so guarded in front of her friend before.

But Jacqui was saved the embarrassment of confessing by two loud, long beeps from the driveway.

"WHERE ARE MY HARAJUKU GIRLS?" Eliza bellowed from the front door of the house.

reunited once again, the three musketeers take a cigarette break

ELIZA CLIMBED OUT OF HER CAR. SHE WORE A WHITE strapless, empire-waist floor-length smocked jersey cotton dress that showed off her jutting collarbone and tanned shoulders. Perched on her button nose was a pair of oversized Dita sunglasses, the latest celebrity fashion obsession, the provenance of which she had tracked down to a boutique in West Hollywood. They were so big they obscured half of her face, but she had to have them. (Everyone else could wear run-of-the-mill Chanel and Gucci, but to be in the know, it was all about Dita!) Her hair was twisted into a long sexy French braid down her back. Her cheeks glowed and her teeth shone. She was the picture of summer, and the beat-up cowboy boots she wore added just the right edgy note.

Mara and Jacqui admired Eliza's dress and both immediately decided they wanted one too. That was the usual effect Eliza's clothes had on the female gender—you always wanted what she was wearing. Luckily, Eliza was one of those girls who happily shared her shopping secrets.

"It's so cute, no? Planet Blue in the 'bu. I was in Cali with my dad the other week. I have the number, so no panicking!" Eliza enthused as she kissed the two girls effusively on each cheek—a habit she'd picked up after a day working in the fashion studio. "Jacqui, no one does more to a pair of Bermuda shorts than you. Where did you get them? Old Navy? Are you serious? They look designer! Mar, your haircut is so good! And did you do something to your eyebrows? But before we catch up, can someone please get me a bottled water? I'm parched!"

Mara laughed and fetched a frosty Glaceau Smartwater from the kitchen and handed it to her. When she'd first met Eliza, she had written her off as some kind of princessy brat, but Eliza had certainly proved her wrong. Although Eliza strove to live in a world where the Sub-Zero was always filled with champagne and caviar, she still knew what it was like to eat leftovers out of a ten-year-old Kenmore in Buffalo.

"Check it out!" Eliza said, motioning to the black LR3 parked in the driveway as she twisted off the top of the bottle and took a long chug.

Mara nodded, impressed. Eliza had told them that her family had regained their former affluence, and the car was proof of their ascension. "It's tight," she agreed.

"Where're the rug rats?" Eliza asked.

"At their granny's," Jacqui explained. *"Agradeça o Deus."* Thank the Lord.

"So no one's here? Good. We can smoke," Eliza said, pulling

out a pack from a Chloé Silverado handbag. "You like? I know. I was bad," she admitted, referring to the bag's five-figure price tag.

The three of them made themselves comfortable on the front steps, catching up over cigarettes. It had occurred to all of them that this might be their last summer together—who knew where next year would bring them?—and the thought made them huddle closer together. Without it being said, all three of them were glad they had one more chance to have another sun-kissed season in the Hamptons to shop, play, and party their hearts out before college came calling.

The girly chitchat was momentarily suspended when a clattering taxicab pulled up to the driveway. A tiny girl stepped out of the back. She was a petite thing, an extremely pretty Korean girl with short brown hair in a pixie cut and cat's-eye tortoiseshell glasses. The driver helped her with her luggage—matching olive green Fendi logo suitcases—and she paid him with several crumpled dollar bills from her Gucci bag.

She consulted a piece of paper in her hand before glancing up at the girls. "Excuse me. This is Creek Head Manor, right?"

"Uh-huh." Mara nodded.

"Can I help you?" Jacqui asked.

The girl looked at the three of them intently, as if noticing them for the first time. "Oh my God!" she said. "You're *them*!"

"Them who?" Mara asked, turning to her friends with a confused expression.

"You're *famous!*" the girl shrieked. "You guys are the coolest girls in the Hamptons—I read all about you in *Teen Vogue!*"

Last summer, as a favor to Mitzi Goober, the three of them had been featured in a "Summer Girls" roundup in the magazine. Mara had been pictured on Garrett Reynolds's arm, stepping out of a Bentley. Eliza had been photographed in her sequined Sass & Bide minidress holding a clipboard in front of a nightclub. There'd even been a double-page centerfold of Jacqui in the outfit she'd worn for the finale at the fashion show.

"You're Mara, right?" the girl said, thrusting a hand toward Mara. "I saw you on Sugar Perry's reality show!"

"Oh. Thanks, I guess," Mara said, still a bit confused.

The girl nodded eagerly. "And you must be Eliza—the trendy one," she said, turning to Eliza.

"So that makes you Jacqui—my favorite!" she squealed, throwing her arms around the stunned bombshell.

Mara and Eliza nudged each other while Jacqui politely escaped the hug. "Favorite"? What were they, like characters in a television show?

The new girl looked like she was about to faint. "How cool is it that I'm going to be working with you this summer!"

"Working with us?" Eliza asked, her eyes narrowing, grinding her cigarette butt on the bottom of her shoe.

"I'm Shannon Shin. The new au pair! And I'm ready for the best summer of my life!"

misunderstandings go hand in hand with too many margaritas

OVER BLUE HYPNOTIQ MARGARITAS ON THE PATIO AT THE Sunset Hotel, the girls discussed the latest development in the Perry establishment. Eliza had driven the three of them to Shelter Island for a quick happy hour drink before she had to pick up Jeremy from work. He had started a landscape company that summer and had soon rounded up all his former employers as clients. They were going to rendezvous at his apartment in a few hours, and she wanted to fortify before the big event. Even though she'd decided she was finally going to lose her virginity, she didn't want to lose her nerve.

"Did you know you were getting help?" Eliza asked, lighting a cigarette and propping her feet on the ledge. They were sitting on the bar's wicker chairs that lined up against the low wall that faced toward the ocean.

Jacqui shook her head. "I guess Anna forgot to mention it. Big surprise."

Mara nodded. "The new girl seems very . . . enthusiastic." She was still struck by how Shannon had treated them—like they were celebrities.

"I think it's great," Eliza agreed. "At least you have someone to order around."

The three of them felt a little older—had it really been almost three years ago that they had first met? Seeing Shannon's fresh fifteen-year-old face reminded them of how young and naive they had been when they had accepted the au pair gig. Shannon had been happy enough to stay at the house by herself to wait for the children to get back while Jacqui snuck out for a quick drink with her friends. They found out Anna had hired the new girl the same way she had originally found the three of them—by posting an ad online. Shannon told them she had sent Anna a professional-looking portfolio, including a ten-page dossier of her skills, complete with moving testimonials from the children she had previously babysat. She had been hired immediately.

Jacqui still felt a little guilty about leaving her there alone on her first day, but then again, Eliza was right. She was in charge, and it would be good to have an extra pair of hands for the summer.

"So we need to have an awesome summer before we start college in the fall," Eliza said. "We need to be at the polo every Saturday afternoon. No exceptions. I hear it's going to blow up this year. Major, major people hosting the VIP tent."

"I've got a press pass," Mara said. "I'm covering it." She still couldn't believe she had merited one—but Sam Davis had handed it to her that afternoon. It was a laminated ID card that read PRESS in red capital letters above her name. Just looking at it gave Mara a thrill.

"Cool. I'm on the list. I'll get you on too, Jac," Eliza promised. Now that her family was back on their high perch, Eliza was confident in her ability to navigate the social stream. "Then there's the Art for Life benefit and the AIDS Luau. Maybe one weekend we should drive out to the North Fork to the vineyards for some wine-tasting?"

"*Perfeito.*" Jacqui nodded.

"How about a party on the boat, Mar?" Eliza asked.

"Sure. Maybe for the Fourth of July?" Mara said, thinking how pretty the sparklers would look off the deck. They could get a cooler full of beer and a few bottle rockets and Roman candles for the boys. Jeremy could probably hook them up if Ryan didn't know where to get them in town.

"I'll do the barbecue," Jacqui offered. "You guys have a grill on the boat, yes?"

"I'll ask Ryan, but I think I saw one," Mara said.

"How is Ryan?" Eliza asked, exhaling a smoke ring and keeping her voice light. She fiddled with the Claddagh ring Jeremy had given her for her birthday. It was an Irish wedding ring, and Eliza wore it with the heart facing inward to show that her heart was already spoken for.

"The boy surfs twenty-four seven. It's like there's salt water in his brain," Mara joked.

"So I've already been asked to join this eating club at Princeton," Eliza said.

"Are you going to do it? I heard they're so snobby," Mara chided.

"You *have* to—it's the only way to eat," Eliza replied. "Nobody eats in the cafeteria. Please!" Eliza didn't think it was being snobby, merely being practical. The eating clubs had better chefs, organic food; one even offered a vegan/macrobiotic diet. She didn't plan on gaining the freshman fifteen. She told them how she'd mapped out the next four years with the help of an insider's guide to the easiest classes and professors who were the most generous with grades. Cruise through the requirements the first two years, take a junior year abroad in Paris, then graduate. Nothing too taxing, since she was certain to take over her dad's company one day. It was what everyone expected her to do, especially her parents.

"Wow, you have it all worked out," Jacqui said admiringly. She felt a little sadness at that, since, for once in her life, she'd made plans as well, except hers hadn't quite panned out.

"I do like to plan, yes," Eliza said modestly. "How 'bout you, Mar? Any word?"

"Not yet." Mara frowned. "It's agonizing. They shouldn't be able to do this to a person! It's not fair."

"I know, that sucks, but Columbia could be awesome. It's in the city."

Mara nodded. "But Ryan won't be there," she said in a tiny, tiny voice. She ground her cigarette out in the plastic ashtray and watched as a group of kids folded up their volleyball net on the beach.

Eliza shrugged. "New Hampshire's not far."

"I suppose." Mara sighed.

"How 'bout you, Jac, what happened with NYU?" Eliza asked.

"Yeah, tell us. At least if I end up at Columbia, I'll know you'll be in the city," Mara prodded.

Jacqui put down her glass and cleared her throat. She felt her cheeks flush with embarrassment as she formed the words. "Yeah . . ."

"Yeah?" Mara echoed, interrupting.

"You got in?" Eliza squealed.

"Congratulations!" the two of them cheered.

Mara and Eliza gave Jacqui sloppy kisses and bear hugs. They knew how much she'd wanted NYU and how hard she'd worked for it.

Jacqui kept smiling. The smile remained frozen on her face long after the subject had switched to what time they would meet up at Sydney Minx's store-opening party the next evening. It was all a misunderstanding—but she hadn't bothered to clear it up. Well, what was the harm? She just didn't want to make it real just yet. Right then, she just wanted another drink with her friends.

temptation wears a bright blue bikini

A FLOCK OF SEAGULLS FLEW IN A TRIANGULAR FORMATION over the sky as Mara drove back to the harbor. Eliza dropped her off with a friendly wave. The three of them had spent the better part of the evening at Sunset Beach and, after waiting an hour for Eliza to sober up, had driven back to the mainland singing along to Gwen Stefani's album with the windows rolled all the way down so that the ocean breeze could blow through their hair.

"Be good!" Eliza called.

"Don't do anything I wouldn't do," Jacqui teased from the shotgun seat.

"That leaves . . . everything!" Mara replied, laughing and waving back.

She heard the sound of Ryan's voice from the deck. He was probably talking to one of his surfing buddies who had stopped by for a visit. Their first houseguests! Mara wondered if there was anything in the fridge she could put together as a snack for them. She felt a Martha Stewart moment coming on. It would be fun to show off their new domesticity.

Mara hurried across their pier and stepped onto the back

deck. She put her bag down in the living area and walked over to the front of the stern, where she found him. Ryan was on his knees, dressed only in his cotton pinstripe boxers, waxing the finish. He was sweaty, and Mara thought he'd never looked sexier in his life. There was only one problem.

This was no surfer dude.

A chick in a turquoise bikini scrubbed down the boat next to theirs. She leaned over her railing and splashed Ryan with suds from her sponge, and Ryan retaliated by throwing his rag at her.

Suddenly, Mara didn't feel very hospitable. The fantasy of serving hors d'oeuvres and cocktails went straight out the porthole.

Throughout the year, Mara had wondered how she would be able to stand it knowing that Ryan was the kind of guy who'd had so many girlfriends, and girls who were friends, and girls who wanted to be more than friends. The problem was he simply adored female company. He was a natural around women, having so many sisters, and was completely oblivious to the fact that Mara felt uncomfortable with how comfortable he was around the opposite sex. Especially those who could fill out a tiny turquoise string bikini.

"I'm just being friendly," Ryan would assure her. "You know you're the only girl for me." But the guy was a natural flirt—it was part of his charm—and as much as Mara didn't want to make him change, seeing him banter so easily with another girl didn't do a lot for her feelings of insecurity and self-esteem. It had been hard enough to get over the Eliza factor.

"Hey, you, have you been standing there for long?" he said.

"Not really," Mara said coolly.

"Tinker, this is my girlfriend, Mara," he said, taking Mara in his arms.

"Oh, hi!" Tinker said. "I've heard all about you," she said in a friendly manner.

"Tinker's in my frat," Ryan explained.

Mara nodded. She knew Ryan was in a coed fraternity at Dartmouth. Somehow, she'd assumed any girl who wanted to join a fraternity would be just one of the guys—but Tinker was one hundred percent babe.

"Anyway, like I told Ryan, my sisters and I are living on my parents' boat this summer," Tinker said.

Mara smiled and tried to look enthusiastic about the situation, then turned back to Ryan. "You stink," she told him.

"I do, do I?" he threatened, and pretended to smother her with his armpits.

"Stop." Mara giggled.

"C'mon," Ryan said. "Why don't we take a shower? We can get all clean . . ." he whispered. "And you can, you know, make up for deserting me last night. . . ."

As Mara's knees turned to jelly, she squeezed his hand tightly. She was going to let him know how sorry she was she'd left him all alone last night. How very, very, very sorry she really was. She shot him a wicked grin. "You are a really dirty boy," she said.

He replied by blowing softly in her ear.

sun-kissed

"Nice to meet you, um, Tinker!" she called, feeling a buzz of anticipation as Ryan led her by the hand down to the master suite, where they would make the most of the rainfall shower-head, the Jacuzzi, the king-size bed. . . .

too close for comfort

WHEN JACQUI ARRIVED BACK IN THE AU PAIR COTTAGE, she was startled to find that most of her belongings had been carelessly shoved into two small drawers and that a strange pillow was lying on the only single bed.

Shannon walked out of the bathroom in a robe, a towel wrapped around her head. "Oh, hi, Jacqui! I had to move some of your stuff since you took the whole closet. You probably didn't know I was going to be here, right? Anna's a bit of a spaz, I can tell."

Jacqui was about to reply, but the girl kept talking. "And I hope you don't mind, but my doctor says I have a back problem and I really can't sleep on the bunk bed. Is that all right?" The tiny girl batted her eyes and left Jacqui momentarily flabbergasted. She was supposed to be the senior au pair here, yet with one breath, Shannon had taken the best benefits of the room.

Jacqui didn't trust herself to reply; she was still tipsy from the margaritas and sour from the misunderstanding she'd left uncorrected. Instead, she started to pull out the drawers so she could fold her clothes more neatly, thinking of a plan.

* * *

An hour later, as they prepared the children's dinner, Jacqui told Shannon about how important the summer was going to be for them. It was certainly going to be an important one for Jacqui because if she was going to spend a fifth year in high school, she would need Anna to hire her for another full year.

"I just want to warn you, the first year I was here, we found out Anna fired the original au pairs before we even arrived. So we can't really slack off. It's not a total party, okay?" Jacqui said. "And the Perry kids can be a little difficult, especially Madison. We have to keep our eye on the basket all the time." Jacqui meant to say "eye on the ball," but she still mixed up her metaphors when she was flustered.

Shannon nodded as she cut up the carrots. "Oh, of course," she said effusively. "I'm really not worried, though. Kids love me."

Jacqui remained silent as she put the pasta pot on the stove to boil, a small smile on her face. With the Perry kids, Shannon had no idea what she was in for. . . .

At dinner, she introduced Shannon to the children. "Everyone, this is Shannon Shin. She's going to help me take care of you this summer."

Shannon got down on her knees and put her face right in front of Zoë's. She affected a high-pitched voice as she asked, "Hewow, Zoey. How are weed too-die?"

Zoë stared back at her balefully. "I'm well, thank you," she said in a clear voice.

Cody screamed when Shannon tried to embrace him and refused to leave Jacqui's side. "I hate you! I hate you! I hate you!" he kept saying, shaking his head at Shannon.

Feeling flummoxed, Shannon tried to befriend the older children. "Hi, I'm Shannon, and Jacqui tells me you're . . . Bill?" she asked, offering a hand to William.

William was rendered practically mute, and his face turned beet red when Shannon spoke to him. He stared at his plate and immediately stuffed his mouth with a spoonful of fettuccine.

Jacqui bit back a laugh. Just as she'd thought, the kids weren't going to be won over that easily. She even felt a little proud of them. She had earned their trust and love through hard work and dedication, and Shannon would have to do the same.

But there was still one more kid at the table. Madison Perry sat in front of a plateful of wilted lettuce leaves that she kept moving around with her fork.

Jacqui nudged Madison to eat, but instead of doing as Jacqui asked, Madison merely glared at Shannon. "Who's that? And what is she doing here?" she asked Jacqui.

"She's the new au pair," Jacqui explained. "Be nice."

Shannon came over to sit next to Madison. "Ooh, you have a TechnoMarine!" she gushed, motioning to Madison's diamond-encrusted pink watch.

"Uh-huh," Madison allowed, holding up her wrist so Shannon could examine it more closely. "My dad bought it at a fund-raiser.

It used to be Paris Hilton's. It comes with five different straps. My favorite's the pink alligator."

"That is so cool," she said. "I've always wanted one. I'm Shannon. You're Madison, right? I love your hair. Do you get it straightened? I'm can't wait to grow mine out so I can get it done too."

Madison beamed. The two of them bent their heads together, admiring Madison's watch. "You're twelve? You look older, so mature. I just turned fifteen," Shannon said. "We're practically like sisters!"

With one flattering compliment after another, soon Madison and Shannon were chatting just like two old friends. As Jacqui helped Cody cut his carrots, she couldn't help feeling a bit cheated.

eliza puts out an APB on a dress

THE PHONE WAS RINGING. *NOW-I-AIN'T-SAYIN'-SHE-A-GOLD-digger-but-she-ain't-messin'-wit'-no-broke-* . . . Eliza opened one eye. Jeremy groaned. She reached over his chest and rummaged on her bedside drawer for her cell.

"Uhloo?" she said while Jeremy buried his head underneath her pillow.

"Hmpprff," Jeremy complained.

"Shh!" she said, jokingly pressing the pillow onto his face but half terrified someone would hear him. She'd snuck him in late last night when he'd gotten off from work and she'd come back from drinks with the girls, but Assignment: Expiration Date hadn't quite gone as planned. Jeremy had spent the whole day planting Japanese maple trees and was so tired he could hardly keep his eyes open. They'd barely gotten to second base before Jeremy began snoring.

Eliza thought they could try again this morning. She was counting on her dad leaving early for his golf game and her mother for her charity committee meeting. Then she and Jeremy could have the rest of the house to themselves. She had meant to discreetly slip out of bed, brush her teeth, change into the lingerie set, and slide back under the covers so she could look perfect before he awoke. But she hadn't counted on an early-morning wake-up call from her least favorite person throwing her off schedule.

"Eliza!" a frantic voice exclaimed.

"Paige? What is it?" Eliza asked, immediately sitting up.

"It's an emergency!"

"What's wrong?" Eliza asked, her heart beating rapidly. Numerous dire scenarios filled her head: Sydney had changed his mind, he hated all the outfits she'd styled. Or the clothes had arrived and all the spray-painted parts had stained parts of the fabric that weren't meant to be painted. The paint had dried the wrong color.

"An outfit is missing," Paige said with panic-stricken urgency. "The one Vidalia is supposed to wear for the finale. I'm here at the boutique on Main Street with Sydney and we've unpacked everything, but we can't find it. It's not here."

"But I packed it myself," Eliza argued. "It has to be there."

"Well, it's not and Sydney's having a heart attack. You know it's the most important outfit in the show. The whole thing is ruined without it."

"I know. I know."

"You need to fix this. You packed that box," Paige insisted. "It's your fault if it's not at the show tonight. . . ."

"All right, don't worry. I'll take care of it," Eliza promised, trying not to panic herself. She clicked off the phone and sat pensively by the side of the bed. All thoughts of early-morning seduction were completely dismissed.

Think, Eliza, think, she admonished herself as she tried to remember the details of the previous night . . . the chronology of events . . . and tried to figure out what had happened: she'd asked Vidalia to remove the dress and put it in the hanger to be wrapped, but in all the frenzy, Eliza had forgotten to check whether the model had done so. She remembered Vidalia saying how she was going to some fancy dinner party that night and needed something fabulous to wear so the cosmetics executives at Estée Lauder would take her seriously and offer her an exclusive contract.

Eliza gasped. The damn model had snuck out in the outfit! She'd worn it to the Lauder dinner! Eliza was sure of it.

"What's happened? Everything okay?" Jeremy asked.

"Everything is going to be fine," Eliza said just as a Black Hawk helicopter thundered overhead. She looked out the window and wondered about the two-fingered logo painted on the side. It disappeared into the clouds, blasting hip-hop music.

Eliza picked up her purse from the side of the bed and fingered her titanium AmEx card. . . .

is there such a thing as an early-life crisis?

SHANNON WAS ALREADY IN THE SCREENING ROOM WHEN Jacqui arrived that morning. The new au pair was sitting at the head of the gaming table, chatting happily with Anna Perry.

"Oh, Jacqui, there you are. You know we do try to run these things on time, dear," Anna said, waving Jacqui toward the nearest seat.

Jacqui glared. "The, uh, hot water was out at the cottage," she explained.

"I should have warned you," Shannon said, an innocent look on her face. "I have to take really long showers because of my back condition. . . ."

Jacqui nodded curtly. That morning, she had woken up to find the bathroom door locked for a solid hour. She had decided to give the kids breakfast without the benefit of bathing and had returned to find only cold, freezing water coming out of the pipes for her own shower.

"I'm glad you guys have met. Shannon has a lot of experience and excellent references," Anna explained.

Jacqui gave the younger girl a sideways glance. Last night,

Shannon had admitted to Jacqui that despite her impressive resume, the only kids she'd ever babysat were her younger siblings. Still, Shannon looked the picture of innocence.

Anna clasped her hands. "So, here we are, another summer in the Hamptons!" she said, mustering a cheerful tone even though Jacqui had heard her and Kevin battling over the credit card bills last night. Anna was already on her third cup of coffee, and it was obvious the strain of her crumbling marriage was getting to her.

Jacqui opened her notebook, her pen poised to take notes on Anna's list of expectations for the children's educational, spiritual, and physical activities for the next three months.

"This year, I have nothing planned for the children," Anna announced.

Jacqui almost fell out of her chair. Every summer, Anna planned a strict, hour-by-hour regimented schedule and a list of unachievable goals she expected the children to accomplish and the au pairs to facilitate. Last year, there had even been an hour-long PowerPoint presentation.

"Nothing?" Jacqui asked, mouth agape.

"I've been reading a lot lately about 'mini-midlife crises'— about kids who are so thoroughly scheduled that they experience undue anxiety and juvenile stress syndrome. You know, like those Japanese kids who throw themselves out the window during finals," she said with a meaningful look toward Shannon.

"They call it *karoshi*," Shannon replied cheerfully. "Suicide due to overwork. It's rising among grade-schoolers especially."

"Right," Anna said a little nervously. "Anyway, I don't want that for the kids. Therefore, this summer is all about play. I want them to relax, enjoy themselves. Let them be free . . ."

"To do what they want," Shannon finished.

"Exactly. I think that's about it."

"That's it?" Jacqui asked, still incredulous.

"That's it," Anna said.

Jacqui couldn't believe it. No riding lessons, no surfing lessons, no kabala camp, no krav maga, no conversational French, Italian, and Cantonese? No ballet, no yoga, no Pilates, no Yogalates? The kids free to do whatever they wanted? Play video games, watch movies, go to the mall, swim, hang out with their friends . . . nothing educational or aspirational at all?

As they walked out of the screening room, Jacqui couldn't help but share with Shannon how different this summer was going to be compared to the ones before.

Shannon smiled craftily. "Who do you think sent her the *Time* article on stressed-out grade-schoolers? I know what these alpha moms are like. I'm here at the Hamptons for some fun, hello! By the way, you don't need to thank me."

Jacqui granted her new coworker a respectful nod. Shannon Shin might be a manipulative little wench, but one day at the Perrys' and she already knew how to work Anna. . . . Well, she might just come in handy.

"Did you get an invitation to the Sydney Minx opening?"

Jacqui asked her. "It's tonight, and it's supposed to be the best party of the summer."

"No," Shannon said, her face dropping. "I don't know anyone here but you, really."

"Don't worry."

"Is that an invitation?"

"I think it's a truce," Jacqui said, sotto voce.

"Excuse me?"

"Nothing. Now, let's decide what you should wear. . . ."

underneath ryan's perfect exterior lies the soul of pigpen

RYAN ASSURED MARA THAT AFTER A COUPLE OF DAYS, SHE wouldn't even notice the rocking of the boat, but Mara woke up from her afternoon nap feeling cranky and like she hadn't slept at all.

She'd spent the morning at the *Hamptons* office, tracking down background information for the Sydney Minx piece and calling in gift bag requests for Sam. Her editor demanded a gift bag from every event featured in the magazine even if she hadn't attended it personally. Sometimes, Sam called in gift bags from as far away as Europe if she heard the contents were particularly choice.

After work, Mara returned to the Catalina for a short nap before the evening's festivities. When she awoke, she realized she had only a half hour to get ready for the fashion show.

She walked out to the living room and found all of Ryan's gear haphazardly strewn around the room. His boxes had arrived by UPS truck from Hanover that morning, and the living room

111

looked like a branch of the Sports Authority. There were a wake-board, several snowboards, tennis and badminton rackets, lacrosse and hockey sticks, basketballs, golf balls, footballs. Ryan had once told her calling him a "jock" was an insult. The proper term, he'd explained, was *athlete*, since *jock* connoted a level of brutal small-mindedness to which Ryan certainly did not sub-scribe. His best friend from prep school was gay. All right, Mara thought, looking at all the sports paraphernalia. So he wasn't a jock . . . but he was certainly *athletic*.

One of the boxes was open, and Mara saw that it contained all manner of clothing, from clean T-shirts to dirty socks and towels to suit jackets that were still on hangers and wrapped in dry-cleaner's plastic. It appeared that Ryan had just tossed anything and everything into the nearest box without bothering to separate anything. Nestled in the pile of clothing, Mara saw CD jewel cases, cigarette boxes, an ashtray (dirty), a beer mug (clean), and even a trash can, complete with balled-up scraps of his term papers. Mara shook her head—she hadn't known Ryan was such a slob. Ryan had promised to get his stuff in order, but he'd apparently abandoned the project to hit the waves. Typical.

He sauntered in just as she was trying to excavate her second suitcase from underneath yet another one of his surfboards.

"Let me get that," he said, easily pulling up the board so she could reach for her bag.

"Sweetie, do you think we could kind of—well, clean up here a little bit?" Mara fretted.

"Sure, sure," he said, coming over to kiss her. He was wet with sand and smelled like the sea. His dark hair was plastered slick against his forehead. Normally, the sight of him in his black wet suit would have made her melt—but she was more interested in finding her invitation to the party and the list of people she had to get interviews with for her story.

"I can't find anything in this mess!" she complained. There were a ton of empties around the room from a night when his friends had stopped by. Mara's Martha Stewart fantasies of elegant entertaining had been quickly shattered, since the boys had preferred to eat cold pizza and drink cheap beer.

"Why are you getting all worked up over this fashion show?" Ryan asked.

Mara was beginning to get the impression he thought her job was pretty trivial, especially since several of the girls in his circle had penned the column in the past. It bothered her that he didn't understand that it was a big deal for her.

"Ryan, I'm not sure where the boutique is. And I don't even know how I'm getting there. Are you going to come with me?" she asked.

Ryan sank down onto the couch. Even though Mara didn't own it, she felt irritated to see the water from his suit seep into the Italian leather, where it would definitely leave a stain. It bothered her that Ryan wasn't even aware of things like that—the couch probably cost thousands of dollars, but what was such a small amount to a guy who already owned everything?

"Can I meet you there?" he asked, hooking a hand behind his back and unzipping the suit. "I need to shower and change."

"I guess I could get a ride," Mara conceded. She quickly dialed Lucky, who was fortunately not too far from Sag Harbor and was able to swing by.

"Cool," Ryan said, planting a kiss on her forehead before he walked, whistling, into the shower.

Mara shrugged as she unzipped her suitcase. He was the love of her life, but sometimes it was maddening how careless he could be. . . . Mara was starting to discover that the path of love wasn't always smooth.

Sometimes, it was littered with dirty beer cans.

working hard or hardly working?

NOW, *THIS* WAS WHAT SUMMER WAS SUPPOSED TO BE LIKE. . . .

With Anna's decree of full summer freedom ringing in their heads, Jacqui had decided that she and Shannon would just hang out by the pool the whole day. William was absorbed in a book, Madison was tanning on a raft floating lazily in the middle of the pool, and Zoë and Cody were hanging out in the shallows, practicing headstands in the water.

Shannon was zoned out underneath the umbrella, wearing a skimpy black maillot one-piece, and Jacqui sat beside her in her new red French-cut bikini. That morning, she had purchased her new swimwear at one of the mobile J. Crew trucks that roamed the Hamptons for just this kind of emergency. Jacqui liked how the trunks on her suit could switch from boy shorts to a sexy high cut with just a few twists to the sides of the fabric.

Jacqui closed her eyes and felt the sun warm her face and relax her tense muscles. After a few minutes, she sat up on the chair and flipped through the latest issue of *W*. This was the life—the kids entertained, her coworker now a friend, a pitcher of icy lemonade by her side. She settled in for a good juicy read on the latest socialite scandals.

Then from the other side of the pool, behind the tall hedges, she heard a *thump, thump, thump.* Silence. Then *thump, thump, thump.* The noise was distracting, and she couldn't concentrate on her magazine. Finally, she got up to investigate.

She walked past the thick greenery that separated the house from the Reynolds eyesore, the hundred-thousand-square-foot monstrosity erected by the Perrys' bombastic neighbors. Rising above the hedges was a huge inflatable plastic jumping castle, a puffed-out balloonlike structure that contained three tumbling, jumping, and laughing guys inside it. Guys who looked really familiar . . .

"Excuse me!" Jacqui yelled.

The tumbling abruptly stopped as all three boys looked her way, each wearing a goofy smile. She couldn't help but grin back. In the light of day, these boys were seriously handsome. This time, NYU completely faded to the back of her mind. Who needed to worry about college when there were hotties around?

"Greetings and salutations," Grant Kotack said, making an impressive leap from the air mattress to the ground in front of her. "If I'm not mistaken, I do believe we've met before," he said in his silky southern accent.

"It was a very short meeting—unfortunately," Duffy pointed out, taking huge steps on the billowing plastic and ending with a cartwheel onto the grass.

"Almost broke our hearts," Ben agreed, following his friends out of the tumbling castle.

Jacqui wasn't embarrassed about what had happened during her midnight swim— she was proud of her body and didn't think there was anything to be ashamed about.

"I'm Jacqui Velasco. I work for the Perrys," she said, offering a hand to the nearest boy, the shaggy-haired one with the sideburns.

"Grant Kotack," Grant smiled, pleased that she'd come up to him first. He kissed the back of her hand with courtly, old-fashioned grace, which was pleasing to see in a boy who wore painter's pants and an oversized T-shirt with a Reese's peanut butter cup logo emblazoned on it. "A pleasure."

"John Duffy," said the tall, lanky, towheaded one, interrupting their greeting. He was WB-star cute, with a square jaw, ashy-white blond hair falling in his eyes, and the kind of grin that grew slowly from his lips and lit up his whole face. "You can call me Duffy or Duff. Everyone does."

"Ben Defever." The third guy nodded. He'd put on a pair of thick black glasses and looked not unlike Rivers Cuomo from Weezer, one of Jacqui's favorite bands. "Can we help you?"

"Do you guys work for the Reynoldes?" she asked.

"The who?" Duffy asked with a wide smile.

"The uptight bastards who own this joint," Grant said, winking at Jacqui.

"We rented it this summer. It's insane. Do you know there's a saltwater pool stocked with tropical fish in the back? With a

117

grotto?" Ben asked, adding shyly, "You'll have to check it out with us sometime."

"How about now?" Duffy suggested. "Now's a good time, right? I'll get the scuba masks!"

"Only if you want to," Ben assured in a sincere tone.

"Maybe later," Jacqui said, still smiling. Mara had told her all about it last summer. She blushed—Duffy was so cute and boy-ish, Grant the image of an indie-rock guitar god, and Ben just adorable with those glasses. And there it was—a definite tingle up her spine, the feeling she'd been missing all year.

"What about a jump?" Grant asked, jerking a thumb in the direction of the inflatable castle.

"Sure, but I've got a couple of kids here too—can they come?" Jacqui asked.

"Yours?" Duffy asked, looking perplexed.

"No, I'm the au pair." Jacqui laughed.

"Oh, good, because for a while there, you scared us," Grant teased, which let Jacqui know that Duffy had just been fooling with her.

"The more the merrier!" Ben offered. "Bring them on!"

Jacqui smiled her thanks and ran to tell the kids the good news. She brought them over, along with Shannon, whose eyes grew wide at the sight of the three cute boys.

"What's going on? Hi, I'm Shannon!" she said, smiling broadly at the three guys, her hands on her slim hips. "Cool castle!"

But when Jacqui was around, like all boys, Grant, Ben, and Duffy could hardly see, much less hear, anyone else.

nobody ever said college humor was mature

SYDNEY MINX'S BOUTIQUE WAS IN THE MIDDLE OF THE EAST
Hampton main street, lit up with two spotlights that beamed
Sydney's initials into the sky. There was the typical crush of people
attempting to gain entrance, waving their pink-and-gold invita-
tions vainly at the phalanx of unsmiling PR girls who were only
letting in the press and VIPs.

Mara flashed her pass and was immediately ushered inside.
She spotted Jacqui at the bar, trying to get the attention of the
bartender.

"Where's Eliza?" Mara asked, yelling over the blaring techno
music. She looked around—for the party of the season it was surprisingly low-key, or maybe Mara had attended enough of these
events over previous summers to finally feel jaded by them—a
few socialites here, a few B-list celebrities there, a goodie bag . . .
ho hum. All in all, it wasn't that much different from the standard boutique opening. It was possibly even just a teeny bit boring. Hopefully the fashion show would change that. In the
middle of the store stood a raised runway covered in plastic.

Jacqui shrugged. She craned her neck and tried to catch the

bartender's eye, feeling slightly irritated. She usually had no problem getting a guy's attention, but the bar was mobbed and Jacqui's request barely registered.

"Champagne, madam?" Duffy asked, suddenly appearing with a flute and placing it in Jacqui's hand.

"Oh, thanks! And one for my friend too?" she asked.

"Not a problem," Ben said, appearing with another flute. Jacqui passed it to Mara. They toasted quickly and took long sips from their respective glasses.

"There's more where that came from," Grant assured them, topping off their glasses with a bottle of Veuve Clicquot hidden underneath his arm.

"Where'd you get that?" Jacqui asked.

"We have our ways," Ben said mysteriously.

"Nicked it from the kitchen." Duffy grinned, revealing two more bottles underneath his canvas coat.

"With a healthy bribe to the bartender," Grant explained. "Hey, you two clowns owe me, by the way."

Mara and Jacqui giggled. The three boys formed a protective half circle around them.

"Guys, this is Mara. Mar, these are the guys," Jacqui said, introducing them. Mara smiled and thanked them for the drinks.

"Where's Shannon?" Mara asked. She'd heard the latest about the au pair's machinations concerning the bed and the closet but agreed with Jacqui that as long as Shannon had been responsible for Anna's change of heart, it was worth a few inconveniences.

"Over there," Jacqui said, and Mara looked over to where the dark-haired girl was ferociously going through the racks of clothing one by one. Shannon reminded her of someone, Mara thought. Someone who shopped as if executing a military operation. It struck her—Shannon was a lot like Eliza. Or at least, shopped a lot like Eliza: as if her life depended on it.

"It's kind of hot in here, isn't it?" Jacqui said to no one in particular as she fanned the neckline of her vintage Oscar de la Renta dress.

"I'll take care of it!" Duffy exclaimed, quickly springing into action. He was so thrilled to have a task he almost knocked over a nearby mannequin. "Hey, buddy!" he called to the nearest cater-waiter. "Turn up the air, yo!" he called as he ran after the guy.

"Don't bother—I know where the HVAC is!" Ben argued, nudging Duffy to the side so *he* could fulfill Jacqui's latest request.

"Stay right here," Grant whispered, giving her arm a squeeze. "I know the guy who's running the party. I'll get it done."

"Who are they?" Mara asked when the three boys disappeared into the throng. "Your slaves?"

Jacqui laughed. "They're cute, aren't they?"

"Not bad."

"They're the guys who started DormDebauchery.com—there was a big piece in the Sunday Styles section about them a few months ago, remember? They started the web site their freshman year at Harvard, and last spring their IPO took them to, like, several hundred million dollars."

Mara nodded in recognition. The web site was a paean to college humor—selling T-shirts screen-printed with slogans like the
punch line to a famous *SNL* skit, "More Cowbell," and jokes
concerning teenage abstinence, proclaiming, "I gave my word to
stop at third." They were famous for their "Shocker" logo—a vul-
gar hand gesture (not the usual one) of two fingers held up in a
crooked *V*, which they'd made into the huge foam fingers normally found at football games. Ryan had once explained to Mara
what "The Shocker" was, and she'd been disgusted for a day and
then amazed at how dirty boys' minds could be. But what was
most amazing was how young and rich they were. None of them
was over twenty-one.

"Anyway, they rented out the Reynolds castle this summer. It's
their first summer in the Hamptons, so I told them I'd show
them around," Jacqui explained.

Mara raised an eyebrow. "All three of them?"

"I'm just having some harmless fun." Jacqui laughed.

"Oh, wait, there's Sydney. I should go—I need to get an interview," Mara said, spying the designer mingling in the crowd.

She passed her champagne glass into Jacqui's hand, almost
running over a tuxedoed waiter bearing a tray of canapés as she
chased the rotund designer around the crowded room.

"Sydney, hi! Mara Waters from *Hamptons*; we're doing a story
on you. . . . Can I ask you a few questions?" she asked, thrusting
her iPod voice recorder in his face. She'd bought it soon after
finding out about the assignment.

"Not right now," Sydney said, hiding his face behind his black fan. "As you can see, I'm extremely busy."

"I know, I'm so sorry to bother you, Mr. Minx, but if I could just get some quotes?" Mara asked, feeling intimidated by Sydney's imperiousness.

"Paige! Paige!" Sydney suddenly shouted, taking no notice of Mara. "Talk to my assistant, Paige. She'll take care of what you need. . . ."

"Oh, okay. I guess," Mara said, defeated, as she switched off her recorder. "Do you think you'll have time after the show to chat?"

"Regina, darling! You look fabulous! Yes, thank you. It's crazy, right? And Cecily! You're wearing it! Love!" Sydney said, disappearing into a crowd of socialites congratulating him on the opening and taking no further notice of Mara.

Mara stood to the side, patiently waiting for him to finish his conversation. "Mr. Minx, do you think—"

"Can you move? You're blocking my light," Sydney ordered, cutting her off before she could finish her sentence. "Paige!" he yelled. "What's the ETA on that dress?"

"Eliza said she'd be here any minute now," Paige assured him, looking harried.

"She better be," Sydney threatened. "The show starts in minutes!"

Mara felt upset and flustered. She'd been brushed aside like an inconsequential minion, like someone who didn't have her own column in the area's most popular magazine. Maybe Eliza could help get her on the inside track—but Eliza was nowhere to be found.

Mara tried not to panic, but if she didn't get an interview with Sydney, how on earth was she going to file the story?

eliza turns main street into an haute couture drop zone

MARA WAS STILL CHEWING ON HER NAILS, WORRIED ABOUT the fate of her assignment and wondering where the hell Ryan was. She'd tried calling him on the boat, but he hadn't picked up the phone. He really should have arrived at the party by now. She was contemplating calling him again when the lights in the store dimmed and the raised runway was illuminated in a pink glow. The guests' conversations hushed, and they clapped halfheartedly, manicured fingernails clinking against the crystal.

Runway-staple French techno music wailed from the overhead speakers, and the first model, dressed in a spray-painted tiger-print caftan, walked out of the back room and onto the platform. Model after model followed, each wearing a variation on the jungle theme, and Mara noticed that the clothes were actually interesting to look at. With their tie-dyed and spray-painted details, they represented a radical and slightly avant-garde departure for the Sydney Minx line.

Mara took copious notes while Jacqui chugged champagne.

125

After fifteen minutes, the final model, wearing a tangerine tunic and turquoise hot pants airbrushed with gold flecks, abruptly stopped mid-walk. The music was suddenly drowned by an ear-splitting noise coming from outside the store. The audience turned away from the runway and crowded to the front of the store to look out the window to find out what had caused the interruption.

Hovering above the store was an ominous-looking black army helicopter.

"Is that our Black Hawk?" Duffy asked.

"Nah—no logo. Must be a rental."

Mara and Jacqui followed the crowd outside. A rope ladder was being lowered from the helicopter, and a familiar figure was climbing down toward the sidewalk.

"Oh my God! It's Eliza!" Mara gasped.

So it was. Eliza descended from the rope ladder wearing a daringly cut, shredded chiffon dress and thigh-high crocodile boots. She had several chunky interlocked gold chain rope necklaces around her neck. As the wind kicked up by the helicopter blades whipped the dress around, Eliza sauntered straight from the rope ladder to the sidewalk, into the store, and onto the runway stage without breaking her confident stride.

The photographers rewarded her with a shower of flashbulbs—and the momentarily stunned crowd broke into enthusiastic cheers and wolf whistles. They had seen a lot of things in the Hamptons—but a fashion show finale via helicopter was a definite first.

Eliza grinned as she posed for the camera, bathed in the klieg lights. It had worked! She'd made it happen! She'd managed to track down Vidalia at the model's fifth-floor walk-up in the East Village. At first, she had planned on having Vidalia do the honors, but the model had been so hung over from the party the night before, there was no way she was going to look presentable for the fashion show. So Eliza put the dress on herself and thanked God she was a sample size. Then she chartered a helicopter flight on her new Marquis Jet Card (thank you, AmEx!) that took her from New York to the Hamptons in a snap. Those nifty little Black Hawks sure came in handy.

She looked toward where Paige and Sydney were standing in the corner. She couldn't see that well because the flashbulbs blinded her, but she was certain they were going to congratulate her on a job well done. She'd pulled it off all by herself—this was surely a spectacle that the Hamptons would be talking about for the rest of the summer.

mayday! mayday!

"WE DID IT!" ELIZA CROWED, STEPPING OFF THE RUNWAY and holding out her arms to envelop Paige and Sydney in a hug. "Isn't this amazing?" she cried as the photographers continued to snap her picture.

Only when the flashbulbs died down did Eliza realize that Sydney and Paige did not share in her happiness one bit. She'd expected Paige to be a little jealous, sure, but wasn't she the one who'd told Eliza she had to "fix" it or else? Why couldn't she at least look a tiny bit happy that she'd pulled it off? Instead, Paige looked like she was going to vomit, and Sydney's eyes were murderous. Hello, had she missed something here?

The smile evaporated from Eliza's face. "What's wrong? Did you guys not like the helicopter? Don't worry, I've got it covered. I have a Marquis Jet Card. I won't charge it to the company—my treat."

"Paige, you know what you have to do," Sydney said ominously before turning his back without even acknowledging Eliza's presence.

"Eliza, can I have a word?" Paige asked coldly.

What now? She'd managed to save the evening—and they

were acting like she'd done something terrible. As if she'd failed to deliver the goods instead of coming through with a bang. This was so not what she expected. She followed Paige to the back room.

"What's going on?" she asked. Her face glistened from the heat of the photographer's lights.

"You're fired," Paige said flatly. Eliza noticed Paige couldn't quite conceal a note of glee in her voice. Paige had wanted this all along. The little brownnoser, who couldn't style an outfit if you put a Bedazzler to her head, had just been waiting for Eliza to trip up. Eliza just wasn't sure how she'd managed to make such a mess of things. Something didn't compute.

"But I don't understand. . . ."

"This night was about *Sydney*. Sydney Minx. And you know what's going on out there? What people are talking about?"

"What?" Eliza asked, still confused.

"You. That's who. Who's the girl from the helicopter? Who's the model who flew down? Who's the girl in the dress? Who's *the girl*. It's all about you. I had to teach a couple of reporters from the *New York Post* how to spell your name!"

Eliza almost said, "They know exactly how to spell my name at the *Post*!" She wisely kept her mouth shut. "C'mon, Paige, cut me some slack," Eliza pleaded. "Talk to Sydney. He listens to you. I mean, I got the dress back, didn't I?"

"You *got* the dress, but you *took* the press," Paige replied.

As if on cue, a tall reporter from the *East Hampton Star* gossip column tapped on the side door. "Hey—chopper girl. Can I get a quote?"

Paige rolled her eyes.

"Sure—be with you in a bit." Eliza smiled. When the reporter left, she grabbed Paige's arm. "You can't be serious. You guys can't do this to me. This is my internship for the summer. My parents will freak if they find out!"

Eliza was devastated. She had just found her passion, found that there was more to life than a MasterCard. She was really looking forward to learning more about the fashion industry. How could they take it away from her now?

"You're fired, Eliza. Please remove that dress and vacate the premises immediately."

And just like that, chopper girl went down in flames.

in celebrity journalism, noncooperation is never a problem

THE PARTY WAS OVER, AND JACQUI AND THE THREE GUYS from the web site had departed to continue the hoopla at the Reynolds castle. Mara caught a ride with them and asked them to drop her off at the Starbucks a few blocks from the harbor. She could grab a double latte to fuel up, and the coffee counter was close enough to the dock that she could walk home.

She was totally screwed. She had no story. Sydney Minx had completely ignored her the whole evening and refused to give her an interview. And she had four pages to fill! Dozens of column inches! The story had already been laid out by the art department; they were just waiting for her text to arrive.

What was she going to do . . . ? This time, she was going to get canned for sure. Sam Davis had handed her a plum assignment—but Mara had ended up with egg in her face. It wasn't even as if she were trying to nail an interview with the president, for God's sake. Sydney Minx was a fashion designer! Fashion designers lived for press! Yet somehow she had bungled it again.

At this rate, Mara decided she should forget about becoming a serious journalist, since she couldn't even hack it as a celebrity reporter.

A few people were idling by the coffee shop, and after Mara collected her double-shot no-fat venti cup, she took a seat by the window, BlackBerry in her clammy hand. Better to do it now than later . . .

"Hi, Sam? It's Mara."

"Hey, there." The noise of a squalling infant filled the background.

"I'm so sorry to call so late. . . ."

"Not a worry at all. What's up?" Sam asked, sounding chipper and professional.

"It's just, about the Sydney Minx cover," Mara hedged.

"Uh-huh? Heathcliff, put down the baby, put down baby Kathy right now! Mommy says!" Sam ordered.

"I didn't get—" Mara said hesitantly.

"I said listen to Mommy! Bad Heathcliff! Bad boy!" Sam screeched.

"I didn't—"

"What did you say?" Sam asked, a little breathlessly. "Sorry, it's a madhouse around here. Three kids under the age of five, and the nanny's gone for the day."

Mara made a sympathetic noise. "Sydney wouldn't do the interview—I don't have anything for the piece. I'm so sorry," Mara confessed, gripping her coffee cup tightly.

"The old diva is still holding that *Them* piece against me, huh?" Sam asked, a trace of amusement in her voice.

Mara was surprised to hear her boss laugh as if nothing was wrong.

"Well . . . that's okay. We'll just do a write-around."

"What's that?"

"You call people close to Sydney to give you quotes—people who knew him back then, people who know him now, people who know how his mind works and what he's like in private. We need at least two to go on the record, and everyone else can be "a close source" or an "insider." You did some research today, right? Go back to LexisNexis, use our account—and we'll just write the story around him without his input."

"We can do that?"

"We do it all the time," Sam assured her. "Standard practice."

"Oh."

"So, three thousand words by tomorrow morning?"

"Right," Mara promised, grateful to have been saved from a future of arranging canapés on a platter. She was so glad not to have been fired she didn't realize she still didn't know exactly where to begin. But that was okay. She'd just realized she had a friend who was *very* close to the story indeed.

playing designer deep throat

FIRED.

Given the boot.

Voted off the island.

Torch extinguished.

Like a failed contender on one of those reality shows wherein the steely-eyed, pompadoured billionaire or the former supermodel or the convicted lifestyle guru or the flak-jacketed adventure guide somberly handed you your butt on a platter and ushered you to the nearest exit and confessional cam.

She stood alone in the cramped quarters of the staff bathroom in the back of the store and tried not to cry. Instead, she took off the gold chains one by one and hung them on the door hook. She unzipped the crocodile boots and unbuttoned the chiffon dress, then hung it carefully on a padded hanger. Paige had barked her orders without even pausing to wonder what Eliza would wear once she took it off. Thankfully, Eliza had been able to grab a goodie bag before they were all gone. She put on one of the complimentary Sydney Minx T-shirts. It was a size large, so it fell all the way down her thighs, as big as a dress. It would do.

She walked out of the bathroom barefoot, wearing only the T-shirt. In her handbag, her Treo rang. What now?

This-shit-is-bananas, B-A-N-A-N-A-S . . . her Treo chirped.

Mara.

"'Lo?" Eliza greeted.

She listened while her friend told her tale. Mara was having some problem with her article since Sydney wouldn't give the interview.

"So I need some names, people who will talk about him, what he's like to work with, where he gets his ideas, that sort of thing," Mara said. "And anyone who can give us any juicy insider stuff. Do you think you can help?"

Even through her cloud of humiliation, Eliza spotted clearly an opportunity for revenge.

"No problem," she said. "You should talk to his former partner, Richard Mendelsohn—he financed the line until they parted ways last year. And a few of his design associates; some of them don't work there anymore. His socialite friends. He used to hang out with my friend Taylor's mom, Pringle. Oh, and Anna Perry too. She knows him from way back. They'll have tons of scandalous stories, I'm sure." A vindictive smile appeared on Eliza's face.

"You are the best!" Mara said gratefully.

"Yeah, that's me. The best." Eliza sighed.

"Liza, is something wrong? You sound weird."

"No—it's nothing. I'm just tired," Eliza dismissed. Revenge was sweet, but it offered little consolation. Getting Sydney crucified in print wouldn't do much to get her job back. She suddenly wished she hadn't been so backstabbing but justified her snarkiness by telling herself she was helping a friend.

"Okay," Mara said doubtfully. "Insane entrance, by the way. It's all everybody's talking about."

That's the problem, Eliza thought, but she didn't say anything to Mara. They said their good-byes and Eliza hung up. She walked out to the front of the store, looking for Jeremy. He had texted earlier to say he was running late because of a client meeting but that he would meet her outside as soon as it was over.

She found him standing in front of his truck, talking animatedly to Paige on the now-deserted red carpet. Come again? How and why did they know each other? She saw him give Paige a kiss on the cheek. Eliza hung back in the shadows, feeling like an intruder.

When Paige finally disappeared in a taxi, Eliza walked up to him, careful about where to step.

"Hey, babe." Jeremy grinned, giving her a quick hug. "Is this what the beautiful people are wearing this summer? T-shirts? What happened to your shoes?"

"How do you know her?" Eliza asked, climbing up into the truck without bantering back.

"Who?" Jeremy asked, backing out from the curb and putting an arm around Eliza's headrest.

"That girl you were just talking to. Paige McGinley."

"Oh, Paige. We grew up on the island together," he said. "Old friend of mine. She really climbed up the corporate ladder quick, huh? Pretty impressive. Do you work for her?"

Great, Eliza thought. Just what she needed to hear. Jeremy was fraternizing with the enemy. "It's a long story."

"Oh yeah? What'd I miss?" he asked, since he'd arrived at the party too late to witness her star-making entrance.

"Nothing," she replied, shaking her head. She didn't want to get into it just then.

mara's sense of humor floats away with the tide

THE FOAMY LATTE WAS A WELCOME PICK-ME-UP, AND, ARMED with the data from Eliza's e-mail, Mara felt pumped and ready to pull an all-nighter and write her article. She walked from the Starbucks back to the Sag Harbor dock. The boats were rocking gently, and Mara walked down the length of the pier until she realized she'd passed their spot—where was the *Malpractice*? She walked back and forth until she finally realized: it was just not there.

The boat—and, more importantly, her computer—were gone!

Stolen! was the first thing that came to mind. . . . Call 911! Ryan hadn't made it to the event, so something terrible must have happened! She had to report a boat-jacking! Her imagination ran wild with Colombian drug dealers and illegal arms merchants hijacking the yacht for their dire purposes—for a moment, she was utterly convinced Ryan had been kidnapped!

A minute later, she realized she was being completely ridiculous. The boat hadn't been pirated or stolen. Ryan had obviously gone for a midnight sail. She guessed he felt that was more important than meeting her at the party.

She punched his number frantically on her BlackBerry. Her

computer was on that boat, and her article was due in a couple of hours. But there was no service in the bay, and the closest Mara got to reaching him was when an automated voice informed her, "The number you are trying to reach cannot be completed as dialed. Please check the number and try again."

Shit.

She looked around frantically and noticed a couple of kids from the boat across the way pulling out of their dock on two Seadoo jet skis. "You guys going out to the bay?" she asked.

"Yeah, someone's throwing a huge bash on a yacht."

That sounded like Ryan, all right.

"Can I get a ride?"

"Hop on."

They cruised the water until they spotted the *Malpractice*. Its floodlights were on, a wild party in full swing, the boat's speakers thumping out bass lines. Several people were bobbing by the side of the water in lifesaver vests, making use of the diving board off the port side. Another kid was scaling the masthead to run up a pirate flag.

The jet ski pulled up by the side of the boat, and Mara hoisted herself on deck, her blood boiling. When she found him, she swore she would . . . she would . . .

"Mara!"

Ryan scooped her up in his arms. "You made it! I left you all these messages."

He had a big grin on his face and an even bigger beer stein in his hand. "I was worried you'd miss the first big bash of the summer." He looked absolutely psyched to see her and planted a big smooch on her lips.

What messages? Mara wondered. She hadn't received one call from him. "You didn't come to the show," she accused.

"I fell asleep," he said sheepishly. "By the time I got up, I knew it would be over. And then Tinker and her sisters came by, and then we called some people . . . and we got some beer . . . and . . ."

And decided to have the party of the century, Mara thought. It did look pretty fun, but she didn't have time for socializing. She was on deadline.

"C'mon, let's get you a drink," Ryan said.

"You *left* me," Mara said, her anger not so easily assuaged.

"What are you talking about?"

"I got to the dock and it was gone—this boat is *my home*, Ryan, don't you understand? For the summer. Where I *live*. My computer is here. And I have a job. And I got there and the boat was missing and—"

"Hold on—hold on—I left the number for a water taxi on your phone," he said. "Didn't you get my voice mails?"

"No," she said.

"I kept calling," he insisted, looking perplexed.

"Did you call my BlackBerry or my old number?" she asked. "Because I told you to only call me on the work phone. I'm not using the old one anymore."

"Oh," he said, smiling sheepishly. "I forgot."

She turned away from him. Didn't he ever listen to her? And where did he get off hanging out with cute girls when she was at work? Did he even know how bad it sounded?

She stormed down to the main cabin without another word, leaving Ryan looking hurt and irritated on the deck. "Mara, c'mon, don't be that way!"

A couple of guests were making out on the couch in the living room, but she hardly noticed them as she walked straight into the captain's quarters. She slammed the door with a bang and walked over to her desk. She turned on her computer with a vengeance.

When she was done with the piece, she would *kill* him. But first, she had to make a few phone calls.

to whom much is given, much can be taken away. . . .

"C'MON, WHAT'S WRONG?" JEREMY RAN A HAND THROUGH his curly chestnut hair and stuck his upper lip out at Eliza. "What did I do to get the silent treatment?" he asked, mystified by her actions. "I thought you were going to spend the night at my place," he added, a little hurt at the change of plans.

Eliza remained silent, thinking, *Paige McGinley. Just an old friend. We grew up here on the island.* Terrific. The woman who'd just handed her the biggest humiliation of her life was an "old pal" of her boyfriend's. Nothing could have made Eliza feel worse.

She'd planned to spend the night with Jeremy at his apartment in Montauk—she'd already told her parents she was going to sleep over at a friend's house, and her ass was covered. She'd even stashed an overnight bag with her lingerie set in the back of his truck that morning.

She'd thought that after making such a triumphant splash at the fashion show, she would cap off the evening by handing over her V card. And she had wanted to—*really* wanted to—but after having her ego stomped on, she just didn't feel like it tonight. All she wanted to do now was hoover a tub of Ben & Jerry's and fall asleep watching *Room Raiders*.

Jeremy's truck idled on her driveway with the lights off. "Are you sure you don't want to come over?" He put a hand on her knee and began to massage it. His strong fingers worked their way down to her calf muscles, kneading them gently.

Eliza hesitated. She did want to—but she wanted their first time to be perfect, and the evening was already ruined for her.

"I wish I could, but I forgot, I told my parents I would go to some bird-watching thing with them tomorrow, and I need to get up early," she said reluctantly. It was a white lie—her dad had invited her to join them, except she'd already said no.

He lifted his hand from her knee and put it around her shoulders, drawing her close so that she was pressed against his chest. His fingers lightly caressed her arm, sending electric currents up her spine. "C'mon, stay. I want to show you my new apartment. I cleaned up just for you," he said huskily.

Eliza melted a little at that. She should just go with him—who cared about Paige? But then the memory of Jeremy kissing Paige on the cheek soured the moment and strengthened her decision.

"I can't. I wish I could. Next time, okay?" she said, kissing him quickly on the lips. "I'll call you."

She waved at him from the front steps, watching as the truck disappeared beyond the hedges to the private easement on the property. She walked into the house and found her parents in the kitchen, waiting for her. Her dad was holding a stack of credit card bills in his hands.

"Hi, Mom, hi, Dad," she said, giving them quick pecks on the cheek.

"I thought you were spending the night at Taylor's," her mother said.

"Change o' plans," Eliza said breezily. "What are you guys still doing up?"

"We received a phone call today from American Express."

Eliza nodded as she opened the stainless steel freezer drawer and poked around for the cartons of ice cream she knew were inside. She found a pint of Phish Food and began digging into it with a spoon, straight from the carton.

"Did you buy a Marquis Jet Card?" her mother asked. "And please, use a bowl. Were you brought up in a barn?"

"Uh-huh." She nodded, shoving a heaping spoonful into her mouth.

"The barn or the jet card?"

"Jet," Eliza said, her voice muffled by the ice cream.

"And you chartered a helicopter from New York to East Hampton today?"

"Uh-huh," she repeated, licking the spoon.

"Who told you to be so extravagant? That card is for *emergencies*," her mother emphasized.

But it *was* an emergency . . . at least, it had seemed like one that morning. "You and Daddy have NetJets, and I thought . . ." Eliza said in her defense, reminding her parents that they were subscribers to a private jet service as well.

"Eliza, we already bought you a car for the summer. This is outrageous. Eighteen-year-old girls do not charter private helicopter flights. We've canceled the account," her mother told her, her tone dropping low and cold. "And Daddy and I found out that all of your other credit cards are already maxed out. Those cards were your allowance for the summer."

Uh-oh.

"You really need to learn the value of things. You can't spend money like water. This kind of behavior is what got us into trouble in the first place. I'll need the cards back," her mother said sternly.

"Every one?" Eliza asked, stricken. She looked plaintively at her father. Her dad always let her do whatever she wanted, and money was never an object when it came to his little girl. But this time he merely shook his head and didn't look her in the eye. This totally *blew*. Usually her mother was the strict one, but if her father was also upset, then she was definitely in the doghouse. Make that the poorhouse. How was she supposed to get by without the help of her friends Visa and MasterCard?

"Every one," her mother repeated, holding out her palm.

"But what am I going to do for cash?" Eliza asked, reaching into her purse and relinquishing her treasured cards.

"You have your internship stipend," her mother reminded.

"I don't anymore," Eliza confessed, her stomach twisting in disappointment and frustration. She stabbed the ice cream hard with the spoon, and a huge chunk of it flew out of the pint and on the terrazzo floor. "Shit," she cursed.

"What happened?" her mother asked, looking genuinely concerned. "I thought you said that it was going so well and that you were really enjoying yourself."

"I'd rather not talk about it right now," Eliza said quietly. "It's complicated." She returned to ferociously shoveling in the ice cream.

"Well, dear, you are going to have to find a new job if you want money for the summer," her mother said. Her tone of voice indicated that the parental court had made its decision, and no further appeal would be heard by the two justices.

anna is the wife who cried wolf!

SHORTLY AFTER HALF-PAST FOUR O'CLOCK THE NEXT afternoon, Jacqui, Shannon, and the children had just returned from Main Beach when Laurie walked into the kitchen, looking nervous. "There's someone at the door," she said.

Jacqui was helping Cody remove a scuba mask and Shannon was collecting wet towels. They both looked up at the sound of Laurie's voice. The kids dispersed into their rooms, leaving trails of wet sand on the zebrawood floors.

"Who's here?" Jacqui asked.

"A man. He wants to see Anna."

Jacqui shrugged. "Did you tell her someone wants to see her?"

"She's having her facial," Laurie explained. Anna had recently gotten into the habit of having costly at-home spa treatments. Once a week, a facialist, a masseuse, and a manicurist visited the house to pamper her with their services. "I told him to come back in an hour, but he won't go away." Laurie nervously twisted the ends of her plain cotton blouse. "He said it's important."

"You want me to tell her?" Jacqui asked, finally understanding what Laurie was asking her to do.

Laurie nodded in relief. "Would you? She told me no visitors, and I'm worried if I say anything, she'll . . ."

Jacqui stood up and shrugged. "All right. No skin off my back."

"Nose." Shannon giggled. "No skin off your nose."

Jacqui tapped on Anna's bedroom door softly. The sound of tinkling water, wind chimes, and whale songs drifted from behind the door. "Anna—there's someone at the door who needs to see you."

There was no answer.

"Anna? Anna?"

With a start, the door banged open, and Anna stood in the doorway in a white terry-cloth bathrobe, her face covered in a chunky green avocado mask. "What is it? I told Laurie I was not to be disturbed!" she hissed.

"There's a man . . . a man at the door . . . says he has to see you. . . . We told him to come back, but he won't go," Jacqui explained, suddenly feeling as nervous as Laurie.

"Who does he think he is?" Anna whispered viciously, stomping down the stairs to the foyer. She opened the door, where a man in a dark suit and sunglasses stood patiently.

"Yes?"

"Anna Perry?" he asked.

"That's me," she replied haughtily.

"You've just been served," he said, handing her a thick yellow envelope. "Good afternoon." He tipped her a salute and walked away.

"What?" Anna asked, whatever color was left in her face draining. She ripped open the envelope and pulled out several pages of a thick document. "THAT BASTARD!" she yelled. Anna threw the papers in the air and stormed through her own ticker-tape parade back to her spa treatment room. "I can't believe he took me seriously!"

Jacqui winced.

Shannon, huddled in the kitchen doorway, looked at Jacqui with questioning eyes. "What just happened?"

"I think Kevin just asked Anna for a divorce," Jacqui said, collecting the scattered papers. "Go outside and watch the kids. Don't you say a word!"

She skimmed a page. *Contract for the predetermined division of assets, arrangement of alimony or other support, and/or allocation of attorney's fees associated with the termination of marriage,* she read.

She flipped through the second bundle of papers, and only when she found the signatures on the last page did it slowly dawn on her what she was reading. Anna and Kevin Perry's prenuptial agreement!

Her eyes scanned down, and Jacqui found a section circled and marked with an arrow, with notations from a lawyer. *Until August 26th,* the lawyer had scribbled in the margin.

The circled clause stipulated that if Kevin and Anna were married for less than five years, Anna wouldn't receive a penny in the event of a divorce. In New York, it was called the "Trump clause"—after Donald Trump, who'd famously ditched Marla

Maples a month before their five-year anniversary so that he wouldn't be required to give her a bigger settlement. If Anna was able to stick it out beyond five years, she got half of everything, but if the marriage ended before they made it to the five-year mark, she got nothing.

Jacqui felt her stomach clench. Anna was about to get Trumped!

Kevin had actually done it! She read the first paragraph—under *cause for dissolution*, the lawyer had checked *physical abuse* and cited Anna's *use of excessive force* (um, an ear flick) that had led to *massive trauma* (i.e., broken cartilage) and *physical endangerment* (but it was just a little infection!).

Then the reality hit her: if the Perrys got divorced, Kevin would take the children (most of them were his), and if Anna was left broke, Jacqui would be out of a job. She wouldn't be able to complete a fifth year of high school and would have to move back to Brazil instead. No more New York, and certainly no more NYU. So much for a stress-free, careless summer. A divorce would totally suck. Not only would it render Jacqui homeless in the fall, the kids would never get over it—they'd already gone through so much when Kevin split up with his first wife.

She'd heard that Zoë had refused to speak for six months. Madison had retreated into overeating, and that was when William had begun to show symptoms of hyperactive disorder. They were finally settled in with Anna as their stepmother—what would they do when Kevin pushed her out of their lives? And poor Cody, who wouldn't be able to see his half brothers and sisters. Jacqui felt a pit forming in her stomach. She didn't know who she felt more sorry for—the kids or herself. Jacqui could see the kids playing happily outside through a large bay window, without a clue as to the impending destruction of their family unit.

She slipped the papers back in their envelope and walked back toward the pool, her mind a whirl. Her problem was no longer just that she hadn't gotten into college—now she would have to fight just to keep her life afloat. Jacqui took a deep breath. Thankfully, she'd always been a strong swimmer.

mara is big green with envy

A FEW WEEKS AFTER THE FASHION SHOW, JACQUI, MARA, AND Eliza went out to dinner so that Jacqui could celebrate getting paid. Mara remembered those thick, cash-filled envelopes with affection. She'd traded them in for the skimpy direct-deposit payments due a cub reporter. Even though the perks made up for it, part of her did miss receiving those thick tax-free wads of cash every three weeks.

The three girls were sitting in a booth at Lunch and had ordered the restaurant's famous lobster rolls and a pitcher of beer to share. Jacqui did most of the talking, since Eliza was uncharacteristically quiet and wasn't her usual boisterous self and Mara's thoughts were preoccupied with her relationship with Ryan.

They were still having some bad feeling over the other morning, when Mara had woken up and found that they were drifting from the dock. Ryan had forgotten to check on the knots that held them to the pier, and they had come loose in the middle of the night. They'd had to call the someone at the yacht club to give them a tug back to land, and Mara had come in late for work and had been yelled at by her boss.

A formal politeness had descended on their relationship, with the two of them walking on eggshells around each other. The frosty atmosphere worried her. Being in a relationship was really hard work. It wasn't the honeymoon she'd been expecting. Mara was stressed over the situation. Ryan was the best thing that had ever happened to her, but it bothered her that he couldn't understand why she was so upset.

She'd managed to work her way back into Sam Davis's good graces by filing a great column on the Writers versus Actors softball championship, where she'd given the celebrities funny nicknames (portly Alec Baldwin was "Cake Batter"). Mara knew a thing or two about the game, and her trenchant observations on how a backyard activity had grown to have corporate sponsors and coverage on ESPN simply due to its participants were funny and wellput.

Jacqui was telling them about how the web site guys had chartered a plane to write her name in the sky when Mara noticed a familiar figure stroll into the restaurant. Her neighbor wasn't wearing her signature blue bikini this time, but Tinker was outfitted in a very tight halter top and cutoff Daisy Dukes.

She walked by Mara's table and said hello. "Mind if I join you guys?" she asked with a friendly smile. "I think my sis is running late."

"Sure," Mara said tightly before taking a huge bite from her lobster roll. She wiped off the excess mayo on her lips with a gingham napkin. "Guys, this is Tinker. She's living on the boat next to ours on Sag. Tinker, this is Jacqui and Eliza."

"Cool," Tinker said. "How do you all know each other?"

"We au-paired together a couple of years ago," Eliza replied.

"Oh, right," Tinker said, turning to Mara. "Ryan told me he was dating his little brothers' and sisters' nanny."

Mara colored. The way Tinker said *nanny* sounded like Mara had only taken the job to seduce the rich kids' hot older brother.

"How do you know Ryan?" Jacqui asked curiously.

"We're in the same coed fraternity at Dartmouth," Tinker explained, taking a handful of Mara's fries. "It's so fun. Ryan's president."

"Which one?" Eliza wanted to know.

Tinker told her.

"Do you guys still have Naked Night?" asked Eliza, who knew a thing or two about Ivy League Greek culture.

"Naked Night?" Mara asked, almost choking on her beer.

"Yeah, it's like one night of the year when all the members hang out in the nude all evening. It's really trippy, I heard. Lindsay's older brother went to Dartmouth. He told us about it," Eliza explained, scooping up the chunks of lobster salad that had fallen onto her plastic plate.

"Oh God, it's so wild." Tinker laughed, as if thinking about a very naughty secret.

"Really," Mara said icily. "Tell us more."

"Well, first we streak the campus, and then there's a hot tub in the basement of the house and we all get sudsy in the bubbles.

The pictures are absolutely hysterical." Tinker giggled. "We get so drunk, it's scary. It's a miracle no one's drowned in the Jacuzzi."

"I'm sure," Mara said sarcastically. "So what else do you guys do in this frat?"

"In the winter, there's a big scavenger hunt in the woods. Every item we find is some kind of alcohol. By the end of it, everyone's so drunk some of us write our addresses on our arms. *If found, please return to Animal House.* I woke up in a pasture once. I had no idea how I got there. Anyway, I'm organizing it with Ryan this year." Tinker rolled her eyes. "Sadly, there's not much to do in New Hampshire, so we basically have to make our own fun. Which means a lot of beer and planning road trips."

"Oh."

"Last winter, we all went to Stowe. A couple of us are on the ski team. We all snowboarded on the mountains together. Ryan's really good. But you know that," Tinker said. "Ryan's good at everything."

Right, Mara thought. It was a trip he'd invited her to. But she'd bowed out of it since she couldn't ski and hadn't looked forward to making a fool of herself on the mountain.

She looked at Tinker. She was one of the prettiest girls she'd ever seen—tall, long-limbed, with fine Scandinavian features— the high forehead, the silver blond hair and cornflower blue eyes. A hot girl who was in Ryan's frat, who could ski and snowboard and liked to plan scavenger hunts in the woods. Beautiful . . . and *athletic.* It sounded like Tinker did a lot of things that Ryan always wanted Mara to do. Mara couldn't share in any of Ryan's sports activities, since she had the coordination of a lobster.

What exactly had happened in Vermont on the ski trip? Not to mention Naked Night? *In the hot tub?*

She wondered if she should be worried. *But you're the one spending the summer with him on the boat,* she reminded herself. Not Tinker. And even if she and Ryan weren't getting along right then, they would make up. They always did.

Tinker's sister finally arrived, and Tinker waved her good-byes to the three girls and made Mara promise that she and Ryan would visit their boat that weekend.

"She seems nice," Jacqui hedged.

Mara made a face.

"C'mon," Eliza assured. "You're so much prettier than she is. And I bet her chest isn't real. Silicone City."

There were times when Mara was glad Eliza was so sharp-tongued, and this was one of them.

"You know, there really is nothing to worry about. She doesn't seem like Ryan's type at all," Jacqui observed.

"Really, why not?" Mara asked, skeptical.

"Well, for one, she's nothing like you," Jacqui said wisely.

The check came, and Mara plunked down her plastic. Eliza rummaged in her purse, and she looked up at them, empty-handed, her face red. "Guys, can you spot me this one?"

"Of course." Mara nodded. "Why, did you lose your credit card?"

"No need, I've got it," Jacqui said, handing Mara her card back. She pulled out a hundred-dollar bill from the fat envelope. "*Chicas*, this is my treat."

When the waitress had taken their bill, Eliza told them her sad story.

"They fired you?" Jacqui asked, aghast.

"But you were on the cover of *Dan's Papers*!" Mara argued.

"They *fired* you?" Jacqui repeated again, still shocked.

Eliza nodded. "And after they found out about the chopper rental, my parents took away the plastic. I'm officially broke."

"What are you going to do?"

Eliza held up an application form. She had picked one up from the reception desk when they had walked inside the restaurant.

"You're going to work *here*? At Lunch?" Mara gasped. Eliza Thompson, the girl who was a waitress's nightmare with her picky salad instructions, was going to be serving customers herself? Or, even more unlikely, working in a hot kitchen?

"Well, they're hiring . . . and beggars can't be choosers." She laughed hollowly. "At least I won't starve."

looking to get lost

LATER THAT NIGHT, THE THREE WEB SITE HONCHOS INVITED Jacqui to a party they were throwing at the castle to celebrate their latest triumph—their stock had split and they were now worth double what they used to be. The guys had outdone themselves: the house was packed with glamorous revelers, there were three different full cocktail bars set up in the patio with massive "Shocker" ice sculptures, and the Killers were scheduled to play a set in the ballroom.

Jacqui rang the doorbell, but not even the promise of a fun night of partying could make her feel better just then. It was too late. Kevin had made good on his promise, had filed papers and sent an assistant to the Hamptons to bring his things back to their town house in the city. He had been gone for two weeks.

Anna had asked Jacqui to keep it a secret from the kids. She didn't want to upset them, and she wanted some time to ponder what she was going to do now. "Don't worry, I'll think of something," Anna had told her.

But for the most part, Anna didn't seem to be doing anything to save her marriage. Instead, she hit the boutiques with a vengeance. Not a day went by that Anna didn't come home loaded with shopping bags. When the kids asked Jacqui why their dad was never home, she had to lie and tell them he was away on business. The atmosphere in the house was becoming strained, with Anna locking herself in her room for hours and then coming out red-eyed and sniffing and the children demanding to see their father.

Thank God for the three guys—their fun-loving antics made her forget all of her problems. It was obvious all three of them were attracted to her, and it was entertaining to watch them jockey for the key position, but since the three of them shadowed her constantly, she didn't know which one of the three was the boy who made her heart skip faster.

She rang the bell again, impatient to get inside and grab a drink to drown her sorrows.

The door opened, and Ben Defever stood in the doorway. His good-looking face broke into a sweet smile when he saw her, but his forehead soon creased in concern. "What's wrong?" he asked, noticing her agitation.

"It's nothing—oh, Ben," Jacqui said in a wretched tone.

"C'mon," he said "let's go somewhere quiet, where we can talk."

Jacqui nodded, and they slipped through the crowd to the back staircase. Ben put a light hand on her back as he led her up to the top floor of the house. His room was in the northern end.

She sat on the edge of his bed and put her head in her hands.

"Now, tell me what's bothering you," Ben said, handing her a glass of sangria.

"I just can't take it anymore," she said mournfully, thinking about the Perrys' impending divorce and her fifth-year issues. She took a long gulp from the glass and looked around, as if the answer to all her problems could be found nearby. His room was unexpectedly neat for a boy's, spartan and immaculate, with nary a dirty sock or a wet towel in sight. A few guitars were stacked against the wall.

"Boss trouble?" Ben asked.

Jacqui turned to him with a wan smile. "Yeah, kind of. It's a lot of pressure working for them. And there's only so much one person can do, you know? But they expect me to do everything. Sometimes I feel like I'm the only person keeping that family together, and it's not even my family. *Merda*."

Ben nodded sympathetically. "I know. It sucks. I feel the same way—not about my family, but about the business. The site was my idea and I write a lot of it, on top of overseeing the marketing stuff, and I can't bring myself to delegate. I get kind of burnt out sometimes."

"Me too."

"But it'll get better. You just need to take a second to breathe." Ben took a deep breath and exhaled. "Just let it in, then push it out."

Jacqui followed his lead. For a few minutes, the room was quiet except for the sound of their breathing exercises. "You're right—it does help."

"Anytime you ever need to talk, you can come to me, you know," he said shyly.

"You're so sweet," Jacqui said, impulsively putting her arms around him. She put her face in the warm cotton of his shirt and felt his heart beat through the fabric. It was just nice to be next to someone. Ben was such a great guy—he really understood her feelings. He held her for a while and then cleared his throat. He looked at her hesitantly, as if he'd just realized she was clinging to him.

"This is nice," Jacqui whispered.

"Sorry," Ben said. "I . . ." He meant to apologize for holding her for so long, but soon, there was no need for any apology as Jacqui had brought her face close to his and he decided to kiss her instead, removing his glasses before doing so.

Jacqui closed her eyes and put a warm hand on his hot cheek, rubbing his stubble. His lips were soft and warm, and he smelled like strawberries and heather. *Strong and sensitive—just what the doctor ordered,* Jacqui thought.

They jumped apart when someone knocked on the door.

"Yo, Defever! Jacqui in there? Someone said they saw her comin' up," Duffy's deep voice called. "You hidin' her?"

Jacqui and Ben exchanged guilty looks. "Yeah, she's in here," Ben said reluctantly.

Duffy stormed in, his eyebrows wagging. "What've you two been up to?" he asked suspiciously.

"I was just, uh—showing Jacqui my telescope. Venus is rising," Ben lied, motioning to the telescope planted by the window.

Jacqui nodded. Venus? Was that some kind of pun? The

goddess of love? Ben winked at her and she winked back, but Duffy was already pulling her up from the bed.

"C'mon, the party's downstairs," Duffy urged.

"All right!" Jacqui agreed. Feeling so much better after talking to Ben, she was ready for some of Duffy's wild antics.

Duffy galloped down the stairs, but instead of bringing her to the hubbub of the party, he led her past the ballroom, through the back patio, and to a golf cart parked behind the main house.

"Hop on," he urged, sliding into the driver's seat.

"Where are we going?" she asked, a little amused.

"You'll see." He grinned, revving up the engine.

"All right, be that way," she teased. They zipped across the Reynolds estate, the golf cart bouncing over the grass.

He turned to her and offered her a thermos from his jacket. "Drink?"

Jacqui sipped from it. Rum-spiked punch. She snuggled happily against him on the cart. He reminded her of a frisky, overeager puppy, and Jacqui had a soft spot for friendly creatures.

"How fast can this thing go?"

In answer, Duffy floored the gas pedal, and Jacqui squealed as they zoomed by the tennis courts and the guest bungalows over to the private beach on the property.

"Wanna drive?" he asked over the sound of the waves crashing on the beach.

"What? No!" But it was too late. Duffy had taken his hands off the wheel, and Jacqui screamed as she tried to steer the cart.

"You're crazy!" she yelled, but she was having too much fun to be upset, and they bounced along until Duffy finally put on the brakes. They stopped so abruptly Jacqui was thrown into his arms, and they tumbled out of the cart, falling onto the sand, entangled in each other. They were both laughing as they rolled on the shore.

"You almost got us killed!" she cried, pretending to be furious.

"Oh, c'mon! You loved it!" he teased.

The moon was full, and the beach was deserted. Their only companions were a bunch of seagulls flying low over the water or walking slowly on the sand.

"It's so peaceful out here," she said, still lying on top of him.

"Yeah, I don't like crowds much myself." He smiled, looking up at her. Her hair was windblown and her cheeks were red from the cold.

"You are such a liar! You guys are always having parties," she reminded him, but she was charmed nonetheless. She punched him on the shoulder.

"*Ow!*" he yelped. "You . . ." And before she knew it, he was tickling her, and she was laughing so hard she got the hiccups.

"Oops," she said, feeling embarrassed.

"Just hold your nose. Here, I'll do it for you," he said, pinching her nose with his thumb and index finger.

"I cand breed," she gasped, still giggling. She pulled his hand away, and then he was holding it tightly in his.

"If you say so," he said, leaning over to give her a kiss, and she met his lips with her open mouth, tasting the mix of salt and sweet liquor in his kiss. As he kissed her, his hand smoothed her hair ever so gently.

A loud honking interrupted them, and they pulled away just in time to see another golf cart pull up next to their overturned one. Grant was sitting in the front seat, and he looked genuinely pained to see his friend alone with Jacqui.

"Jac, you're missing the Killers. And you, my friend, have got a phone call," Grant told Duffy pointedly. "Your girlfriend's on the line."

"So, you've got a girlfriend?" Jacqui said to Duffy, her arms crossed. She got up to sit next to Grant and let him drive her back to the party.

"*Ex*-girlfriend. We broke up six months ago!" Duffy pleaded. He looked so crushed that Jacqui immediately forgave him. But the golf cart sped back to the house anyway.

She danced with Grant in the middle of the mosh pit, the two of them mangling the lyrics to "Mr. Brightside." He made sure she was relatively unharmed within the circle of slam dancers, but a beefy kid broke through, knocking right into them, and Jacqui stumbled to the ground. She lost Grant in the pushing, milling crowd, and for a moment she was worried she was going to be trampled.

But a strong hand pulled her up to her feet, and she was relieved to find Grant's tall form standing protectively above her once more. He cleared a path through the dance floor to the kitchen. "C'mon, let me get you some ice for that cut," he said. "Sorry about that. I'll have that kid beaten behind the shed," he said in his laconic southern manner. He was Rhett Butler in a Death Cab for Cutie T-shirt.

"I'm all right, really," Jacqui said, touched by his concern.

Grant pulled out a medical-grade ice pack from the fridge, twisted it to release the chemical reaction that created the ice, and held it against Jacqui's forehead gently.

She put a hand over his, pressing it closer to the wound. He was such a gentleman. A ministering angel. They stood like that for a long time without speaking, and part of Jacqui wanted to never stop bleeding. Grant pulled his hand away and assessed the cut on her forehead. "I think you're okay now."

Jacqui nodded, a bit speechless. Grant was so handsome, with his striking eyebrows and gray eyes. The sideburns gave him a rockabilly edge that she found immensely appealing. He was just so sexy—there was an animal magnetism to him that she couldn't resist. The heat of the dance floor had made her blood run quickly, and she looked at him hopefully.

That was all he needed, and without warning, he pinned her against the sink, looked deep into her eyes, and kissed her urgently. There were a few people milling about in the kitchen who soon fled when they noticed what was going on. Jacqui kissed him furiously back, embracing him tightly.

She pulled him closer to her, and when his warm hands

slipped up the back of her shirt and down her jeans, she wanted nothing more than to feel his body next to hers.

"They're all in love with you, you know," Mara warned Jacqui when they bumped into each other at the party after Jacqui had stumbled out of the kitchen alone, trying to get her bearings. She and Grant had quickly separated when Duffy walked in, complaining to Grant that the bars were short of mixers.

"They're just having fun," Jacqui demurred, stirring her drink.

"Are *you* having fun?" Mara asked pointedly. She was covering the party for her column, had already leveled her steady gaze on the trio, and had described them in print as *the kind of fellows from my high school who would sit in the back of the class throwing spitballs and clapping erasers but who secretly earned straight A's. Smart boys can play dumb too.*

Jacqui blushed, thinking of kissing Ben in his room, Duffy by the beach, and Grant in the kitchen. The truth was that when they kissed, she forgot about all the Perrys' divorce as well as the fact that she had kissed one of each guy's best friends a few minutes before. Oh, well, she was just having fun, right?

Later, when Jacqui returned to the main party, she received knowing secret smiles from all three boys.

"This is such a great party," Jacqui said, watching members of the Killers push each other into the pool.

"This is just the beginning, my friend. In the fall, we're having this huge party at the Rainbow Room to launch a couple of new sites we've developed. You've got to be there," Duffy said, handing her a marijuana pipe. "You're in New York, right?"

"What's wrong?" Ben asked, noticing her face fall.

"I might not be," Jacqui confessed, exhaling and coughing.

"Why not?" Grant asked, accepting the pipe and taking a huge hit of his own.

"My bosses are getting a divorce," she blurted. She hadn't been able to tell Mara about it because of Ryan, but she felt safe telling the guys. It wasn't as if they could do anything about it anyway. "And if they get a divorce, I have to leave New York and go back to São Paulo in September."

All three guys looked like they had just been told their stock had dropped three hundred points.

a team of horses can't drag ryan away from the waves

"YOU'RE LEAVING?" MARA ASKED, TRYING NOT TO SOUND TOO disappointed.

Ryan shrugged. He looked around the crowded VIP tent at the Bridgehampton Polo Club, frowning. He'd agreed to accompany her to the polo, something he wouldn't have been caught dead at otherwise.

The traditional afternoon event had become a commercial circus. It was little more than a platform for corporate advertising—one week, a telecom company, the next, a tropical island tourism authority, their logos draped all over the tents. He cringed in distaste as a pinched-faced woman walked through the crowd, draped in several hundred carats' worth of diamonds.

Mara was pleased that he had accompanied her to the event but had become distressed when, after the first chukker, he'd become completely bored with the constant posturing of the crowd. He'd stood in a corner by himself, looking restless and nursing his drink.

sun-kissed

She knew there was nothing Ryan disliked more than having to attend some snobby social event. He liked nightclubs fine but had no particular interest in spending an afternoon watching wealthy old men hit a ball across a field. During the first summer she'd spent in the Hamptons, he'd only attended the polo because he'd heard she would be there. Later, he'd confided that he thought polo was the most pretentious sport: since it cost so much money to play, it was just about showing off.

"You know this isn't my scene. Besides, you're busy," he said, trying not to make it sound like an accusation. "Don't you have to get that guy to give you a sound bite?" he asked, nodding toward the back of the tent, where, bordered by a velvet rope and several menacing bodyguards (the VIP tent?), stood Boris Carter, the arrogant celebrity host everyone was gawking at shamelessly. Boris was the star of such movies as *No Guts, No Glory 1, 2,* and *3*—a trilogy based on a popular video game.

So far, the actor, famous for his squinty-eyed Texan stare and broken nose, had rebuffed all of Mara's attempts to nail a few quotes. He'd had the temerity to tell Mara that "talking to her was not part of his job." Apparently, the self-important Hollywood star had been paid a princely sum to attend the event but explained to Mara through his bodyguards that his appearance fee did not include having to grant interviews to the press. Mara had been in the middle of arguing with his publicist on the phone from Los Angeles when Ryan tapped her on the shoulder.

"I think I'm gonna take off. You seem pretty busy, like always."

"I'm not *always* busy," Mara replied. "You make it sound like all I do is work."

"Well, don't you?" Ryan asked. Mara's Diary column was a huge hit, having quickly turned into a Hamptons must-read. Her outsider-turned-insider tone hit a comic nerve with loyal readers. Her mailbox was stuffed with invites, and her presence was requested at a fabulous bash every night of the week.

Already, her busy schedule had driven a bit of a wedge between them—Ryan was always trying to get Mara to blow off her job so they could spend more time together. "It's not like you're writing for *Newsweek*," he'd said under his breath the other evening when he'd wanted her to hang out with him and his friends and Mara had chosen to stay at home to bang out an assignment. "It's superficial celeb gossip stuff—you can do it in your sleep."

Mara tried not to feel too insulted. Why couldn't he just chill? Just the week before, they'd been getting along so well. Then they'd hosted a kick-ass Fourth of July bash on the boat. The party had been the first time they had entertained friends together as a couple, and the evening had been perfect. Eliza had brought Jeremy, and Jacqui had brought not one but three dates. All eight of them had had a blast.

"If you can just wait, I'll be done in a few minutes, I swear," she promised, holding up her BlackBerry. "I finally got Boris's rep to look up his contract to see if it includes interviews. He's going to make Boris talk to me. Right, Lucky?" she asked, looking for backup from the photographer, who was standing next to them.

"Oh, sure." Lucky nodded.

"Wish I could, but the group's doing a paddle-out in a half hour. Why don't you come by afterward?" Ryan asked.

"All right," Mara said, feeling dejected. Ryan had told her about the paddle-out earlier. It was a surfer thing—a big deal with the community, Ryan had explained—surfers liked to commemorate events by gathering together and paddling out on their boards into the ocean as a group activity. This one was for Tinker's twenty-first birthday. Mara couldn't decide if she was more upset that Ryan was leaving the reception or that he was leaving to attend a paddle-out for Tinker.

"Great! See you later." Ryan smiled as he made his way toward the exit.

"Let him go," Lucky said sympathetically. "If you love someone, set them free."

"Lucky, Sting is so over," Mara chided.

But Lucky was right. She couldn't put Ryan on a tight leash. He was his own person and free to do whatever he wanted. If she let him go freely, he would come back to her.

mara is a righteous betty

MARA HIT THE SEND BUTTON ON THE SCREEN. SHE'D SPENT the last hour polishing her copy on the polo reception. The actor had finally consented to give her a brief interview after his publicist had convinced the party's sponsor to kick in a free trip on the company jet to St. Thomas, a fact that she hadn't left out of her column. Her readers loved that sort of insider dish, and she had managed to pull off writing about the celebrity as both an idol and an object of ridicule—no mean task. She stretched and yawned, then checked her watch. Eleven-thirty in the evening.

Ryan still hadn't returned from the paddle-out. He'd said they would be down at the cove. Maybe she should join him. He'd gotten a ride with his friends, so the car was available.

She took the Ferrari down to the beach. She couldn't see very well in the dark, but as she rounded a sand dune, she came upon a brightly lit bonfire. People were sitting around it, and she heard the sound of laughter and a guitar being strummed. An Igloo cooler filled with frosty Coronas was planted in the sand.

Mara took off her shoes and walked barefoot on the cold, wet sand as she approached the merry group.

The surfers were hanging out in front of the bonfire, their boards stuck perpendicular on the sand behind them. Ryan was seated in the middle. He'd put a sweatshirt over his wet suit, and he was strumming a guitar. Next to him was Tinker, in the tiniest bikini imaginable, a black one that looked like it was held up by shoelaces, the straps were so thin. Even though it was goose-bump cold and everyone else was huddled in blankets and wearing sweaters. Mara herself shivered in her cotton yoga pants and terry-cloth sweatshirt.

She walked up to the group and cleared her throat. Ryan looked up. His handsome features broke into a huge grin that melted her heart.

"Mar—you're here!" he said, putting aside his guitar.

She nodded. "I got the story done."

"Hey, guys! You remember Mara, my girlfriend," Ryan said.

"Sure enough." Several of the guys smiled.

Of course they remembered her. She was the one who'd gone totally ballistic when she'd found all of them hanging out on their boat when she had to write a story. She'd practically chased them off the port side. But they smiled at her in a friendly fashion nonetheless.

"Make room, bro," Ryan ordered. The guy next to Ryan moved a foot, but Mara squeezed herself between her boyfriend and the bikini-wearing wannabe home wrecker instead.

"Happy birthday, Tinker," she said.

"Glad you could make it," Tinker said coolly.

Ryan kept strumming his guitar.

Conversation veered toward the experience of the paddle-out—how amazing it was to be one with the ocean at sunset. "I, like, felt so small, man, like a grain of sand, a drop of water. . . . Mind-blowing, brah," the boy next to Ryan was saying. *"Respect."*

"I've never felt so self-actualized," Tinker agreed.

Mara raised a skeptical eyebrow. The most New Age she ever got was burning a stick of incense in an ashtray. *Self-actualized?* What the hell was Tinker talking about? It all sounded hokey to her. She found she enjoyed the surfers' company—they were all laid-back and mellow—but she couldn't stomach all the beach-side philosophy they espoused.

Still, it was nice to sit next to Ryan. He was playing her favorite song on his guitar, "Wonderful Tonight." She knew it was a code for how happy he was that she had come to the beach.

"We're going out tomorrow, killer waves off the point, get inside the pope's living room," a dreadlocked surfer enthused, meaning the swells were so huge, they would be able to surf inside the barrell of the waves.

Mara smiled. "Maybe I'll go too."

"You will?" Ryan asked, surprised. It was the first time Mara had offered to join him all summer. "Are you sure?"

"Yeah." She nodded, reaching over to hold his hand.

"Cool," he said, giving hers a warm squeeze. He went back to strumming on his guitar, a small smile playing on his lips, and she knew they were all right again. They might not see eye to eye on how they were going to spend the summer (Ryan seemed to want to carry on his hard-core Dartmouth partying, while Mara wanted to jump-start her career), but there was one thing they agreed on: they were crazy for each other.

around and around they go

THERE WAS A BRIGHT YELLOW SCHOOL BUS PARKED IN front of the Perry mansion the next morning. The driver of the bus honked the horn several times until Jacqui walked outside. She found Grant and Ben hanging out of the bus window. Duffy was sitting in the driver's seat. "*Bom dia*, Jacarei. Get in! We rented Great Adventure for the day," he said, bidding her a good morning. "Everyone on board!"

"You what?" Jacqui asked.

"You looked so down the other day, we thought we should try to make you feel better. And what's better than a day at an amusement park?" Ben asked.

"Your chariot, madam." Grant smiled as Duffy opened the door.

Jacqui helped the Perry kids aboard. As they pulled out of the driveway, she saw a dejected Anna Perry looking at them from her bedroom window.

The drive out to New Jersey took several hours, but the guys kept the kids entertained by cracking jokes and telling them about their latest silly videos on their web site. "There's one

176

where these two dudes are doing a choreographed karaoke of *NSync. It's hilarious."

True to their word, the company had rented out the entire amusement park for a staff "family day." They had the whole place to themselves, and the two-thousand-acre park had an almost ghost-town-like quality, since fewer than a hundred of them were in a place that could hold thousands. Jacqui couldn't even imagine how much this excursion had cost—the boys seemed to have no concerns in that area. It was all play money to them.

"Hey, Jac, should we check out the Batman ride? The centrifugal force is excellent. It'll make your hair stand on end, a real rush!" Ben cajoled.

"No way, we've got to check out the Haunted Tunnel. Don't worry, I'll keep you safe." Grant smiled. He had a high appreciation for campy pleasures, and Jacqui knew he was looking forward to snuggling on the small creaky boat.

"It's bumper cars all the way!" Duffy urged, hopping up and down like a little boy.

The three boys stood in front of her, eager faces aglow, each convinced that only he was the one who had kissed Jacqui the night before.

"I—I . . ." she said, flustered. "Give me a minute," she pleaded. She sat down on a nearby bench and clutched her forehead.

"Still worried about the divorce?" Ben whispered out of earshot of the Perry kids.

"Yeah, I'm sorry, guys. Can we just sit down for a moment?" she asked, Cody and Zoë at her side. Shannon had run after Madison and William, who were hell-bent on riding the upside-down roller coaster until they both puked.

"Look, Jac, if you're really concerned, you have to do something about it. You can't just sit around letting it happen," Duffy declared.

"What do you mean?" Jacqui asked, wondering if she should feel offended. Cody and Zoë stepped away to throw coins in a fountain.

"Well, you know, we built a multimillion-dollar business from our dorm rooms. Surely we can help you keep one dinky marriage together," Ben said.

"True dat, true dat." Grant nodded.

In the end, since they had two kids under the height limit to entertain, the three boys and Jacqui ended up spending the day on the slow, pokey kids' rides, which Cody and Zoë enjoyed. As they went around and around the two-mile-an-hour choo-choo, long legs folded with knees pressed up against the seat in front of them, the boys looked longingly at the high-flying, technologically advanced roller coasters that thundered across the park. But not one of them would give up being by Jacqui's side.

out of the frying pan and into the fire

ELIZA MOPPED UP THE COUNTER DEJECTEDLY. IT WAS HER first day of work at Lunch, and so far, it had been an unmitigated disaster. She was dressed in the uniform Lunch T-shirt with the screen-printed logo of the diner on the front (available at the gift shop for fifteen dollars) and white shorts with a jaunty red apron around her waist. During her brief stint as a waitress, she'd spilled a pitcher of iced tea on a customer as well as herself (although the customer had borne the brunt of it). Her T-shirt was splattered with grease from the kitchen, where she'd been posted even more briefly. She was quickly relieved of that duty after she accidentally upset a vat of clam chowder while attempting to place an angry lobster in a boiling pot. She'd lost control of the crustacean, and the lobster had hightailed it to freedom through the swinging doors into the restaurant, to the applause of all the patrons. And the kitchen floor was now wet and chunky with the creamy soup.

Hence the cash register. Her employers thought she couldn't possibly do any harm there. So far, they had been correct. But Eliza spotted a threat to this balance out of the corner of her eye.

179

She kept mopping up, trying to look busy so that the customer would choose to be served by the other cashier. But no such luck.

Paige was headed her way.

The designer's assistant looked chic and polished in a black Lacoste shirt and colorful Sydney Minx capris. She rapped her fingernails on the table. "Eliza," she said, in that condescending tone.

"Oh, hi, Paige," Eliza said, trying to look like manning the cash register at the lobster shack was the most normal thing in the world. "Did you enjoy your lunch?"

"I did indeed." Paige smiled thinly, handing Eliza her corporate credit card. "Although I would have enjoyed it more if Sydney hadn't called me in the middle of it, screaming that none of the T-shirts that were supposed to go to the other stores had arrived."

"What do you mean?"

"All eight hundred T-shirts were sent to East Hampton. I told you to send half to the boutiques in Miami, Chicago, and Los Angeles."

"Oh," Eliza said. In the middle of the frenzy of that night, she had completely forgotten that only half the T-shirts were to be sent to the store opening. Damn! She handed Paige her card back and a pen to sign the receipt.

"God, Eliza. I mean, seriously. You couldn't even fill out a T-shirt order correctly." Paige accepted her credit card receipt and checked it, her eyes narrowing. "Nor did you calculate the tax correctly on this bill."

"Jesus, I'm sorry," Eliza said, her fingers shaking as she punched in the numbers again. The credit card machine beeped angrily. "I just learned how to work this. . . ."

Paige sighed loudly. "Can someone else help me? This girl here doesn't seem to know how to do anything."

The other cashier walked over, took Paige's card, and helped Eliza void the earlier transaction. "Sorry about that, miss. She's a new trainee."

"Maybe you should just give up. You're a pampered rich girl, and that's the only thing you can do right," Paige hissed. "And by the way, next time you want to give out our clients' personal information to the media, you should think twice, because next time, we'll sue your ass."

Eliza stood back, stung.

"What do you mean?"

Paige thrust the infamous issue of *Hamptons* toward Eliza. "This is what I mean." She sneered before stomping out of the restaurant.

Eliza flipped through the magazine and found Mara's profile on the designer. Oops—she had completely forgotten about the write-around. The anonymous "sources" Eliza had given Mara had gleefully stuck their knives in Sydney's back. There were a lot of passive-aggressive comments from Sydney's "friends," and the story was an all-out bitch fest. His former assistants said that Sydney took all the credit for their designs or ripped off other designers' work, his partner said that Sydney had cheated on their financial arrangement, and his clients complained of double-charging on their bills.

She couldn't help but laugh when she read that "someone" had leaked to Mara that Sydney wore a toupee. (That would have been Eliza.) Paige could complain all she wanted, but the damage had already been done, and there was nothing to prove that Eliza had been the one to spill the beans. Eliza closed the magazine and resumed wiping down the counter, whistling a merry tune.

whoever said "practice makes perfect" is a liar

JUST KEEP YOUR HEAD DOWN AND THEN PULL YOURSELF UP, pull yourself up on the board! C'mon, now! You can do it, you can do it! One! Two! Three! And— Mara flopped back into the water, hanging for dear life to the side of her surfboard.

Ryan paddled up next to her, grimacing with concern. "Hey, babe, you all right there?"

She sputtered up some salt water that had gone into her nose and managed a weak smile. Her swimsuit was giving her a painful wedgie. She should have worn a wet suit like Ryan had suggested, but with the image of Tinker in her minuscule bikini in mind, Mara had opted for sexy instead of sensible. Alas, when she'd arrived at the beach, she'd found Tinker looking trim and athletic in a full-body wet suit. Several times, the force of the waves had almost pulled off Mara's bikini top.

Another large wave crashed into them, and Ryan dove into it, emerging from the crest, a tall, graceful figure on his surfboard. All around him, his friends were similarly positioned, including Tinker, who was a demon on the water (she rose elegantly from her board as if pulled by strings), but Mara couldn't even get her body *on* her surfboard, let alone try to *stand* on it. Every time the waves rolled, she was buffeted by the crash, and she was pulled farther and farther back toward the shore.

It wasn't enough that she had woken up at daybreak to do this. It wasn't enough that her eyes hurt, her joints hurt, and she couldn't breathe. She couldn't even see, since one of her contacts had floated away, and her arms were red from scraping on the sand. To add insult to injury, Tinker had had the audacity to actually make fun of her surfboard.

"Oh, that's so cute! You have a foamy!" Tinker cooed when she saw Mara's board as she and Ryan arrived at the beach.

"No need for that," Ryan said good-naturedly. "It's Mara's first time."

"What's a foamy?" Mara asked when Tinker was out of earshot. She was using one of Ryan's old boards, one he'd picked himself for Mara to use, so she didn't understand the mockery.

"It's a beginner board. Most surfers use fiberglass, like mine," he said, motioning to his sleek Ferrari Challenge Stradale, a limited-edition five-thousand-dollar surfboard with the distinctive stallion logo.

"Hey, who's the baby with the foamy?" another one of Ryan's surfer friends called, hooting at the sight of Mara's yellow surfboard.

"Knock it off," Ryan called back. "Ignore them, they're just a bunch of Barneys," he told Mara.

Ryan spent the better part of the morning trying to teach her the fundamentals of surfing. Either he was a really bad teacher or Mara was just an awful student. The closest she had gotten to her surfboard was when it hit her on the head when the waves rolled in.

She'd told Ryan to let her practice alone. She didn't mind, since it looked like he really wanted to hit the big waves that were breaking down the beach.

"You sure?" he'd asked. "I can stay. I'm just glad you're here." He was sitting on top of his surfboard as naturally as if he were sitting on the couch, while Mara was barely clinging to the side of hers, frantically dog-paddling with her feet underneath the water.

So much for her fantasy of re-creating that Justin-Cameron smooch—the two of them on their surfboards locking lips on the water. Not going to happen.

Especially if she was half drowning.

"No, go ahead—I'll get the hang of it sooner or later. I don't want to keep you," she urged him, feeling guilty.

"Okay," Ryan said reluctantly. "I really don't mind. I want to stay."

But Mara thought she'd rather he didn't see her fall flat on her face again while the surfboard whacked her on the head, especially since that bitch Tinker was cruising on her board doing her best imitation of Kate Bosworth in *Blue Crush*.

"No, really. Go. I want you to go," she said.

So he'd left her, and Mara had spent the rest of the morning bobbing up and down beside her surfboard, trying not to choke on the ocean water.

As she floated away from the rest of the surfers, she caught sight of Ryan on his board again, a striking, slim figure crouched in the peak position to get maximum speed, getting up on the plane above the waves. She loved him so much. . . . If only she could share this with him . . .

After a few minutes, Mara swam back to shore. She waved to Ryan from the beach and then walked away. She had to be at work in an hour.

jacqui springs a parent trap

IN THE MOVIE, LINDSAY LOHAN WAS STILL A CUTE NINE-YEAR-old with freckles and a sunny smile, not a stick-thin lollipop-headed starlet notorious for her after-hours antics in a host of Hollywood nightspots. Jacqui grasped a handful of popcorn and stared reflectively at the screen. She had rented the Disney remake to pick up a few tips from the twin Lindsays' attempts to get their parents back together. It was a bonus that Cody and Zoë loved the movie.

The web site guys had suggested trying to talk Anna and Kevin into counseling, but nothing as practical as therapy would ever appeal to Anna. And it wasn't as if Jacqui could just give Kevin a call and suggest such a thing—they hardly spoke to each other, because things had been a bit awkward between them ever since Kevin had tried to hit on her the first summer she was working for the family.

Anna's behavior was also becoming more erratic—the other day she'd asked Jacqui if she could tag along when Jacqui was going out after work to meet Mara and Eliza at Tavern. She had tried to talk Anna out of it, but Anna had insisted. Eliza and

Mara exchanged alarmed looks when they saw Anna, but Jacqui merely shrugged. Their former and Jacqui's present employer had quickly downed four shots of Jägermeister and spent the evening draped over the twenty-two-year-old DJ. "Your mom is hot!" several guys told Jacqui. "She's not my mom; she's my—oh, never mind," Jacqui had said.

The next morning, Anna, still reeling from the effects of a brutal hangover, had asked Jacqui when they were going to do that again.

Never, Jacqui had thought. Anna's partying like a teenager sure didn't seem like the actions of a woman desperate to save her marriage.

But what if instead of making them *figure out* if they were still in love with each other, Jacqui could make them *believe* that they had never fallen out of love? After all, even though they hated each other's guts right now, like Dennis Quaid and Natasha Richardson in the movie, Anna and Kevin belonged together. Anna was the only woman who thought Kevin's law puns were funny (he liked to say that he had a "sunny deposition"), and Kevin was the only man who thought Anna looked hot in a billowing African muumuu.

Jacqui knew that Anna was still in love with her husband—her demand for a divorce had just been a way to make him notice her, and even though Kevin was a workaholic, he did love his wife; he just never tried to show it. So what if she, Jacqui, orchestrated a courtship of sorts—doing nice things for each of them in secret, which they would assume the other person had done for them?

Where would she start? First, she needed a recruit. She couldn't do this alone.

"So, you want me to help you send Anna romantic gifts but pretend they're from Kevin even though they're not?" Shannon asked when the two of them were in the laundry room sorting through the children's dirty clothing. "I mean, I know divorce is a sad thing and all, but I guess I don't understand why you'd want to be so involved."

Jacqui bit her lip. Could she really trust Shannon? She had no choice, really. She took a deep breath and told the younger girl the whole story—about the apartment in New York, the NYU rejection, how she needed the Perrys to stay together so she could finish her fifth year of high school and stay in New York.

"But remember, you can't tell Madison, okay? Anna doesn't want the kids to know," Jacqui warned. She knew how close Shannon and Madison had become. The two girls were glued together at the hip, and Madison was really blossoming under the friendship, looking up to Shannon like the big sister she'd never had.

"I guess I won't," Shannon said reluctantly, feeling bad about keeping something from a friend. She tossed a folded T-shirt into the laundry basket. "I'll help you, but."

"But?"

Shannon broke into a wide grin. "But you have to promise me you'll invite me to stay with you in the city at your apartment sometime. I live in Jersey, and it's sooo boring. My parents would never let me stay in the city, but if I told them I had a friend . . ."

Jacqui contemplated Shannon's proposal. She could see where this was leading—Shannon turning Jacqui's sweet studio into a New York City crash pad of her own—inviting friends over, sneaking in beer, forcing Jaqui to host a bunch of fifteen-year-old brats in her private abode. In the end, it would be a small price to pay for living in the city, and Shannon couldn't come over every weekend, could she?

"All right. It's a deal." She nodded grimly.

"Cool. And remember, I need to sleep in the bed. No pullout couch for me. My back problem, you know."

The next day, Anna Perry discovered that someone had sent her an iPod programmed with all of her favorite Matchbox Twenty love songs. ("Matchbox Twenty?" Shannon had asked, wrinkling her nose in distaste when Jacqui had told her what to put on the MP3 player. "Ew!" "Just do it!" Jacqui had laughed.)

Anna and Kevin had not said a word to each other since he had served her papers. Kevin was still bunkered back in the city. Jacqui knew that Anna had tried calling him on his cell and at the office, but he never returned her calls. Perhaps the black iPod nano would give her a sign that he was having second thoughts. Of course, gifts wouldn't be enough in the long run. Jacqui knew she would have to engage Kevin in some way to make Anna believe he wanted her back, through a more personal approach, like actually asking her out on a date.

But for now, Jacqui noticed Anna was in a good mood all afternoon, humming "Push" as she went about the house. Score one for the plan. She ushered the kids into the Range Rover.

"Where are we going today?" Zoë squealed. After the excitement of yesterday's impromptu trip to Great Adventure, the kids expected something as fun every day.

"Just the beach. Sorry." Jacqui smiled. "Zoë, is this your book?" she asked, picking up a copy of V. C. Andrews's *Flowers in the Attic*. "You're reading this?"

Zoë nodded.

It was a book for twelve-year-olds, and Zoë was eight. Two summers ago, the kid hadn't even been able to recognize letters. But now she was reading at an advanced level! Okay, so maybe Zoë shouldn't be reading that book (blond incestuous twins?)—but hey, at least she was reading! It looked like the "summer off" plan was working. With Kevin out of the house, the daily battles had ceased, and the environment was peaceful for once. William had decided to be an amateur geologist and was collecting stones and seashells on the beach and doing research on their provenance. Free from a fully regimented schedule, Cody had stopped having his "accidents" and was finally properly toilet-trained. Madison had even (grudgingly) started eating again. She looked red-cheeked and happy.

Even Jacqui was benefiting from the new relaxed approach to the summer. If her plan didn't work, at least she'd return to Brazil in September with a killer tan.

blue-collar blues

TALK ABOUT A SIGHT FOR SORE EYES. ELIZA UNTIED HER
apron and stuffed it in the laundry basket underneath the
counter, smiling as she saw Jeremy walk inside the door. Her spirits lifted the minute their eyes met. He looked so adorable in his
blue uniform work shirt with STONE CONTRACTING scripted on
the front pocket. His jeans were dusty and muddy, but Eliza
thought she had never seen him look cuter.

"Can I help you?" she asked flirtatiously.

Jeremy pretended to scan the menu underneath the glass
counter. "I'm not sure. I'm looking for an Eliza Thompson? You
might know her—about so high," he said, motioning under his
chin. "The prettiest girl in the Hamptons, kind of high-
maintenance?" He leaned over the counter. "Do you know what
time she gets off work?"

Eliza threw her arms around him and gave him a kiss.

"So, do you want to eat here?" he asked.

"Are you kidding? I can't get out of this place fast enough."

They drove to the nearest sushi restaurant, and over shrimp tem-
pura rolls, Eliza unburdened her tale of woe. Jeremy knew that

she'd lost her job working for Sydney's showroom but not that Paige had fired her. She'd kept that detail out of it, not wanting to bring up memories of his old "friend."

"I can't even walk, my knee hurts, and I think I'm breaking out from all the stress!" she said, dipping a piece of sushi into the wasabi-spiked soy sauce. "And I almost burnt my fingers when I tried to get the corncobs out of the oven!"

Jeremy was silent as he picked at his chicken teriyaki. It had been Eliza's idea to get Japanese, and it was obvious he didn't share her enthusiasm for the cuisine.

She continued her tirade, complaining about customers who didn't tip, waitresses who stole her stations, and an abusive and mocking kitchen staff. Jeremy grunted in response but didn't interrupt her self-pitying monologue.

Finally, he threw his napkin on the table. "So what?"

"What do you mean, so what?" Eliza asked, taken aback by his harsh tone.

He shrugged and took a swig of his Sapporo. "People *work*, Eliza. I know it's hard to imagine, but some people have to work hard to get where they are; they don't just inherit it. I've worked hard all my life. . . . I started out as a gardener, a groundskeeper, and I worked all through high school and college and every summer. And even now, even though I have my own landscape company, it's not easy. Nothing's easy. You just need to get used to it."

Eliza started to protest, but he didn't let her get a word in.

"Some people think money's just handed to them; they don't

realize how much hard work really goes toward earning it. You've got to get your hands dirty, you know? It's not just about cruising through life. It really makes me sick how entitled some of my clients act," he said, furiously taking another swig from his beer glass.

"I mean, I know you're not used to it. But it's like, my friend Paige—she and I used to cut lawns together, and we had to get in the dirt and pull weeds, and we made, like, minimum wage, but she was always there, and she never complained."

"Oh, really. So you want me to be more like Paige, is that it?" she asked snippily, trying not to show him how much he'd hurt her with his unsympathetic comments. And to bring Paige into it as well—that really stung.

"Well, not everyone can be like Paige—"

"Of course not. Paige is perfect," Eliza said bitterly.

When the check came, Eliza grabbed it.

"Hey, c'mon, I got you," Jeremy argued.

"No, no. I don't take any handouts," she snapped. It had been her decision to eat at Mount Fuji, even though the bill was equal to her full day's pay, which meant she'd basically worked eight hours for a few sushi rolls. "*I* don't expect a free ride."

They drove back to Eliza's house in silence, and when he dropped her off at her driveway, she slammed the door so hard it shook on its hinges.

trouble in paradise

THE DISHES IN THE SINK HAD BEEN UNDISTURBED FOR A whole week, sitting in tepid water, crusty and dirty. As Mara rinsed them off and began to stack them in the dishwasher, she wondered why Ryan never even bothered to try to make the place neater. All of his boxes were still unpacked in the living room, and the dozens of empty beer cans, dirty paper cups, cigarette butts, and empty vodka and gin bottles from the assorted parties added to the general detritus. He'd promised to clean up after each get-together, and Mara would have cleaned up herself except she had to be at work so early and she arrived home so late, there never seemed to be enough time to try to get the place in order.

She had to face it: Ryan was a terrific slob without a live-in maid.

Mara pulled the vacuum cleaner out of the utility closet and began to sweep, picking up pieces of paper and throwing all the empties into a big black trash bag. A small nagging voice in her head wondered if they had rushed into this too soon. Sure, they'd been together all year, but they'd hardly been in the same city for more than a few days. The transition from long distance to close quarters was a rocky one.

Ryan was so used to having people pick up after him. There was a reason why his room at home was always clean and his bed there was always made—it was called hired help. He didn't even notice that they were practically living in a trash dump. The other day she'd found a half-eaten bag of potato chips underneath the bed, along with an empty pizza box and a bong.

Not that she could talk—she wasn't the neatest person in the world—but at least she tried to put things away in their proper place. And what did he do all day? He was always surfing—either on the water or on the Internet. He could have at least begun to unpack.

Plus, all of Tinker's talk about what she and Ryan did at Dartmouth was really starting to grate on Mara. The other day, Tinker had come over to hang out, and every other sentence that had come out of her mouth began, "Me and Ryan used to . . ." The litany was endless: Ski trips. Keg stands. Greek Week. Rush parties.

Still, Dartmouth was where she wanted to be—especially because that was where Ryan was. She tried to put her doubts out of her head. She couldn't hold his messiness against him. He couldn't help it that he was used to living in a household with a staff of nine. It was the way he'd been raised. She had seen his room at the frat and shuddered to think what kind of mold had seeped into the beer-soaked walls. But for some reason, she had assumed that when they lived together, he would clean up his act. She had obviously assumed incorrectly.

She couldn't even be that mad at him, because whenever she pointed out how gross the boat was, he was always so cheerful and apologetic about it. Not that it ever amounted to actual cleaning on his part.

Mara pressed the lever and switched off the vacuum. The room didn't look any tidier. She sighed. It was the most she could do for now, since she had to meet Jacqui and Eliza at the premiere of the new feel-good Cameron Diaz movie in an hour.

She arrived a few minutes late and found Eliza waiting by herself in front of the theater. The red carpet was empty, since the stars had yet to arrive. A small group of photographers stood around chatting. A few of them took casual shots of Mara and Eliza to fill the time. Nothing reduced a person to celebutante status faster than the sight of a real celebrity. As soon as tousle-headed Cameron arrived, the photographers forgot all about Mara and Eliza. Not that either minded. They had both gone through the PR rinse cycle and had come out of it a little worse for wear.

"Where's Jeremy?" Mara asked.

Eliza shrugged, and Mara didn't push. It wasn't as if Ryan was there with her either. It turned out Jacqui was the only one who brought a date. She arrived holding hands with Duffy, the tall blond one with the Heath Ledger smile.

"What's the story?" Eliza whispered when Duffy excused himself to collect the complimentary popcorn and snacks.

"He's nice," Jacqui allowed, smiling.

"So is he the one?" Mara teased. "What about the other two?"

Jacqui shrugged. She'd asked Duffy on impulse since she had seen him first—bumping into him at the tennis courts that afternoon. Not that she was neglecting the other two—she was supposed to go parasailing with Grant tomorrow, and Ben had asked her to accompany him to a reggae festival in Quogue later that week.

If the three boys knew they were all dating the same girl, they never mentioned it to her, and for now, Jacqui gave no indication of her actions. Each boy had declared it was best not to let the other two find out about the relationship, and there had been many close calls already—she and Duffy sneaking out of the Jacuzzi just as Grant walked out to the patio, hiding in Ben's closet when Duffy suddenly walked in asking for a light, she and Grant getting his sailboat stuck among some rocks off the bay one afternoon and hoping they'd be rescued by the Coast Guard before Ben and Duffy figured out they were missing.

The last thing Jacqui wanted was for her good time to go bad. She'd promised herself she would come clean once she figured out which one of the boys she really wanted to be with. The problem stemmed from the fact that whenever she was with each of them individually, she was convinced he was the one. Duffy made her laugh, Grant was hands-down the best kisser, and Ben, the most romantic of the three, wrote her love songs on his guitar.

"I'm just having fun," Jacqui insisted. "It's harmless."

Mara shook her head as the lights dimmed. She already had enough trouble with one boyfriend; she couldn't even begin to imagine juggling the affections of three. "I hope you know what you're doing," she told her friend.

and then she moved on to quarters. . . .

THE REYNOLDS CASTLE WAS SHAKING WITH THE SOUND OF a blistering bass line, and the whole house was packed with people gathered for what had now become the weekly "DormDebauchery debauchery." Jacqui was picking her way through the crowd, looking for one of the guys, when she chanced upon the person she would have thought least likely to attend one of these parties.

In the middle of the room, where a Ping-Pong table was littered with empty paper cups, was Anna Perry, intensely taking part in a no-holds-barred Beirut tournament. The guys had explained the rules of the game to Jacqui—but all she understood was that whenever the ball bounced, it meant the participants drank.

"Anna?" Jacqui asked, aghast, just as Anna slammed a Ping-Pong ball on the table and watched it hop around, finally landing in a cup. Jacqui shouldn't have been surprised, considering last weekend she'd bumped into Anna at the VIP lounge at the Star Room.

Anna jumped when she saw Jacqui. "Oh! Hi!"

"What are you doing here?" Jacqui asked. *With a bunch of teenagers?* was the unspoken part of the question.

"Give me a sec," Anna called to the gathering, stepping away from the table, her pint of beer in its plastic cup in hand.

They walked over to a quieter corner, next to one of Chelsea Reynolds's prized Aztec sun calendars that the boys were using for target practice.

Jacqui noticed that there was something different about her boss—for one thing, Anna was wearing her hair long and loose in waves, like a lot of girls were doing now, including Jacqui. And her clothes! Gone were the embellished, structured, proper Michael Kors and Carolina Herrera ensembles. Anna was wearing a tight Skull and Bones polo shirt over a denim mini. The label was the most popular one in the Hamptons that summer—a line of preppy staples emblazoned with a Jolly Roger–like skull-and-bones logo. Anna Perry looked like she was thirty-three going on sixteen. . . . It was a little disturbing.

"What's going on?"

Anna sighed loudly and took a big gulp from her beer cup. "I'm depressed. The lawyer's pressuring me to sign. He told me Kevin wants custody of Cody as well, since he's taking the rest of the kids when he moves out—can you believe it?"

"But didn't he send you a gift certificate to a spa the other day?" Jacqui asked, trying to rally. Her instincts had been right— Kevin would be taking the kids. She would be out of a job for sure!

"He did, but I'm sure his secretary just ordered it. He never buys gifts himself," Anna noted shrewdly.

Jacqui tried not to blush, since she herself had ordered the certificate but had put it under Kevin's name.

"But what about the iPod with all those songs?" Jacqui asked urgently.

Anna shrugged. "I guess."

"He can't want a divorce. I think he's just playing games—he wants you to think he wants out so he can win you back," Jacqui said.

"What are you talking about?" Anna asked. "I'm confused."

"Sometimes, asking for a divorce is just a sign of love," Jacqui said desperately, trying to channel Dr. Phil–like mumbo jumbo. She had to make Anna believe it.

"I don't know. Maybe it's for the best." Anna sighed. "Maybe I should just sign the papers, take Cody, and move back to Jersey. I just want to feel young again. All the passion is gone from our marriage. In the beginning—oh, it was crazy. He was crazy about me. Couldn't divorce Brigitte fast enough. But now . . ." Her voice trailed off. They heard the pounding sound of Kanye West snarling about gold diggers in the background.

"I think the divorce is just a smoke screen. I think Kevin's planning something really special for the two of you," Jacqui said, as sincerely as she could. This was terrible. Operation Parent Trap was a bust—Kevin's "gifts" hadn't seemed to make an impression. And so far, Jacqui hadn't been able to come up with a way to get the two of them in the same city.

"You think so?" Anna asked hopefully.

"Trust me. It's just a sign that he's serious about you. He loves you."

"He used to, anyway," Anna said doubtfully.

Their conversation was cut short when cries of, "*Anna! Anna! Anna's turn!*" arose from the Beirut table.

"Oh, I should go—it's my turn!" Anna said, skipping happily back to the drinking game.

Jacqui bit her lip. She would have to find another way to really convince Anna that Kevin was still in love with her short of Kevin actually coming out and saying so. Although that seemed to be the only way Anna would ever believe her husband was still interested in her. Suddenly, the prospect of going back to São Paulo at the end of the summer seemed inevitable, and Jacqui felt the mean reds coming on—if only she could find someone to talk to, to make her feel better, the way Ben had the night they had first kissed.

"We get all kinds here," Grant mused, coming up behind Jacqui and watching Anna funnel three pints of beer at once. "Your boss, right?"

"Uh-huh." Jacqui nodded, still thinking about the disappointment her grandmother would feel once she found out Jacqui had failed to get accepted into an American college like she had planned. But Grant was still talking and had put his arms around her waist, pulling her close.

"She came over the other night complaining about the noise.

But then she realized she'd met us before—at that club, with you. So Duffy just invited her in—and, well, she's come over every night of the week now."

"Don't you think that's weird? I mean, she's, like, forty." Anna was actually a few years shy of that date, but she might as well have been retirement age to Jacqui, who at seventeen thought twenty-five ancient.

"Yeah, but Duffy thinks she's a MILF. So, there you go." Grant shrugged, leading her to the den off the living room where they could be alone. He locked the door behind them and returned to nuzzle her neck briefly, planting soft butterfly kisses. Kisses that normally would make her knees weak and her heart melt, but when he started unbuttoning her shirt, Jacqui didn't feel like making out just then.

She pushed his hands away and removed herself from his embrace, holding her shirt closed and looking him in the eye. The guys probably thought it was hilarious that their uptight neighbor was playing drinking games, but Jacqui didn't think it was that funny. "I just don't think it's such a good idea to encourage her to visit. I mean, how can she get her marriage back on track if all she's doing is hanging out here?"

"Huh?" Grant had already forgotten the topic of conversation. "Who cares?" he asked, putting his arms around her again and kissing her forehead, then her nose, and finally her lips. He gently pulled her arms away so that he could finish removing her top. His fingers stroked her bare stomach.

Jacqui sighed and rolled over. There were worse things one could do to pass the time than fool around with a cute boy, but just then, it was the last thing she felt like doing.

sometimes, manhattan can be an escape from the hamptons. . . .

BY NOW, MARA WAS SO USED TO GETTING IN EVERYWHERE in the Hamptons that when the PR girl at the door stopped her friends from entering the CD release party for some new hip-hop act, she was momentarily blindsided.

"But they're with me," she argued. "I'm with *Hamptons*. Lucky's already here?"

"I know, Mara, and we're really glad to have you, but we're oversubscribed right now. I'm sorry. I can only get you in plus one," Mitzi's assistant said. "Not plus two."

"It's not a big deal." Jacqui shrugged. "I can go."

"No, stay where you are," Mara ordered.

"Forget it—let's go," Eliza said. "I don't want to stand around and argue with the clipboard patrol all night. Let's just get a drink across the street. We *can* pay for our drinks sometimes, you know."

"But my column," Mara protested, thinking she still needed a few items for the piece.

"Oh, Mara, c'mon. One night off? All you do is run around with your notepad and recorder. Didn't Sam Davis already say you were doing such a great job, you remind her of her when she was young? Can't you just kick back and forget about your column for one night? Just hang out with us; no getting up to talk to celebrities. Okay?" Eliza asked.

"All right," Mara conceded. "I guess I could just write from the pictures tomorrow." She'd quickly become a pro at structuring her column to highlight Lucky's candid photographs.

"That's the spirit." Eliza smiled.

They settled into a couch near the door and ordered drinks. Jacqui was just telling them about the latest Anna Perry transformation when Taylor and Lindsay walked inside the bar. The two used to be Eliza's best friends, back when she was still the most popular girl at Spence, but they had dropped her like last year's Uggs when they discovered Eliza's family had lost all their money and Eliza had been reduced to working as an au pair.

"Oh, hey," Eliza said. Since her family was back in the black, her old friends from New York were cordial. Not that she cared one bit.

Lindsay merely shrugged, but Taylor's response was warmer. "Hey, E., I heard you got into Princeton—good job," she said.

"Thanks. Where are you headed?"

"I got rejected from Yale. Can you believe? My grandfather threatened to revoke his donation. But I got into Brown, thank

God. So it's all good. Providence can't be any worse than New Haven anyway."

"How about you, Linds?"

"Oh, NYU for me," Lindsay said, exhaling a plume of cigarette smoke. "Close to home. I gotta get back to the city next weekend for some pre-frosh event."

"Anyway, see you around, Eliza," Taylor said.

"Hey, aren't you working at Lunch these days?" Lindsay smirked.

Eliza ignored the question, turning to Jacqui instead. "Are you going back for the pre-frosh thing? You should go. They, like, give tours of the campus and talk about the classes and stuff. I'm sure Anna will give you the weekend off. Shannon can take care of the kids."

"Oh, me? I, uh, I don't know," Jacqui said weakly.

"You have to go," Eliza insisted. "You need to scope out the boys and stake out the best dorms. Otherwise, you might end up in social Siberia."

"Yeah, Jac, you know what? We should all go!" Mara piped up. A weekend in New York sounded like an excellent plan.

"Oh my God. What a great idea! Totally!" Eliza nodded. "The three of us haven't been in the city all at the same time—how awesome will that be?"

"Work has been crazy—I totally need a break from Sam Davis. Today she made me hunt down a milk chocolate Mounds bar. And after searching everywhere, I finally found out they only make them in dark chocolate. *There is no such thing as a milk chocolate Mounds.* But do you think she believed me? Plus, a bunch of people from Ryan's frat are coming in and staying with us next weekend. I think I'll avoid getting on that train." Mara shuddered. Ryan's friends from college were nice enough individually, but as a group, they devolved into meathead city. What was it about boys that reduced them to video-game-playing, beer-swilling, immature, testosterone-pumped adolescents when they were all together? "Anyway, maybe while I'm there, I can get a tour of Columbia as well. I still haven't heard from Dartmouth."

"It's settled, then: we're going. Jacqui can do the NYU thing, Mara can visit Columbia, and all of us can hang out and shop," Eliza decided.

They high-fived each other giddily. Jacqui's heart sank. How could she tell them she wasn't going to NYU? She couldn't. As for watching the kids, Shannon could hold down the fort at home as well as keep Operation Parent Trap going. The spa certificate had been Shannon's idea—not that it had done much good. Plus, a weekend in the city would be a much-needed break from Anna, who seemed to want Jacqui's social life for her own.

It would be yet another escape.

She downed her drink quickly and looked longingly at the crowd mingling by the jukebox. She tapped her foot impatiently, thinking it would be fun to join them. As if on cue, she spotted a familiar face by the bar and waved him over.

"Hello, ladies," Ben Defever said, looking adorably owlish

behind his square-rimmed glasses. "Mind if I steal Jacqui away for a moment?"

Eliza and Mara traded knowing smiles. "Go ahead," Mara urged.

Jacqui practically leaped off her seat and followed Ben to the impromptu dance floor. She began shaking her hips wildly to an infectious Outkast hit, but Ben just stood aside, nursing his drink.

"Don't you want to dance?" she pleaded.

"It's so loud in here. Let's go find somewhere we can really talk," Ben suggested, cupping his mouth and yelling so that he could be heard above the music.

"Oh, all right." Jacqui sighed and let him lead her to a quiet corner. Talking just didn't hold the same appeal as dancing did right then. If only she'd bumped into Duffy instead—he could always be counted on for a hilarious Napoleon Dynamite impersonation on the dance floor.

But when you're dating three boys at the same time, sometimes you end up in the right place with the wrong boy.

shannon tries her hand at a little identity theft

THE LIGHTS IN THE AU PAIRS' ROOM WERE STILL SHINING when Jacqui returned later that evening from a grueling conversation with Ben in a coffee shop next to the bar. All she'd wanted to do was chill out, but Ben had been more interested in really delving into a serious discussion on her feelings. He'd dropped her off at the main house, and she had barely made her way to the au pairs' cottage when she bumped into Duffy, who was bouncing by on a pogo stick on the way to the beach.

But after the caffeine-and-analysis session with Ben, Duffy's crazy antics left her cold, and all she wanted to do was lie on the beach and let him hold her.

Sadly, Duffy had other ideas. He couldn't keep still, and for a moment Jacqui wished she were with Grant, who really knew how to make a girl feel good. Finally, she'd said good night after Duffy slightly twisted his ankle on a hard landing and had to limp back home. Jacqui shook her head: boys. They offered so much and too little at the same time.

"You're still up?" Jacqui asked, noticing Shannon sitting

upright in the middle of the single bed, tapping on a laptop computer.

"Wait till you see what I found," Shannon crowed, excitement in her voice. The newest au pair had thrown herself into Operation Parent Trap with gusto and enjoyed coming up with schemes to manipulate the Perrys into thinking they were in love.

"Come look," Shannon said, and Jacqui sat down on the bed next to her.

Jacqui looked at the screen. "Isn't that . . . ?"

"Anna's. I know. I took it from her office. Laurie left the key in the kitchen the other day and I swiped it."

Shannon typed a bunch of keystrokes and Anna's e-mail outbox came up.

"How'd you get her password?" Jacqui asked.

"Easy, it's all stored in the memory. I'm Korean; we're, like, computer geniuses, right?" Shannon smirked. "A kid could figure it out."

Shannon clicked on an envelope icon, launching an e-mail, and filled in Kevin's e-mail address in the "to" box.

"I think it's time Kevin got a love letter from his wife, don't you think?" the younger girl asked.

Jacqui was impressed. Faking e-mail love notes certainly ratcheted up the game. Shannon typed:

Dear Kevin, I'm so sorry I've been so crazy. I can't bear to be apart from you. You know you're the only one for me. This has gone far enough. I miss you and can't fall asleep without knowing you are by my side. I hope your ear is okay. I can't live with knowing I've hurt you. Call off the dogs and let's get back together again. Yours always, Snugglepuss. It was the nickname everyone in the house knew Kevin called Anna. Anna had even had it embroidered on one of her boudoir pillows.

"Nice, huh?" Shannon asked with a cheeky grin. She clicked on the send icon and sent the love note whizzing into cyberspace. Afterward, she went to the sent-mail folder and deleted the e-mail so that Anna would never see it.

Jacqui was still marveling at the younger au pair's creativity when Shannon launched another window. This time, she typed in the mobile address for Kevin's law firm. With speedy efficiency, Shannon accessed his e-mail account as well. "He uses her laptop sometimes. All I needed to do was find all the cookies, and the computer had stored all his passwords, too."

Jacqui nodded, watching over Shannon's shoulder as she began typing:

Dearest Anna, I think I made a mistake. Please forgive me. I'm lost without you. You're as beautiful as you were when I first saw you in my office and we snuck off to the Regency Hotel. Remember those days? You were my secret and now you are my future. I still love you. Your own, Kevinbear. P.S: My ear is healing nicely.

"Kevinbear?" Jacqui gagged.

"I saw it in some old e-mails." Shannon snickered. Like all the staff in the Perry household, Shannon was caught up in the history of her employers' marriage and knew that Anna was the secretary with whom Kevin had been having an affair before she became his wife.

They checked Anna's account. Kevin's e-mail appeared in the new-mail folder.

"Do you think it'll work?" Shannon asked.

Jacqui nodded. "Pretty sure it will on Anna's side, at least. All she needs is a couple of groveling e-mails from him and she'll start sending love notes on her own. The only problem is Kevin. What if he doesn't want to get back together and sends e-mails saying so?"

"Well, I fixed it so that I get a text message whenever Anna gets a new mail from his account so that I can delete his real e-mails if they're nasty," Shannon explained. "I'm sure he'll come around in time and send mushy notes of his own. You said yourself that he still loves her. In the meantime, we'll just write them for him."

Jacqui looked at Shannon in awe. "You're a genius!"

"I know," Shannon said modestly. "Just call me Kevinbear."

That did it. They started laughing hysterically. Faking a romance between their two warring employers was just too much—Jacqui felt tears coming to her eyes, and Shannon laughed so hard her shoulders shook and she almost dropped Anna's laptop. Their mirth was interrupted when Madison suddenly appeared in the doorway. Jacqui had forgotten to lock the door when she entered.

Madison explained that she couldn't sleep and was looking to see if Shannon was still up and interested in watching a movie in the screening room.

"What's so funny?" Madison asked. She looked from Jacqui to Madison expectantly. "Tell me!"

Jacqui stopped laughing immediately and Shannon suddenly looked really guilty. To them, it was a bit of entertainment, but these were Madison's parents they were talking about.

"Nothing—there's, uh, a really funny video on Dorm-Debauchery.com," Shannon said, quickly covering up.

"Let me see," Madison urged.

Shannon quickly closed all the windows and brought up the boys' web site.

"That's it?" Madison asked, unimpressed, when Shannon clicked on a video of a guy falling off his skateboard. She looked quizzically at the two of them. Shannon quickly looked away and didn't meet her friend's eyes.

Jacqui shrugged. "Mad, it's past my bedtime, but if you and Shannon want to see *Titanic* again on the big screen, go ahead."

"I think I'll just go to bed," Madison said coldly.

"I feel bad," Shannon said when Madison had left. "We should tell her."

"I know," Jacqui agreed. "But she'll tell the other kids, and then Anna will freak. Besides, once our plan works, she'll never have to find out anything. They'll be going off on a second honeymoon in no time. We're giving them what they want most from each other—an apology."

"Right." Shannon nodded.

The two girls felt very pleased with the fake e-mail love letters. Operation Parent Trap would soon be a mission accomplished.

Shannon stowed the laptop away and said good night, turning out the lights. Jacqui climbed up on the top bunk, and for a moment, the room was quiet as the two girls drifted off to sleep. Until Shannon whispered, "Snugglepuss," and that set them off once again.

scientists confirm what girls already know: dopamine levels spike when shopping

JULY IN NEW YORK WAS HOTTER THAN USUAL, AND ELIZA cranked up the AC in the Land Rover as high as it would go. They made good time on the highway and arrived in Greenwich Village a little before noon. Most of New York University was situated around Washington Square Park, a small patch of green in the dense urban neighborhood.

Eliza pulled over to the curb next to the stone arch, a small replica of the Arc de Triomphe in Paris. The arch bore a huge purple banner with the NYU logo and the words WELCOME PROSPECTIVE FIRST-YEAR STUDENTS! Several booths and registration tables were set up, and the park was lively with NYU students in purple T-shirts leading around excitable high school seniors. Purple balloons were everywhere. It was a cheerful, vibrant day, and already several students had started an Ultimate Frisbee game in the southeast corner.

"So what do you think? It should end at about four or five? We can pick you up then," Eliza said, unlocking the doors.

"Sure." Jacqui nodded, climbing out. She waved to the two of them from the sidewalk and watched as the car disappeared down the street. When they were definitely out of sight, Jacqui lost her ebullient facade, and her hand fell limp at her side.

Why couldn't she tell the truth? It wasn't like they would judge her or anything. They were her friends. But admitting to Mara and Eliza that she had failed would be like admitting to herself that she had fallen far short of her goal. And she just wasn't ready to do that.

A cute freckled boy wearing an NYU T-shirt found Jacqui walking furtively past the fringes of the event.

"Hey! Welcome to NYU. Will we be seeing you in the fall?" he asked, handing Jacqui an NYU button.

Jacqui colored. "Oh, oh no—no, you won't!" she said, before running past the arch and bursting into tears.

She furiously wiped her face with the back of her hand. This was no way to act. She was in New York, and there was absolutely no reason to cry. Okay, so she might have to go back to Brazil at the end of the summer, and maybe she'd have to be some kind of salesgirl all her life, but she didn't have to think about it right then. As she walked down Bleecker Street, she passed by the Marc Jacobs store.

The mannequin in the front window was wearing a cute pink bikini with purple hearts.

Jacqui stopped sniffing and walked inside, pushing open the glass door, which tinkled to announce her arrival.

"Hi, can I help you?" a cheerful salesgirl asked.

Jacqui nodded. Okay, so every time she was depressed, she bought another bikini. But somehow, handing over the plastic made her feel better. That's why they call it retail therapy.

mara visits the ivy in the apple

THE COLUMBIA CAMPUS WAS LOCATED FAR UPTOWN, ON the other side of the city. Eliza dropped Mara off right on 116th and Broadway, in front of College Walk—a pretty brick-lined street bordered by a row of trees on each side. Unlike NYU, Columbia had a proper campus. There were two green lawns in the middle of a square bordered by Low Library, a domed Palladian building on the north side, and on the south by Butler Library, which housed the university's book collection (one of the largest in the world, next to the Library of Congress). Etched in the pediments of both Low and Butler libraries were the names of Greek writers and philosophers in a majestic array: SOPHOCLES, SOCRATES, HERODOTUS, HOMER.

Mara walked around, impressed by the scale and feeling of scholarship the architecture inspired. She hadn't expected Columbia to be so beautiful. She had visited Dartmouth and had immediately fallen in love with its leafy, colonial New England atmosphere, but Columbia had a different feel—it was an urban campus; New York was just outside the gates. It felt like a genteel sanctuary in a vibrant metropolis, offering the best of both worlds.

Not that it mattered. Columbia might have classical architecture and a New York address, but it didn't have Ryan. She checked into a modern glass-and-steel building with crisscrossing entrance ramps. The admissions office had told her to meet her student guide in front of Ferris Booth Hall. Mara noticed how modern the café inside the building was and how chic the students looked—unlike at Dartmouth, where a slouchy preppy homogeneity prevailed, with everyone wearing J. Crew sweaters or dressed down in slouchy sweatpants. The Columbia kids were a lot more dressed up, in fashionable jeans and hipster shades of black.

She approached a girl in low-rise jeans wearing a worn, vintage Skid Row band T-shirt and Puma sneakers. "Hi, are you Danielle?" she asked.

"I surely am. And that makes you Mara?"

Mara nodded. "Thanks so much for giving me the tour."

"Not a problem at all; I'm happy to show you around." Danielle smiled. She wore her hair in a ponytail, and Mara noticed she didn't wear a speck of makeup. None of the clothes she wore were trendy or expensive, but there was something fresh-faced, practical, and undeniably cool about her. Mara liked her on sight.

Danielle explained that she was a sophomore and from California. She was working in the dorms that summer and was a film and gender studies major. She chattered happily about her classes, Columbia's core curriculum, and the advantages and disadvantages of several first-year dorms.

"So, Carmen is the most popular. It's, like, the classic Columbia freshman experience. You get a suite, four roommates sharing two rooms, and a bathroom. It's nice, like a little apartment, so you don't have to share a bathroom with boys. The other buildings can be a little scary. A lot of the dorms have coed bathrooms, and my friend who was in one last year said she was constipated for a year!"

As Danielle showed her around, Mara noticed that the curly-haired girl said hello to a diverse group of people—from a tall guy in a basketball jersey, to a girl in a printed granny dress and hiking boots, to a boy in a tight white tank top with a rainbow flag pin, denim short-shorts, and black combat boots.

"So what do you do for fun?" Mara asked.

"Oh, there's tons of things. I mostly go out downtown. I like to go clubbing. And, of course, the Angelika—the art cinema. The restaurants in New York are just amazing. Have you ever had Ethiopian food? There's a really great Ethiopian restaurant on 115th. And what's cool is you can use your dining card at a bunch of places on Broadway."

"Is it very social here?"

"How do you mean?"

Mara shrugged, feeling embarrassed. "Are there a lot of frat parties?"

Danielle wrinkled her nose. They walked down 114th Street, past a row of brownstones, each door decorated with a letter of the Greek alphabet. "Yeah, we do have frats. But it's not a big part of Columbia life. Our football team sucks. The typical notion of Greek life here is pretty atypical. Like the frat for poets. Every year, they host this really groovy party called Hot Jazz and Cool Champagne. Girls wear cocktail dresses and this great jazz band plays Billie Holiday. It's really fun."

Mara thought that sounded really cool . . . and extremely different from everything she'd heard from Tinker about social life at Dartmouth.

"So, what are you doing with your summer? Hanging out?"

Mara told her about her column in *Hamptons* magazine.

Danielle immediately lit up. "That is fantastic. Wow. Good for you. Columbia is the place to be for aspiring journalists, you know. Sam Davis—who used to edit all those big magazines? She's an alum. So are a lot of people in publishing. We have an Art Suite, a Writers' Suite, and a Nonfiction Writers' Suite, and the *Spectator* is one of the country's best college papers."

Mara's head was swimming. Columbia sounded really, really great. And the writing program—along with its list of prestigious alumni—was very tempting. Plus, she'd already gotten in. The school actually wanted her—it didn't still have to make up its mind, like Dartmouth.

Maybe she didn't even want to go to Dartmouth anymore. But that was crazy, wasn't it? What about Ryan? She felt bad thinking like that, especially since they'd been fighting so much lately.

After the tour, she said good-bye to Danielle and promised to

look her up if she made it on campus in the fall. Then she hailed
a cab to take her downtown to meet the girls in the Meatpacking
District to check out the new boutiques. One advantage of moving to New York City—the shopping would certainly be a lot
better than in New Hampshire.

you always need to be armed in a food fight

TAKING CARE OF THE KIDS WAS HARDER THAN SHANNON HAD thought. With Jacqui away, Shannon had assumed it would be a breeze. In fact, she had been looking forward to the weekend— how hard could it be?

But Eliza's Land Rover had barely turned the corner when it started. Zoë looked across the breakfast table at the new au pair with a skeptical eye.

"I don't eat pancakes," she informed her.

"You do when Jacqui makes them," Shannon pointed out.

"These are gross," Zoë said, pushing her plate away.

Seeing his sister resist, Cody did the same. "No eat," he said. "I hate you! I hate you! I hate you!"

"C'mon, you guys, these are good, see?" Shannon said, forking up a piece and putting it in her mouth. "Yum."

"No, Zoë's right, these *are* gross. They're, like, the grossest pancakes in the world," William agreed. An evil smile came onto his face. If Jacqui had been there, she would have recognized that smile. It meant that mayhem was about to erupt.

William picked up a pancake and threw it across the table, hitting Zoë in the face.

"Ow!" the little girl screamed. She picked up a handful of berries from a bowl and pelted them at her older brother.

Chortling, Cody did the same, upturning the jug of maple syrup on the walnut table.

"Stop it! Stop it!" Shannon yelled.

"Food fight!" William cheered.

"Nooo!" Shannon yelled as Cody spilled his glass of milk on the floor.

Madison walked in, sweaty and red-cheeked from an early tennis game. Since the other night, when she had walked in on Jacqui and Shannon laughing about something they hadn't shared with her, things had been a little frosty between the two insta-friends. Shannon knew Madison thought she was keeping something from her, and since Madison was right about that, Shannon didn't know what to do about it.

"Uh—I just—they won't stop," Shannon said as a banana flew by, hitting the microwave.

"Yeah, I can see that." Madison shrugged. "Zoë, Bill, quit it. Leave Shannon alone. Come on, now. Clean up this mess. You know you're both being bad."

"You can't do that," Zoë said. "You can't tell us what to do."

"Yeah, you're not Jacqui," William said.

"So what? I'm older than all of you. You have to listen to me. You guys listen to Ryan, Sugar, and Poppy," Madison pointed out.

In answer, William kicked his chair and Zoë knocked her plate to the floor. Cody giggled and did the same, shattering the porcelain.

"*Stop it!* Everyone stop or I'll sell all your toys and give them to children who'll appreciate them!" Madison demanded, letting them know she wasn't fooling around.

The kids shuddered, and one by one they ran off to their rooms to clean themselves up and do as they were told. They had no idea if Madison would carry out her threat, but they weren't sticking around to find out.

"Thanks," Shannon said.

Madison helped pick up the thrown fruit and handed Shannon a roll of paper towels so she could mop up the floor. "It's nothing. You just need to show them who's boss. I think they're all a little antsy since we haven't seen Dad in a while, and the last time that happened, he and Mom had split up."

Shannon was kneeling on the floor, scrubbing, and didn't reply.

"Do you know anything? Are Dad and Anna getting divorced?" Madison asked directly. "Anna's been acting really strange lately, and Dad hasn't been around all summer."

"I don't know," Shannon lied, wishing she could tell Madison the truth. "I think everything's okay."

Anna walked in as Madison was walking out. "Oh, Shannon, I do hope this isn't the way every breakfast is going to be," she said, noticing the stains on the slate counter. She was uncharacteristically cheerful and wearing a tight halter dress. Anna checked her reflection in the beveled mirror by the entryway.

"Are you meeting someone?" Shannon asked, smiling knowingly. According to the e-mail plan, Jacqui and Shannon, posing as Kevin and Anna, had sent e-mail invites from each of their mailboxes to set up a face-to-face appointment. Kevin thought Anna wanted to talk about making up, and Anna in turn was acting under the assumption that Kevin had asked her to lunch to discuss withdrawing the divorce petition.

"Yes, an old friend." Anna smiled mysteriously. "I haven't heard from him in such a long time, but Ward Pershing was one of the cutest young associates in the office. I used to die every time he borrowed my stapler. He said he would love to meet me for lunch at Babette's. How did he know it was my favorite place!"

Who is Ward Pershing? Shannon wondered, panicked.

Something wasn't right. As soon as she could, Shannon stole away to Anna's laptop. She called up the deleted mail, where her fake e-mails were stored. She scrolled to the one labeled *Coffee, Tea or Moi?* that read, *You, me, Babette's, 1 p.m. Be there. Let's make up for lost time.* Alas, the address line didn't read perry@perryassociates.com but pershing@perryassociates.com. Shannon had mistakenly let the automatic function on Anna's mail system fill in Ward Pershing's e-mail rather than Kevin Perry's, and now Anna was going to meet an old crush rather than her husband. Worse, Kevin would be there to see the two of them together and think that Anna was playing a dirty trick and wanted nothing more to do with him!

Shannon groaned. Jacqui was going to *murder* her. And she'd directly lied to Madison, who suspected something.

It was going to be a long weekend.

if the shoe fits . . .

WHEN SHE'D BEEN LIVING IN EXILE IN BUFFALO, ELIZA HAD missed a lot of things about New York City. The food, her friends, their apartment, the way the light reflected off the Hudson River at night. But she hadn't missed anything as much as she'd missed Todd Gillian, her shoe salesman at Jeffrey.

Jeffrey was a candy-colored store on the far west side of lower Manhattan, in the Meatpacking District. Once an outpost of butcher shops and trannie bars, the Meatpacking District was now the trendiest neighborhood in town, filled with designer boutiques and Asian fusion restaurants. Like Barneys, Bergdorf's, and Saks, Jeffrey was a designer emporium—it sold all the majors—Gucci suits, Yves Saint Laurent cocktail gowns, Marni sweaters, Balenciaga shearlings. But what really set Jeffrey apart was its shoe selection. The front tables were all given over to the latest five-inch cork-soled patent leather Christian Louboutin stilettos, mink-lined Manolo Blahnik boots, and spindly Jimmy Choo sandals. It was a temple to designer footwear, the Valhalla of the sole.

Every time Eliza stepped inside its doors, she could hear angels singing. (Okay, so it was in the voice of Sarah Jessica

Parker, but still.) After she'd dropped off Jacqui and Mara, Eliza had driven all the way down to 14th Street to Jeffrey, where Todd was waiting for her.

She had known Todd ever since seventh grade, when he had fitted her with a pair of lime green Jimmy Choo mules for her friend Taylor's bat mitzvah. Todd had seen Eliza through all the important events in her life: her first Gucci loafer, her first Manolo pump, her first Yves Saint Laurent wedge, her first snakeskin Roger Vivier.

He welcomed her now with open arms. "Eliza! Princess!"

"Todd! My love!" It was their usual greeting.

"Wait till you see what I have for you," Todd whispered, disappearing into the storage area. He came back bearing an armful of black shoe boxes.

Eliza took a seat on the suede couch and removed her Clergerie sandals and clasped her hands in anticipation.

She spent several blissful hours trying on every pair. There was a darling one from Marni with pom-poms on the tips, a gorgeous Dries Van Noten—gold, with silver flecks in the heel—a super-sexy Rochas with a Lucite stiletto. She was in shoe heaven. Until a voice interrupted her reverie. *Oh no, not again.* Eliza turned around.

Paige McGinley stood in front of the cashier, berating the salesclerk. She was holding an armful of the latest designer clothes.

"Where is that leather McQueen dress? I specifically ordered it."

"Yes, miss. But you have to prepay and . . ."

Todd saw where Eliza was staring. "It's her again," he whispered. "She's here all the time. At the same time each season. She wants the new line before it's ready to be sold. She wants to see the look books, the samples. You know she works for Sydney Minx? And all he does is copy everyone else's collection. We stopped carrying his line years ago. He had a falling-out with Jeffrey."

Paige noticed Eliza sitting on the couch and walked over with her many white shopping bags. "So, back on the trust fund?" she sneered. "Mommy and Daddy bail you out again? Too hard to work for a living, I know."

Eliza tried to keep a fake smile on her face. "It's the weekend, Paige. I'm off."

Paige didn't notice as her cell phone rang and she struggled to answer it, rooting through her bag. She removed tissues, stacks of business cards, and a vanity case before finding it. Several loose business cards fluttered to the floor. Eliza picked up the cards that fell by her side and saw one that caught her eye. The older girl shrugged her thanks as she flipped open her phone. Too late— she'd missed it.

"Hey, how do you know Jeremy Stone?" she asked as she handed Paige her cards back, Jeremy's brown cardboard one on top of the pile. Eliza couldn't help herself; she had to know the story from Paige's point of view as well. What if Jeremy wasn't telling her something?

Paige's brow crinkled. "Jeremy who?" Then it relaxed. "Oh yeah. I went out with him," she said in a bored voice.

Eliza's face paled, but she kept the smile plastered on her face. "You did?"

"We went out for two years in high school and after college for a bit. He's a sweet guy. He's doing his own landscaping now; good for him. How do you know him?"

Eliza didn't answer. She was mentally calculating the dates—high school and college, which meant . . . Paige was Jeremy's ex-girlfriend. The one he never talked about. The one who'd supposedly broken his heart when they'd broken up. She felt cold suddenly, as if someone had poured a pitcher of margaritas down her back.

Paige and Jeremy had been together. Paige—she was the girl Jeremy had lost his virginity to. It was almost too much to stomach. Jeremy had told her that he'd only fallen in love once before but that it hadn't worked out. Eliza had gotten the impression that it had taken a long time for Jeremy to get over Paige. Maybe he still wasn't over her. Maybe he still loved her. Maybe he thought of Eliza as some consolation prize when all he wanted, really, was Paige.

Eliza noticed something white by the open shoe boxes. It was another piece of paper that had fallen out of Paige's handbag. Eliza picked it up, thinking she'd return it, when she saw what it was. The receipt for the special-order McQueen. Acting quickly, Eliza crumpled it into the toe of one of the shoes she wasn't going to buy and closed the lid tightly. They would never find it now. She knew that by doing so she would cause the order to be delayed and once Sydney got his hands on the dress, it would be too late to manufacture the knockoffs.

But sabotaging Sydney's plan and knowing that Paige would have to face the designer's wrath later didn't do anything to make her feel better.

Paige had been with Jeremy. Jeremy had slept with Paige. The news was even worse than realizing once she'd made her selections that she couldn't even begin to pay for the shoes. It was only then that she remembered her mother had taken away her credit cards and she wasn't getting a paycheck from Lunch until next week.

the girls string up cupid's arrow and aim it at the perrys

MARA AND JACQUI ARRIVED AT PASTIS AT THE SAME TIME to find Eliza glumly sitting by herself in a corner of the bustling restaurant.

"What's wrong?" Mara asked, pulling out a chair.

The three of them quickly ordered mussels, frisée salads, french fries, and a bottle of wine to share. They dug into the food, sopping up the garlicky sauce that came with the seafood with the crusty bread and toasting each other with glasses of wine.

Eliza told them about Paige and Jeremy and how she was worried that he hadn't called her since the night they'd quarreled at Mount Fuji.

"And the worst part of it is, I'm eighteen and I'm still a virgin!" Eliza wailed, trying to make a joke out of the situation.

"It'll happen," Mara assured her. "I'm sure he'll call when you get back."

"*Querida*, so what if you're a virgin? It's better to wait for the right time," Jacqui said wisely.

235

"I guess." Eliza shrugged. She sighed and tried to cheer up. She didn't want to be such a bummer on their weekend in New York. "Whatever. It doesn't matter."

"Of course it does," Mara said, reaching over to squeeze her arm.

It was so nice to have friends who actually cared about her feelings. "I know. But we don't need to talk about it right now. Do you guys want to get another bottle? I parked my car at my garage, so I don't need to drive. And let's move out to a sidewalk table so we can smoke."

Many cigarettes and several bottles of wine later, they caught a cab back up to the Upper East Side, where they were spending the night at Jacqui's apartment. Eliza had invited them all to stay at her place, but they'd decided it would be fun to see where Jacqui lived instead. Besides, Eliza's parents were kind of odd about guests—her mother had almost had a heart attack after finding a greasy handprint on the Regency sofa after a dinner party, and since then they entertained very rarely. Besides, at Jacqui's they could do whatever they wanted.

Jacqui felt the pride of ownership as she unlocked the door. "It's really tiny—but it's all mine." She stopped. Voices were coming from the alcove. *People* were inside.

"Excuse me?" she called.

A dark-suited Corcoran real estate broker stood in the middle of the living room. She was talking to an earnest young couple in their twenties.

"Oh, hello, are you the current tenant? Sorry. Kevin said this afternoon that we could show the place," the broker explained. "We'll get out of your way."

They left, and Jacqui closed the door, totally agitated. "They can't sell this place! They can't! This is my home!" What had happened? Jacqui panicked. Why was Kevin selling the apartment? He and Anna were supposed to have had a romantic lunch at Babette's earlier, making the divorce history.

"Why not?" Mara asked, putting her bag down on the floor and admiring the marble fireplace. The mantel held a bunch of photos of them from summers past and from their spring break in Cabo.

"Hold on a sec," Jacqui said. "I need to call Shannon." She picked up her cell and dialed frantically.

Shannon picked up on the first ring. "Jac, I'm so, so sorry. I tried to call, but it's been so busy here with you gone."

"What happened? Didn't they go to lunch?"

"That's the thing—they didn't," Shannon confessed. "Well, I mean, they were both there, but by the time Kevin arrived, Anna was eating with someone else."

"Excuse me?"

Shannon explained the Pershing/Perry e-mail snafu and how Anna had returned from lunch angrier than ever, since Kevin had

confronted her at the restaurant and accused her of deceiving him
and, worse, having an affair with a much-younger man.

"So the divorce is still on?" Jacqui moaned.

"Totally. Kevin had a fit, said he was going to the judge as
soon as possible, putting it on an express track." Shannon sighed.

"It's not your fault," Jacqui said, even though she wanted to
strangle the girl for making such a sloppy mistake. But that was
the problem with the Cyrano scheme—stealing identities only
led to more confusion. She hung up the phone and looked at
Mara and Eliza, who were waiting patiently for an explanation of
her outburst and the odd phone call.

"What was that all about?" Mara asked.

"Yeah, and why are you so worried about Kevin selling this
place? Won't you be at the dorms?" Eliza asked, poking into the
fridge.

Jacqui looked utterly miserable. "Because . . ."

"Do you want to try and keep this apartment?" Eliza asked,
still not understanding. "You really shouldn't. You'll make more
friends if you stay downtown, you know."

"No, no—I—I'm not going to NYU," Jacqui said, slumping
across the kitchen counter that separated the stove and refrigera-
tor from the rest of the room. She had a stricken look on her
face, and she buried her head in her hands. She'd tried to hide
from the truth all summer by hanging out with the web site guys,
but now that she was with her friends, she couldn't take it alone
anymore. She needed their support.

"You didn't like the tour?" Mara asked, still not comprehending.

"No—I didn't take the tour," Jacqui said, surfacing for a moment "I—I didn't get in."

Mara and Eliza exchanged shocked glances, and Jacqui told them the whole story. The missing math and science requirements, the fifth year of high school program, the Perrys' impending divorce and how if they split up, it meant a one-way ticket back to Brazil. They felt awful for Jacqui—Mara since all she did was talk about college, Eliza because she knew how hard it was to live with a secret.

"I'm so sorry I lied to you guys," Jacqui said. "I just didn't want to deal with it."

"It's okay," Mara said, putting an arm around Jacqui and hugging her. "We understand. I wish there was something we could do to help."

Jacqui sniffed. "I wish there was too. I'll really miss you guys if I end up going home."

"Well, we can't let that happen," Eliza declared in her bossy way.

"No, not at all." Mara nodded. "You're not going anywhere. That's so weird Ryan hasn't mentioned it. But then again, he hardly talks to his dad."

"Anna's keeping it a secret from all the kids. It doesn't look good. He already served her papers and Anna is really close to signing." Jacqui told them about Operation Parent Trap and how she'd been sending romantic gifts to Anna with Kevin's name on them as well as how Shannon's idea to craft lovey-dovey e-mails in Kevin's name had blown up in their faces when an e-mail from "Anna" had gone astray.

"Yikes," Eliza sympathized. "Shannon's a piece of work, isn't she?"

"There's got to be something more we can do," Mara said. "Something to really bring them back together, face-to-face."

"Their anniversary is next month, you said?" Eliza asked, looking thoughtful.

Jacqui nodded.

"What could we do?" Mara asked. "There has to be something Anna would want that would make her change her mind."

"What about a party?" Eliza suggested.

"For who?"

"The two of them. As a surprise," Eliza said, getting excited. "Maybe if they celebrate their anniversary, they won't want to split up. When my parents almost got divorced, my dad threw this huge party at the Frick for my mom. And because of that, they decided to stay together. My mom said that if my dad would rent out an entire museum to keep her, then he was a keeper too."

"I like it," Mara said. "It's romantic."

"Let's do it," Eliza urged.

"Okay," Jacqui said. "It's worth a throw."

"Shot. Worth a shot," Mara automatically corrected.

"Yes, yes." Jacqui nodded impatiently. "You know what I mean. I still don't know if it's going to work, though. We could throw the best party in the world—but what if neither of them shows up?"

"Well, we'll just have to make sure they have no choice but to be there. How hard can it be?" asked Eliza, ever the optimist.

The three of them put their heads together, talking way into the night. Party planners never worked so hard.

is there more to eliza than just a pretty face?

GOING BACK TO WORK AFTER A FUN WEEKEND IN THE CITY was even harder than Eliza had thought. It wasn't that she didn't like working at Lunch—the place was fun, and she liked the camaraderie in the kitchen. They'd warmed up to her when they saw how hard she was trying to do a good job. Her co-workers were mostly Irish kids working illegally or Long Island natives saving up for summer shopping money, like she was. She'd been assigned back to kitchen duty since they were shorthanded after a couple of cooks quit. Thankfully, this time she hadn't upset any soup pots or liberated any two-pound lobsters.

The work was repetitive and demanding—as a sous-chef, it was her responsibility to cut up all the vegetables needed for the varying soups and salads. Everything needed to be diced to the same exact size, and her hand was getting sore from leaning on the knife. Not that she was complaining—she was determined not to act like the princess Jeremy thought she was. She hadn't called him since they'd had their tiff at Mount Fuji, and she had been disheartened to realize he hadn't called her either. It was the longest they had ever gone without talking. All weekend she had checked and re-checked her Treo, but there'd been no missed calls from J. Stone.

"Order!" the waitress called, bursting in through the restaurant door just as another figure walked in through the back way.

Eliza threw some chopped onions into the chowder. When she turned around, she saw Jeremy standing by the metal sinks, his arms crossed.

"You can't be here," she said petulantly, even though her heart was beating with elation.

"Relax, I know these guys," Jeremy said, winking at the Mexican busboys.

"What do you want?"

"C'mon, let's go outside and chat," he said soothingly.

"I can't; I don't have a break."

"Ricardo—okay if Eliza takes fifteen?" he asked.

The chef nodded. Jeremy had grown up in the area and so knew almost everyone who worked at Lunch.

Eliza sighed and followed him to the parking lot.

"I know you're mad," he said. "And I want to say, I thought about it, and I did give you a hard time the other night, and I'm sorry."

"Fine. Is that it?" Eliza said.

"I'm apologizing—isn't that good enough?"

"Okay, but you shouldn't have lied to me," she accused.

Jeremy's forehead crinkled. "What do you mean? What are you talking about?"

"Paige. I know what happened between the two of you. She told me."

He threw his arms up. "What happened between the two of us? I'm confused. What *did* happen between the two of us?"

"She was your girlfriend."

He exhaled. "It was a long time ago. It was nothing," he said, biting the hangnail on his thumb.

"Nothing! You're full of it! She was the one, wasn't she? *The one.*"

"The one?"

Eliza whispered fiercely. "The one you lost your virginity to. Your girlfriend in high school who dumped you in college."

"Hold up! Hold up!" Jeremy said. "First off, okay, yes, she was the one. But it was a long time ago, and seriously, neither of us knew what we were doing. And she didn't break up with me. I broke up with her. C'mon, now. It's ancient history."

"Not to me."

"You're really something you know?" he said, smiling.

"What are you looking so pleased about?" she asked.

"I'm not. You're being silly. Let's not fight."

"I'm not fighting," Eliza said defensively.

But they continued to argue until Jeremy finally lost his temper. "You know what? You're so obsessed with Paige? Then maybe you should be more like her. At least she was passionate about her work. She doesn't just coast on her looks and connections. She never complains! She loves her job, and she does something that she loves doing."

"Oh—you!" Eliza said, smacking him with her apron.

It left a red mark on his cheek.

He raised his eyebrows and shook his head. He left without another word.

Eliza went back to the hot kitchen. She was utterly disgusted. Anyone could be someone's bitch, like Paige was to Sydney, but slaving away for someone didn't equal passion! How did working at Lunch indicate she was "coasting on her looks and connections"? And, she had wanted to say to him, she *had* found something to be passionate about—she'd loved her job at the designer label but had been fired before she could even explore it more thoroughly. She would show them! She would show Jeremy and Paige that she wasn't just some lazy rich girl who didn't do anything but shop.

It was over a hundred and ten degrees in the kitchen, and Eliza wrung sweat from the bottom of her T-shirt. She took a pair of kitchen shears and slashed the collar and the hem to make it vented and more comfortable. Then she rolled up her shorts and pinned them.

"Hey—look at that," said Margie, the Irish girl who manned the fryer station. "Can you do that to mine too?"

Eliza wiped the tears from her eyes. "Sure." She nodded.

who will have the
last laugh?

VISITING THE DORMDEBAUCHERY WEB SITE HAD BECOME one of Jacqui's regular habits since kissing all three of its founders. But when she logged on to the site after arriving back from the city, she found that the home page displayed the same jokes it had shown for the last week. None of the gags had been updated, and the newest video, which showed an intoxicated starlet smiling cluelessly into the camera while her strap fell and exposed her left breast and plastic surgery stitches, was already old news.

She clicked off the screen, wondering if something was wrong.

When she arrived at the Reynolds castle that evening, she was surprised to find that, for the first time that entire summer, it was dark: the lights were off, the windows shuttered. There was no sign of the nightly debauchery—no hordes of Hamptonites angling for entry, no girls engaging in wet T-shirt contests on the lawn, no booming hip-hop music, no Beirut tournament. What was going on? Had somebody died? She opened the door, calling out softly, "Grant? Ben? Duffy? Where are you guys?"

She found the three of them sitting glumly on the sofa, each nursing a can of beer. Grant was listlessly throwing darts at the board across the room but missing the target by miles; the carpet was strewn with fallen darts. Duffy was picking at a crusted wound on his elbow from the pogo-stick fall. Ben was immersed in a video game but didn't seem to be doing very well; the voice on the television kept intoning, "Please reload. Please reload."

Grant stopped mid-throw, and the dart hit Ben on the knee.

"Watch it!" Ben said, annoyed, throwing it back at him, but it hit Duffy's sore elbow instead.

"Hey!" Duffy bellowed.

They all looked up at Jacqui with gloomy faces, a marked contrast to their usual manic excitement.

"Oh, you're here," Duffy said without his usual enthusiasm.

"Jacqui, Jacqui, Jacqui." Grant shook his head.

"What do you want?" Ben asked a bit brusquely.

Jacqui sat on the arm of the sofa. "Everything all right?"

"No." Ben sighed. "The site's tanking. We've got nothing new, no new jokes or videos. And our hits dropped way down. We lost, like, seventy percent of our market share."

"There's some new site now where kids can put up their own videos and jokes. Goddamn Internet economy. Everything moves too fast," Duffy explained.

They explained that the lack of eyeballs had cased their advertising revenues to take a free fall, and the cost of throwing insane weekly parties had almost bankrupted them.

"We might have to sell the Black Hawk!" Grant cried.

"Why don't you put up some new jokes, then?" Jacqui asked.

"We can't think of any." Duffy shrugged. "Nothing's come to mind. Nothing seems funny anymore."

"I'm depressed," Ben admitted.

"We're doomed," Grant declared.

"C'mon, guys, it can't be that bad! It's just a speed bump; you'll think of something. I know you will. Duffy—Ben—Grant—come on—"

"We know, you know," Ben interrupted.

"Excuse me?" she asked, leaning forward.

"We know what you've been doing." Duffy said, looking at her mournfully.

"You deceived us," Ben lamented.

"What?"

"You've hooked up with all three of us—don't try to deny it; we all know," Grant said.

Jacqui blushed. "I didn't mean to. . . ." Really, she didn't. It had just happened—she had found all three of them irresistible, although in the back of her mind, she'd known this day would arrive, and she suddenly felt awful.

"It's okay. We should have known," Ben said. "It's not such a big deal, except that there's three of us and only one of you."

"And we can't live like this," Grant confessed. "So you have to choose."

"One of us," Duffy said soberly. "Only one."

Exchange all three boys for just one? Jacqui turned crimson. How could she ever decide? Because in a way, she loved all three of them . . .

you get what you wish for

WHEN MARA ARRIVED BACK FROM NEW YORK, SHE FULLY expected the *Malpractice* to be messier than ever—after all, several of Ryan's college buddies had descended on the boat for the weekend. Mara steeled herself for the smell of stale beer when she walked inside the main cabin.

She pushed the sliding door aside, but she was assaulted by a strangely pleasing smell. Like roasting vegetables and rosemary. She looked around—there were no boxes on the floor, no cigarette butts, no empty cans, no dust bunnies in the corner. Instead, the boat was clean, its floors shining, the carpets vacuumed. There was a spray of bamboo sticks in a glass vase, emitting a pleasant scent reminiscent of freshly washed laundry.

For a moment, Mara wondered if she should check the boat's transom to see if she was in the right place.

But then Ryan walked out of the kitchen, holding a wooden spoon.

"Taste," he said in greeting, placing the spoon to her lips.

"You cook?" she asked, and took a lick. It was delicious. Marinara sauce.

"Occasionally."

"And you cleaned?"

"Well, Laurie sent someone over," Ryan admitted. "But I figured it was about time. I should have just had someone come every week. You were right: the place was getting disgusting."

"Did you have fun with your friends?" she asked, watching as he uncorked a bottle of wine.

"It was fun," Ryan said. "But I missed you."

"I missed you too," Mara replied, nuzzling him on the cheek. They kissed briefly. Ryan sniffed her hair, breathing in her scent—he hadn't done that in a long time.

She embraced him tightly. Mara was delighted. The show of affection seemed to mean he was ready to be more supportive of her career aspirations. She was tired of feeling guilty for leaving him all the time. "I have the best news!" she said.

"I do too, but you go first," Ryan said, eyes twinkling. He was still holding her close.

"Sam Davis called while I was in New York. The Associated Press is picking up that profile I did on Sydney! They're going to offer it to all their media outlets. It's going to be published nationally! Can you believe that?" Mara was still in shock about the news. Sam had been very complimentary as well and had said that Mara had bona fide "chops."

"That's great." Ryan nodded, but Mara noticed he let go of her ever so slightly. "Good for you."

Her smile faltered a bit. Why didn't Ryan ever seem that excited about her job? He'd once admitted he never even read

Hamptons magazine, although he did make an exception for her column. But only when she reminded him.

"Sam said that they never sell any stories to the AP. And I got a call the other day from an editor at *Harper's Bazaar*—they want me to write a little story about 'Hamptons style.' It's only five hundred words, but still."

"Mmm." Ryan nodded again. "Very cool."

"So what's your news?" Mara asked, suddenly remembering Ryan had mentioned having some glad tidings as well.

Ryan immediately lit up again. "There's something for you. On the table."

Mara walked over to her desk. It was a thick white envelope with the Dartmouth crest. "Oh my God," she whispered.

Ryan's eyes were dancing. "You got in! I *told* you it would happen!"

"I did," Mara breathed, sliding her fingers through the clasp. She removed a package of forms and read the official letter congratulating her on being accepted into Dartmouth's next freshman class.

"Now we can be together!" He enveloped her in a tight hug.

Mara put the forms back in the envelope, feeling conflicted. She should be happy. She had finally gotten what she wanted. She had gotten into Dartmouth. But she remembered the Columbia campus—the energy of the city, the writing program, Danielle's effortless sophistication. Her story was going out on the wires, and she had an assignment from *Harper's Bazaar*. How could she continue to write about fashion if she was stuck in New Hampshire?

She'd wanted Dartmouth so much, but now that she'd gotten it, it felt anticlimactic.

"Well, what are you waiting for?" Ryan exhorted, giving her a pen so that she could sign the acceptance forms.

He looked so eager and excited for her. Mara remembered why she'd wanted to attend Dartmouth so much in the first place. She and Ryan would be together now; their summer wouldn't have to end. Maybe it was only beginning.

Mara signed her name to the statement, promising to attend Dartmouth in the fall. She put it in her purse. She would mail it tomorrow, with a deposit, as soon as possible. Ryan handed her a stamp.

"C'mon," he urged, pulling her to the kitchen. "Dinner's getting cold."

donna karan, eat your heart out

JEREMY DIDN'T THINK SHE HAD PASSION? SHE *HAD* PASSION. She would show him she was more than just some kind of shopping addict. He thought that all she could do was spend money? And obviously, even with the job at Lunch (which left her fingers calloused, hello), she still didn't merit his respect. Paige was doing something she loved, while Eliza was just a wage slave. Well, enough of that. *She* was going to do something she loved.

Everyone always told her she dressed the best—that she had a unique sense of style that everyone wanted to copy, and it was *her* vision that had made Sydney's show a success—she'd even heard that due to the hype that surrounded her helicopter entrance, orders were up and Sydney's line was back in the black. After working for more than a month at Lunch, Eliza wasn't afraid of getting her hands dirty, and she suddenly realized how she could put two and two together—her passion for fashion and her newly acquired work ethic.

She would design her own collection. Just a few pieces, maybe ten outfits total. She just needed one standout piece. Calvin Klein had made his name on the backs of his blue jeans. Donna

Karan on a stretchy bodysuit. Zac Posen on the strength of one slinky party dress.

Fall meant back to school; back to school usually meant uniforms. Inspired, Eliza sketched out plans to do a working-girl glamour collection: "The Uniform of Fall," she would call it—cool, trendy pieces inspired by uniforms of all kinds—school uniforms (plaid, tartan, gray wool, burgundy, rep ties), flight attendant uniforms (pencil skirts, waist-nipping jackets, colorful scarves), military uniforms (brass-buttoned coats, epaulets, camouflage), Wall Street uniforms (bespoke suiting, skinny pants, houndstooth). A working woman's uniform—the height of wearable chic.

Anytime she had a break between shifts at the restaurant, she started drawing in her book, and thanks to her internship at Sydney's office, she knew where to find the best pattern makers and fabric retailers available. Her friend Todd, the shoe salesman at Jeffrey, offered to be her business partner, and Eliza couldn't have been more excited about the prospect of setting up her own label.

She was going to show Paige and Sydney a thing or two about real motivation and creative vision—something they both lacked.

A few days later, her parents were away for the night, so Eliza invited the girls to come over to her house for dinner, thinking it would be fun for the three of them to cook together instead of going out all the time. She'd visited the farmers' market that afternoon and had returned with fresh vegetables and herbs, and her boss at Lunch had given her a few fat trout filets to take home.

Eliza was marinating the fish in olive oil and lemon when Jacqui and Mara entered, bearing wine bottles and fresh bread from Citarella.

"I love your kitchen," Mara said, putting away the groceries and looking over Eliza's shoulder to take a peek at the fish. "This is such a great house." She squeezed Eliza's arm affectionately.

Eliza smiled. "Thanks, it was my grandmother's. They've had it for ages. Dad had to pay double what they sold it for, but it was worth it."

The Thompsons' kitchen had an earthy, comfortable, shabby quality belied by the custom built-in stainless-steel industrial Traulsen refrigerators. Eliza's mom had decorated in a vaguely French country style, with tons of rooster- and hen-shaped crockery and colorful floral towels. Whitewashed floorboards, rusting and paint-scraped window finishes. And every conceivable surface was covered by family photographs. Eliza on her fifth birthday, wearing a pink dress and carrying a parasol. Her parents dancing at the Stork Club. Eliza on skis in Gstaad. Her mother as a debutante at the Waldorf. Photographs from a glamorous yet loving family life.

Mara admired each picture, thinking Eliza led a charmed and charming life—the kitchen hummed with good energy.

"What's this?" Jacqui asked, noticing a thick sketchbook in

the middle of the table. She opened it and began leafing through the pages. "Wow, Liza. Is this your stuff? It's really good."

Eliza nodded as she stuck the fish in the broiler. "Uh-huh." She told them about her idea for setting up her own label, her face aglow.

"It's brilliant," Mara said, looking at the theme that Eliza had put together. "Can we do anything?"

"Thank God you asked—I need so much help," Eliza confessed, outlining the different tasks: cutting fabric, acting as fit models for the patterns, putting together a press release, meeting with boutique owners. "I bought a sewing machine, but I'm going to have the samples made by real garment workers in the city."

"When's the fashion show?" Jacqui asked, taking a sip from her glass. She'd already offered to help Eliza as a sales coordinator—she would tell her bosses at the boutique in Brazil about the new line.

"A show—God, I never even thought of that," Eliza admitted. "But that's a great idea."

"Sydney's showing the last week of August," Mara informed her. "We just got the invitation today. He's not doing Fashion Week in New York; he wants to show early."

"Wouldn't it be funny if I did my show on the same night?" Eliza laughed. Then she realized—that was exactly what she was going to do. "But how am I going to do a show without any money? I'd have to pay to rent a place and everything. I can't afford that."

"Why don't you do it on the beach? The beach is free. There's a really nice stretch over on Flying Point that's pretty far from any houses. You could have it there," Jacqui said, thinking of the night she'd spent with Grant and feeling sad that they had yet to speak to each other. Grant was ignoring her calls. She'd told her friends what had happened, and they'd both told her to give it time.

"I love it. I'm going to do it!" Eliza decided. "Thanks, guys."

They set the table and sat down to dinner. The fish was fresh and wonderfully moist, and they all complimented Eliza on her cooking.

"Jeremy's a lucky guy," Mara said.

Eliza winced. "I don't know. We're not really talking at the moment." She told them about what had happened the other day at Lunch. It made her unhappy. She didn't know if they were still together or just fighting. "Anyway, I guess one of us should apologize, but I can't decide if I'm waiting for him to call me or if I should just call him."

"You should call him," Mara urged. "Summer's almost over. You don't want to waste any more time," she said, thinking more about herself and Ryan. She told them about finally getting into Dartmouth, and they drank to her acceptance.

"But you don't seem happy?" Jacqui noticed.

"I am, but I'm not," Mara admitted. "I kind of feel like I really want to stay in New York, but then there's Ryan. . . ."

"Boys," Eliza summed up. "Can't live with 'em, can't live without 'em."

"I'll toast to that." Jacqui laughed, thinking about how even though the boys had given her an ultimatum, behind each other's backs, they were still trying to sneak some time alone with her—each had taken the "showdown" to mean she would choose him. This insanity had to end before someone really got hurt. And at that very moment, Jacqui made her decision.

They spent the night helping Eliza with the fabric, pinning up a few patterns, acting as fit models for a few of the outfits, and dancing around the room to Gwen Stefani's newest album. Even if the boys were being a pain, it was a comfort to know they could always count on each other.

she's just not that into you

THROWING A SURPRISE ANNIVERSARY PARTY FOR TWO PEOPLE on the brink of divorce was harder than Jacqui had assumed. Especially when one's love life wasn't turning out to be so great either. It was time for the three-ring circus to stop, and when Duffy invited her for a sunset ride in the golf cart one afternoon, she saw a chance to clean the slate. They had parked near the spot where they had first tumbled out of it and kissed.

"You look so serious," Duffy chided after Jacqui told him she needed to tell him something important.

"I've got some bad news," she said gently, brushing the sand from her jeans.

"It's not me, is it?" he asked.

"It's not you," Jacqui said. "It's me." They both cracked up at the clichéd breakup line.

"Ah, Jacarei. We were having so much fun!"

"I hope you're not mad."

Duffy grinned, the same easy grin he'd given her the first time they'd met. "How can I stay mad at such a beautiful girl?"

"Friends?" Jacqui asked, holding up her hand for a high five.

Duffy slapped it affectionately. "Always."

Jacqui exhaled. One down, two to go.

Later, back at Cupid headquarters, Eliza had procured the number of the best wedding planner in town, and that afternoon, the three of were meeting the organizer to go over the event. They had decided that the best place for the anniversary party was in the Perrys' own backyard. Georgina Perkins's office was in a simple low-slung Southampton cottage, filled with comfortable overstuffed linen couches. There were antique floral prints framed on the wall, numerous pastel chenille throws, and mismatched crockery—tasteful country chic.

"So, is this for your parents?" the high-strung blond-bobbed Martha Stewart doppelganger asked, opening up her massive black appointment binder.

"No," Jacqui said quickly.

"Kind of," Eliza replied.

"They're, uh, *like* parents to us," Mara explained with a helpful smile.

"So, you're thinking tent in the backyard, butlered hors d'oeuvres, five courses, a band, fireworks at the end?" Georgina asked, describing the typical hundred-thousand-dollar Hamptons affair.

"Oh yes." The three of them nodded eagerly.

"And a chocolate fountain. We have to have one," Eliza insisted. Her cousin had gotten married over the spring, and the five-foot-tall flowing chocolate extravaganza had been the hit of the evening. "It's romantic," she argued.

"That's extra," Georgina noted.

"And could we have the steaks catered from Delmonico's?" Jacqui asked.

"Sure. But we'll have to get them from the city, so it'll be extra as well."

"Why Delmonico's?" Mara asked.

"I'll explain later," Jacqui said.

"And who are you thinking for a band?" Georgina asked.

"Well—I know it's a stretch, but do you think we could get Matchbox Twenty to sing at the party?" Jacqui asked.

"Matchbox Twenty?" Eliza gagged. "They're, like, so 1998!"

Mara giggled. Even though she had nothing against the band, Eliza did have a point. It was almost as bad as inviting Sheryl Crow.

"Precisely. That's when they met," Jacqui said. "Anna would die."

"I don't know if we could get the band; I think they might have broken up," Georgina said. "But we could maybe get Rob Thomas to sing one song. I know his wife."

"Excelente." Jacqui smiled.

Georgina wrote down notes furiously. Then she pulled out a deposit form. "We'll need fifty percent up front and then the rest the day of the party. Sign here."

"We've got it covered." Jacqui said smoothly.

They left the wedding planner's office and walked over to a nearby coffee shop.

"So, who's paying for this party?" Eliza wondered.

Jacqui looked sheepish. "I put it on Anna's account. I figured, if it works, they'll thank me for it later. If not, I'm fired anyway."

"Nice." Eliza nodded, impressed.

There was just one problem—Jacqui and Shannon couldn't figure out a way to get Kevin Perry to the Hamptons on the day of the party. After the confrontation at the restaurant and the bad feeling it had engendered, the last place he wanted to be was anywhere near his wife. Worse, Shannon had checked his e-mail account and found that Kevin was planning a trip to the Caribbean in late August—the same time as the party. They had to think of something fast; otherwise Rob Thomas would be singing a divorce dirge rather than a love song.

Later that evening, Jacqui and Ben shared a banana split at the Snowflake diner so she could take care of other unfinished business.

Ben reached over to hold her hand, and Jacqui gently but firmly pushed it away.

"Listen, I have to tell you something," she said. She sighed; this was going to be hard.

But Ben, who was always sensitive to her moods, saved her

from the difficult part. "I already know," he said quietly. "I wish we didn't have to make you choose. It was fun while it lasted. I think we all kind of knew what was going on, but we tried to pretend it wasn't."

"Ben—you guys were right. There's not three of me, and it's not fair to you." She scooped up some fudge-covered ice cream, thought better of it, and put her spoon down again. It seemed rude to eat at a time like this. "I'm sorry," Jacqui said.

"Don't be. I had a great time." Ben smiled. He caressed her cheek softly. "It was worth it."

Jacqui leaned over to kiss him sweetly on the cheek. "Every minute."

nicky hilton can do it— why not eliza?

IT WAS THE THIRD WEEK OF AUGUST—SUMMER HAD FLOWN by so quickly. Mara sat at her cubicle at work, marveling at how much she'd learned that year. She was going over the proposed outline for her final column with Sam, who was on the other line yelling at her husband for having bought them tickets to the Caribbean without securing a free first-class upgrade. "Did you tell them who I am? You did? And—they didn't?"

"So, I was thinking, for my final piece—there's this really great new designer who's showing on the beach next week," Mara said when Sam had slammed down the phone. By now, Mara was used to her boss verbally abusing everyone, including her spouse. It was a common occurrence.

"Who is it? Can they send samples?" Sam asked, perking up and sounding completely normal, as if she hadn't been screaming her lungs out just a second ago.

"No, it's her first collection. It's Eliza Thompson. Remember, the girl we put in the socialite centerfold the first week of July?" Each summer, the magazine regularly shot the season's hottest social swans in a three-page foldout. It was a tongue-in-cheek

264

nod to the *Playboy* model, with lists of the socialites' "turn-ons" and "turn-offs." *Turn-ons: Five-hundred-thread-count sheets. Turn-offs: Flying commercial. Eager readers collected them like baseball cards.* ("Oh, you have an Elisabeth Kieselstein-Cord! Trade you for an Ivanka Trump?")

"She has a line?"

Mara nodded eagerly.

"I don't know," Sam said doubtfully. "This is the final issue, so we can only cover the really big names. Sydney Minx is having his show at the same time. Plus, I spoke to his publicist—he's going to give us a full interview this time."

"But I really think Eliza Thompson is going to be more relevant to the column, to the new generation of readers who are her age . . ." Mara argued. After the success of her column and since receiving the attention of the New York media world, Mara was starting to believe she could pull off being a reporter after all. She was eager to flex some of her new journalistic muscle, especially if it meant being able to help a friend.

"Maybe," Sam said. "But the whole socialite-with-a-clothing-line is kind of done, isn't it? Aren't they all DJs now? Or porn stars? Let's stick with Sydney."

"Are you sure? I really feel like Eliza's show will be more dynamic and current," Mara wheedled, thinking of several fabulous outfits Eliza had in store.

"Sydney's show is the biggest thing to hit this town," Sam snapped. "It's going to close the social season. Everyone is going to be there—nobody can stop talking about that show he did earlier this year. And your profile will only made him a bigger deal. People love scandal. It's going to be his comeback."

"But Eliza—"

"Enough. I want you at Sydney's show."

Mara nodded. She'd been shot down, but what could she do? After all, Sam had been in the business twenty years.

She looked at the invitation Eliza had sent—a carefully constructed origami representation of an oversize tote bag ("The Working Woman's New Briefcase")—and put it aside. There was no way she would be able to cover Sydney's show and Eliza's at the same time. Eliza was bound to be so disappointed; she'd already told several prospective buyers that *Hamptons* would be covering the collection. Mara only hoped her friend would understand.

daughter knows best

IN THE MIDDLE OF HER FITTING, JACQUI GOT A CALL FROM the caterer. Bad news. The credit card account that Jacqui had given her at the meeting had been closed. Kevin had already started to freeze all of their mutual assets. *Damn.* Jacqui thought quickly and provided Georgina with Anna's ATM card. She crossed her fingers. Hopefully, the checking account was still working. Georgina called back. It was. They were back on track.

"What's up?" Eliza asked, pinning back the dress on Jacqui's torso. "Does that feel okay?"

Jacqui nodded. She stood in the middle of Eliza's bedroom and looked at herself in the mirror. She still couldn't believe how well the dress fit. It was a cheeky take on a Catholic schoolgirl uniform, with a glen plaid pattern and a Peter Pan collar. But instead of looking . . . well, costumey and pervy, the dress was fresh-looking and fashionable while being incredibly comfortable.

"It's fabulous," she told Eliza. "It feels so good."

"Cotton with a hint of spandex." Eliza grinned. The glamour girl collection had been inspired by her idea—Girls Who Mattered. It was all about making clothes for girls who had other things to think about than clothes. The "uniform" was supposed to take all the angsting out of dressing—just grab a sweater, a shirt, pants, and go.

She had been able to talk a few of her old classmates into modeling at the show as well, and they were all sitting around Eliza's room, waiting their turns.

"I still need two more girls," Eliza fretted.

"What about Shannon and Madison?" Jacqui suggested. "I'm sure they'd love to do it."

Jacqui found Shannon reading a book to Cody in the sunroom. She explained that Eliza needed a few more girls for her show and thought that she and Madison would be ideal.

"Me? In a fashion show? Fantastic," Shannon said, putting down the book. "But . . ."

"But?"

"I don't know about Madison. She's kind of pissed at me right now." Shannon told Jacqui how Madison had asked her point-blank if Anna and Kevin were getting a divorce and how Shannon had lied to her about it. "I think she suspects something."

"Maybe we should just tell her," Jacqui said thoughtfully. It seemed cruel to keep the kid in the dark. They were also still racking their brains on how to get Kevin back to the Hamptons, and maybe Madison, who was the most observant member of the Perry family, could help them figure out a plan.

The two au pairs found Madison in her room, IM'ing friends on her computer. "What?" she asked.

"First of all, Mad, I'm really sorry," Shannon began. She explained how Jacqui had told her about the divorce and how she and Jacqui were trying to get the Perrys back together through some crazy schemes.

Madison's face was a mask. "So they're really splitting up? Anna's going to have to leave? And Cody too?"

"We've been trying our best to keep that from happening," Jacqui said, kneeling down to hug the girl. "I'm really sorry."

"But, it's not over yet," Shannon said. "We're throwing them an anniversary party a couple of days from their real anniversary."

"The only problem is getting your dad out here to attend the party," Jacqui said. "I thought if we could get him to come out for it, the party would make them feel better and then they'd realize they don't want to split up after all."

"Okay," Madison said, not sounding convinced.

Jacqui spied a picture of Madison and Kevin on Madison's desk. It struck her suddenly that Madison looked a lot like her father and that she was stubborn in the same way. Perhaps they wouldn't need to concoct such a complicated deception after all. "You know, you and your dad are pretty close. Maybe you could call him and ask him to come out to the Hamptons next weekend?"

Madison chewed on her bubble gum and blew a big bubble. "I guess. I do miss him a bit. And I have my first tennis tournament the day after."

"He would be so proud of you," Jacqui urged.

"It would be nice," Madison allowed, adding, a little sadly, "He's never even seen me play."

"Have you ever invited him?" Shannon asked.

The young girl shook her head. "Dad's always so busy. But you're right—he should be at the tournament. He always brags about how he won the junior championship one year. I'll do it."

Jacqui clapped her on the back. "Wonderful."

Madison grinned. "Besides, if it doesn't work, I'll just tell Dad that the neighbors are encroaching on his property. That always sets him off. He'll totally come over to check it out."

Jacqui laughed. That sounded like Kevin, all right.

"Are you mad?" Shannon asked tentatively. "I'm really sorry I lied to you."

"A little," Madison admitted. "But you were only trying to help. I don't want Anna and Dad to split up either. She's not great, but you know, she's all we've got," Madison said, showing a vast degree of maturity concerning her stepmother.

"But that's not all we came to say," Jacqui said, beaming.

The two younger girls found themselves in Eliza's bedroom, being fitted by a team of seamstresses. They could hardly contain their excitement. They were going to be models!

"It's nothing big, you know," Eliza told them. "It's not even a real show. It's kind of a guerrilla event. I mean, we're inviting the press, but it's not sanctioned by Fashion Week or anything."

"Who cares?" Shannon asked. "It sounds amazing!"

"Totally," Madison agreed.

They grinned at each other, and the past few weeks of sourness and suspicion completely faded away and they were fast friends all over again.

Later that evening, Grant knocked on the door to the servants' cottage. It had been a habit of his to pop in during the wee hours for a late-night booty call, and for most of the summer Jacqui had been agreeable. But not this time. She walked down the rickety stairs and met him at the doorway.

Grant raised his eyebrows, and Jacqui nodded, and they walked quietly to the beach, where Grant had already dug out the sand and collected wood for a fire. He knelt by it and struck a match. The flames licked the wood and were soon shooting sparks into the air. Jacqui huddled in the blankets Grant always brought for such occasions.

He snuggled next to her and put an arm around her shoulders. Usually this would be the time when Grant would start kissing her, slowly working his way from her mouth to her neck to the deep spot between her shoulder blades, warm hands underneath her shirt, her bra, her jeans. But after a few minutes of breathless, passionate kissing, Jacqui came up for air.

"Grant."

"Huh?"

"We need to stop. I can't do this anymore. I'm so sorry."

"What do you mean?" Grant asked. "I thought—well, Ben and Duff, they said that you'd broken up with them, so I thought . . ."

Oh. Jacqui's strained smile was all he needed to realize his mistake.

He took his hands away and put them around his head. "Man, I feel like a dork."

"Don't," Jacqui said. "It's my fault. I shouldn't have let it go so long." She sighed. The thing was, she liked Grant, but he wasn't the one. Just one of three.

"If that's what you want." Grant exhaled.

Jacqui nodded. "It's what I want."

Grant scratched his right sideburn for a while, looking at her intently. Finally, he spoke. "Well, one thing I always do is give girls what they want." He kissed her softly on the lips one last time. "I'll always think of you," he said. He fixed her with his smoldering, sexy stare, and Jacqui knew he deserved a girl who only had eyes for him.

Jacqui stood by herself on the beach for a while, watching him walk away. She was glad she had done it but felt sad nonetheless. She'd had a fun summer with three boyfriends, but when it came down to it, there'd just been too many people in the relationship. The seagulls' haunting cries filled the air, and Jacqui wondered if every summer would always be bittersweet.

fashion weak

UNLIKE EVERY OTHER MAJOR DESIGNER IN NEW YORK, Sydney Minx decided to stage his show in late August, the week before Fashion Week, when the entire fashion world converged upon the Bryant Park tents in Manhattan. He was determined to make a splash by "showing early" but also to save money on the fees and expense a Manhattan show would entail. Besides, the bulk of his clients were in the Hamptons. He had rented out the entire Volcano nightclub, and there was a terrific buzz as the well-heeled audience gathered in the main room near the lava fountain to take their seats draped in white linen and decorated with fat goodie bags.

They were all there: the international fashion media (annoyed at having their summer vacations cut short), buyers from all the major department stores, coifed socialites, local celebrities and those who had jetted into East Hampton Airport just for the privilege of sitting in the front row.

Thanks to all the hype concerning Eliza's helicopter stunt and the energy she had brought to the styling of the collection, there was palpable excitement and expectation to see what the designer would do next. Almost all of the women in the room were dressed in the distressed, shredded chiffon and metallic spray-painted clothes that Eliza had created. They were eager to find out what they would be wearing for the fall.

Backstage, Mara held up a tape recorder in front of the designer. Sydney had unleashed a torrent of half-baked explanations about his vision. But so far, the only thing Mara had been able to determine was that he didn't have one.

"I think it's all about party girls, girls who dance on tables, girls who get in gossip columns," Sydney said, fluttering his fan. "It girls, it girls, it girls!"

It was a tired cliché, and Mara pitied the old man for trying to keep his pulse on the beat of the culture when it was so obvious he would rather be anywhere than at a fashion show. She noticed a sharp-faced dark-haired girl prepping the models for the show. *That must be Paige*, Mara thought. She thanked Sydney for his time and walked out to the main room.

She took her seat in the second row and rifled through the program, hoping she could find something there she could hang the piece on, something that captured the idea of the collection so she would be able to articulate it to her readers. She felt a stab of guilt at not being at Eliza's show across town. She hadn't had the heart to tell Eliza she wouldn't be covering her debut.

Exactly an hour late, Sydney's show finally started.

The crowd hushed, and all eyes focused on the end of the runway, and the first model appeared from behind the curtain.

Wearing a slashed-to-the-belly-button leather dress and clunky platform heels. It looked like an outfit better suited to dancing on a Vegas stage than to a chic Manhattan cocktail party. It went downhill from there.

The collection was a slew of tarted-up, décolletage-displaying blouses and thigh-skimming skirts that seemed completely out of touch with what women actually wanted to wear.

"Does he think we live in L.A.?" one swan snorted without checking off any of the items on the runway sheet for future purchase.

Dressing for Dinner, the accompanying notes read, while a model pranced out in a see-through feather-trimmed negligee.

"Maybe for dining at the Playboy Mansion!" another appalled blue blood retorted.

That was enough for Mara. She checked her watch. If she didn't encounter any traffic, she would still be able to make it to Eliza's show. She noticed her boss, Sam Davis, across the aisle, grimacing as a model walked out in a bra and skirt.

If she was going to do it, she'd have to do it now. Mara took a deep breath, ducked her head, and excused herself as she walked from her seat down the row and toward the exit.

She turned to look at the runway one last time and accidentally caught Sam's eye.

"Where are you going?" Sam mouthed, looking cross.

Mara shrugged. She just had to trust her instincts, and if it didn't pay off, well, her days at *Hamptons* were almost over anyway. There was no way she was going to miss her friend's first fashion show.

a few technical difficulties

THE MODELS WERE ALL DRESSED AND MADE UP, AND ELIZA was touched to know how many friends she had—her makeup artist had donated his time, and so had her hairdresser. A crew from Lunch had prepared a table of appetizers, and colleagues from last summer at Seventh Circle had swiped alcohol for the pre-show party. Even the DJ had offered his services for free. There was a feeling of camaraderie in the air; the crowd was mostly made up of young people thrilled to be taking part in a real art event instead of a slick corporate presentation. She wondered where Mara was. Mara had told her she would interview Eliza before the show for the piece, but so far, her friend was nowhere to be found.

Eliza was pumped, except for one thing—on the way to her show, she had passed by Volcano and had seen Paige and Jeremy together outside the club. Paige was there to set up for Sydney's show, but why was Jeremy there with her? The two of them were in a deep, intense discussion, and Jeremy even had a hand on Paige's shoulder. The two of them looked up as Eliza drove by, and she caught both of their eyes. Jeremy looked guilty, and Paige looked annoyed. Eliza felt a stab in her stomach. So they

sun-kissed

were together after all. Jeremy was just waiting to get rid of her so he could go back to his former flame.

She tried to put the image out of her mind and went back to checking each model.

"You guys look terrific," Eliza said. Her vision of working-girl "uniform" glamour was really coming to life. She couldn't wait to see the audience reaction. Would they hate it? Would they love it? Did she have a future in this business?

Eliza peeked out from the side of her car. She'd asked her guests to assemble by the shore. A makeshift runway was cordoned off in the sand, and she had rented two spotlights to light the "stage." Once they were switched on, the show could begin.

She waited for the floodlights to illuminate the runway.

And waited . . .

And waited . . .

Finally, a figure ran up from the sand. When he got closer, she recognized Serge, the busboy from the restaurant who'd volunteered to help with the lights.

"They won't go on. I'm not sure what's wrong." Serge shook his head.

"What?" Eliza asked.

"I tried 'em twice, checked the wires; they all looked fine. I don't know. Maybe the bulbs are busted?"

What good was staging a fashion show if the audience couldn't even see the clothes? The beach was covered in darkness, and the audience was getting restless. Eliza saw guests mingling and drinking the purloined vodka martinis. The show was going to turn into nothing more than a cocktail party if she didn't do something fast.

"What are we going to do?" Shannon asked, her eyelashes heavy with mascara.

"We need to start, Eliza. They're already playing the music," Madison said as the opening chant to Gwen Stefani's "Hollaback Girl" played in the background.

"Shit!" Eliza cursed, gnawing on her cuticles until they bled. She had no idea what to do now.

Jacqui noticed they weren't starting and walked out of the line to speak to Eliza. "What's the problem?"

Before Eliza could answer, another figure appeared next to her car.

"Hey, did I miss anything?" Mara asked, walking up to the huddled crowd.

"The spotlights—they won't go on!" Eliza told her friends. "I don't know what to do!"

"I just saw someone working on them," Jacqui remembered. "I thought she was one of your volunteers."

"No, Serge just checked. He said they're busted," Eliza said. "Mar, where have you been?"

Mara blushed deeply. "Sam made me go to Sydney's show. But don't worry—the thing was a total disaster. No one even stayed for the finale. I thought I was the only one walking out early, but when I turned around, I noticed a bunch of people behind me. I think they all followed me here too."

Eliza felt elated at the news. Sydney's show was a bust! Ha! Then she realized. Paige. It had to be. She'd known Eliza was staging a show, and she must have been furious when she noticed that everyone had walked out before the end of Sydney's show to go to Eliza's. Sabotaging the spotlights had to be her revenge.

Eliza started to feel the sweat form in her armpits. She was so done. She could see major editors from *W*, *Vogue*, *Bazaar*, and the *New York Times* out there, as well as several prominent buyers from the best department stores in the country. They would never give her another chance if she messed this up. She would just be another fashion statistic—joining a slew of wannabes whose creations crowded the clearance racks. If she even made it to the clearance racks.

"Okay, what if we gave all the models candles?" she suggested. "I could run to the Stop and Shop on 27 and—"

All of a sudden, there was a hoot from the crowd. Then cheering erupted.

"What's going on?" Eliza craned her neck. She saw the sandy runway ablaze in lights, even though the spotlights were still dark. "How—?"

"Who cares? Let's go!" Jacqui said, stepping out from behind the car and leading the pack of models down the catwalk.

The show finally started, and to the surprise of everyone, most of all Eliza, the "runway" turned out to be lit by two lines of cars parked by the beachhead, their headlights blazing.

jacqui in wonderland

JACQUI WAS STILL WEARING HER FINALE OUTFIT—A DARING three-piece black suit that was perfectly fitted to her proportions—when she saw three guys walking toward her from opposite directions, each holding an enormous bouquet of flowers. They handed them to her one by one, looking adorably sheepish.

"You were great," Duffy said. "It made me want to wear the clothes myself!"

Ben elbowed him away and turned to Jacqui with a somber look on his face. "Are you okay?" he asked, concerned.

"I'm fine." Jacqui nodded. "I really like you guys."

"We really like you too." Grant winked.

"And the site, is everything okay?" she asked.

Ben nodded. "Stock's back to where it was before the fall, a few points higher, even."

"Someone sent in a video of that movie star Boris Carter, you know, Mr. Action Guy—who says he does all his own stunts?—getting a leg cramp from walking his dog. Pretty funny."

Duffy rocked on his heels and put a friendly arm around her shoulders. "Believe us, nothing will stop the Debauchery," he promised.

They all hugged each other fondly, and Jacqui realized that even if she had lost her chance at love, she had at least come out of the summer with three very good friends. Breaking up with all three boys was the best decision she could have made.

The three of them had added up to one great boyfriend, but Jacqui was certain that one day she would meet the *one* boy who had all those qualities—Duffy's energy, Grant's magnetism, and Ben's sensitivity. In the meantime, their friendships would survive, and, by default, Jacqui had become the fourth amigo.

It looked like everything was settling in place. Except the clock was ticking—the anniversary party was tomorrow night. Madison had happily reported that Kevin had postponed his trip to the Caribbean to attend her tennis match and would be in East Hampton to support her as well as to check out the fictional encroachment on his property. He had been incensed when she told him that the Reynolds were building a three-story gazebo in their backyard that was going to look over the Perrys' pool and block their view of the ocean.

There was a new snag, however—Anna still wasn't back from her spa trip. She was supposed to return earlier that evening but had explained she was taking an early-morning flight instead, since she wanted one more night to "commune with the stars." Jacqui hoped her employer's newly rejuvenated self would be on that plane. Otherwise, there was one to São Paulo with her name written all over it.

caught in the high beams

ELIZA CAME OUT TO TAKE HER BOWS AT THE END OF THE show. She looked out at the applauding guests, several of whom cheered and wolf-whistled. They had loved it—but even better, she had never felt so satisfied in her life. The past two weeks, she had worked harder than she had ever done, and she was so proud of herself. Her collection was a success—even if no one ever ordered a single piece or no one ever wrote a single line about it, she was satisfied. She'd done it for herself.

Mara ran up and gave her a big bouquet of tulips. "This is from me and Jac," she said, kissing Eliza on the cheek. "We're so happy for you!"

A man wearing a natty bow tie approached her with his card and introduced himself as the dean at Parsons. "I'd love to talk to you about scholarship opportunities to our freshman class."

Parsons School of Design? The school that counted Marc Jacobs, Donna Karan, and Calvin Klein as alumni? Eliza couldn't believe it. She'd never even thought of applying, because she'd been certain she wouldn't get in—and besides, there was the whole Princeton thing. She'd been working so hard to get into

Princeton all her life. If she told her parents she wanted to go to design school, they would choke on their vichyssoise.

"Thank you," she said.

A slim girl with long dark hair and wearing the season's best jeans joined the throng. "Hey, great collection. We should talk—I'd love to order some for my store."

Eliza recognized her immediately. She'd been shopping at Scoop forever. It was Stefani Greenfield, the store's owner.

"Give my buyer a call," Stefani said.

"Definitely." Eliza grinned.

She looked around happily. Her "models" were mingling with the guests; the buyers were all talking to Todd, her new business partner; and several editors had congratulated her on their way to their cars. Slowly, one by one, the headlights that had lit the catwalk turned and disappeared up the road until the makeshift catwalk was dark again. It would have been the happiest moment of her life—if only . . .

Suddenly, she missed Jeremy with an ache so painful, it hurt to breathe. She had no one to share her success with, no one to rehash every little delicious detail with, no one who would tell her how well she had done. Of course she had her friends, and she smiled to notice Jacqui attempting to make peace with her three suitors and Ryan and Mara walking on the beach holding hands. If only . . .

Eliza sighed. Maybe that was the way life was—it just wasn't perfect. There would always be something missing. She gathered the rest of the clothes, packing them away carefully so that she could ship them to the Italian manufacturers later that week. If they did get as many orders as she thought, they would have to start production on the line as soon as possible.

She was lugging the rolling trunk over to her car when a familiar figure walked up from the shadows.

"Need help with that?" Jeremy asked quietly.

Eliza looked up. It was as if she had been wishing so hard for him to appear and now that her wish had come true, she wasn't quite sure if he was really there, standing in front of her. "I can handle it."

"I know you can," he said, walking over and taking the other end of the trunk. They lifted it into the car together.

"I'm really proud of you," he said. "I always knew you could do it. That was amazing. I don't know anything about fashion, but I think girls will really like it."

Eliza smiled. "I hope so." Then she realized Jeremy had once told her that part of his job as a landscape contractor and designer was to figure out creative lighting schemes for the estates he tended. Some preferred tiki torches, some gas lamplights. He'd once had a commission to light a garden party for a big shipping company and had used truck headlights as an interesting twist.

"It was you, wasn't it?" she asked. "The headlights? Was that your idea?"

Jeremy looked sheepish. "Yeah, I overheard you talking about the busted spotlights, so I checked them out. The wires were cut."

"Bastard!" Eliza swore.

"It's my fault. Paige went a little *Fatal Attraction* tonight. She asked me to meet her at Volcano this afternoon because she said she wanted to tell me something. Turns out she just wanted to get back together again. Then you drove by, and I told her you were the only girl for me, ever. I think it set her off."

"You told her that?"

He nodded. "Eliza, you should have told me Paige had fired you. I knew she would try to do something like that once she found out about us. She tried to get back together with me earlier this year, but I told her I was going out with you."

"She knew I was your girlfriend all along?" Eliza asked, incredulous. No wonder Paige was always giving her a hard time. She'd wanted Jeremy back for herself, but when he'd rebuffed her affections, she'd taken out her anger on her romantic rival—Eliza. It all made sense now.

"So she cut the wires?" Eliza asked.

"Yeah, I think so. She's a bit psycho. The first time I broke up with her, she came by the Perry house at five in the morning every day, and I almost got fired. But don't worry, I don't think she'll bother you anymore. I told her if she ever did anything like that again, I'd tell her family what she's been up to. Her dad's a cop—he won't stand for that sort of thing."

285

"How did you get everyone to agree to turn on their floods?" she asked, stepping into his arms. "Not everyone who's parked up there was here for the show."

"I told them that if they turned on their lights, some beautiful girls would appear," he murmured.

sweeter the second time around

THEY WALKED ON THE BEACH, FEELING THE COLD WATER wash over their bare feet. Mara leaned her head on Ryan's shoulder. The summer was almost over. It wasn't what she'd thought it would be—she'd realized love wasn't enough. There were chores to consider. Perhaps she and Ryan had rushed into it too soon and taken all the mystery out of it. Living together. They were still so young—they had the rest of their lives to fight over who squeezed the toothpaste from the middle. She decided that if she did end up at Dartmouth, she wouldn't move in with him until sophomore year.

Ryan kissed the top of her head. "Guess what I brought," he said, fishing in his Coach wallet.

He handed her a laminated piece of paper.

It read *Washington Post*. BEHIND THE SEAMS: SYDNEY MINX, by Mara Waters. It was the headline of the profile she'd written earlier that summer, which had been picked up by the Associated Press and distributed to their network.

"Oh my God," Mara said. "The *Washington Post*! That's huge. That's a real newspaper," she told him.

"I know," Ryan said, grinning. "You're a rock star."

"When did you see this?" she asked.

"I put in a search the other day. Your piece showed up in about fifty newspapers. This is the biggest one."

They walked a little more, past the fashion show, and found a private spot behind a dune. She was so touched that he would even remember to look up where her article had been published and that he would keep a copy in his wallet.

"This reminds me of something," Mara said wickedly, pulling Ryan down to the sand.

He rolled over on his back and put his arms underneath his head, looking up at the stars. She cuddled next to him, feeling his warm body on the wet sand.

"What?" he asked sleepily.

"That night we slept on the beach? Remember? That first summer?"

"Mmm . . ." Ryan agreed, his eyes closed.

Mara snuggled up under his chin, marveling at how his lashes lay flat against his fair cheek. He was just so handsome. He was the kind of guy she'd never thought would ever, ever, in a million years be interested in someone as ordinary as her. But he had stopped being "that guy" anymore. He was just Ryan. Her Ryan.

He rolled on top of her suddenly, pinning her to the ground with his body. "I wanted to do this that night," he said as he held her arms down with his.

"What stopped you?" Mara asked.

"It was kind of hard to do since you were all zipped up in your own sleeping bag." He laughed.

"What's stopping you now?" she asked, looking at him through half-lidded eyes. The sound of the waves crashed behind them.

"Absolutely nothing," he replied, pulling up his sweater and throwing it over her head so that the two of them disappeared underneath. Thank God it was so roomy. . . .

Later, back at the boat, Mara was trying to wash the sand out of her jeans. *That's what you get for having sex in the sand,* she thought, a bit amused. Her hair was mussed, and her lips were red from his kisses. She had been wrong earlier—love *was* enough. Love was all she would need ever. She didn't want anything else but Ryan. Ryan, Ryan, Ryan. His name was written in the stars above her head in the night sky; she had called his name out again and again.

There was a tap on the bathroom door.

"Come in," she said, smiling up at him. He was wearing only his boxer shorts, his perfectly sculpted lateral muscles shining in the dim light.

"I found this on the kitchen table," he said.

He held up the white envelope with a Dartmouth address. "Why haven't you sent it in yet? Wasn't it due yesterday?"

Mara was momentarily caught off guard. The acceptance form. She had been meaning to mail it in all week and somehow had never gotten around to it.

She didn't know what to say. She'd deliberately forgotten to mail it because she was still on the fence about whether to accept their admission. The prospect of turning down Columbia seemed wrongheaded now, especially in light of how quickly she was amassing press clips.

"Anyway, don't worry about it. I can make another call to the admissions office," Ryan assured her.

"*Another* call? Ryan, did you do something?" she asked, finding it difficult to breathe. She was starting to get really angry.

Earlier that summer, Ryan had offered to ask his dad, a prominent alum, to put in a word for her application—but she had expressly told him not to. Had he ignored her request? How could he not respect her wishes? How could he go behind her back like that?

"Did you ask your dad to help get me off the wait list at Dartmouth?" she asked, fixing him with a glare.

"What are you talking about?" Ryan asked, offended. "Of course not. You told me not to."

"But you just said you were going to 'make another call.' Don't lie to me, Ryan," she threatened. "I'd never lie to you."

Ryan shook his head. "I only wanted to make sure the two of us could be together. Was that so wrong? Don't you want to be together? What's the matter with you?"

"I can't believe it," Mara said. "I just can't believe you would betray me like that."

She stormed out of the cabin. She had to get away from Ryan just then. He had actually called his dad and asked him to pull some strings on her behalf! He'd actually used his connections to get her off the wait list! How could he? He knew she didn't approve of that—she had wanted to get in on her own, not because her boyfriend's dad was golfing buddies with the university president. It was all so . . . so . . . wrong.

He would never understand her.

the runaway bride

"WHAT'S GOING ON?" ZOË ASKED AS A CREW OF WORKERS set up an enormous white tent in the backyard by the pool.

"We're having a party!" Jacqui said merrily. "Now go put on that pretty dress."

"Whose birthday is it?" Zoë asked as Jacqui pulled the smocked French linen dress over the little girl's head.

"It's your mommy and daddy's," Shannon replied, helping Cody into a cute navy blue sailor outfit.

The team from Georgina's firm were putting the final details on the event—the driveway was being lit with tea light candles, a huge bower of roses had been erected above the front door, and in the backyard were three tents—one for staging, the middle one for dinner and dancing, and a third housing a fully equipped trailer with separate men's and women's bathrooms.

Kevin was due to arrive any minute now from Manhattan. He had been so happy to hear that Madison had qualified for the tennis tournament, he had offered to take her out to dinner, just the two of them, for some father-daughter bonding. The kids were all dressed, and Jacqui had succeeded in talking William into wearing a nice shirt and tie.

Unfortunately, they still had no idea where Anna Perry was. She was supposed to have come back from her weeklong trip to the spa in Arizona that morning, but she had yet to arrive.

It was five o'clock in the afternoon. Already the guests were starting to show up: Anna and Kevin's society friends, Kevin's parents, a few gossip columnists from the various newspapers.

Jacqui started to panic. If Anna never appeared, she was looking at a full-scale fiasco. Kevin would not be pleased to learn that "Anna" had orchestrated a hundred-thousand-dollar party and then failed to turn up at the event. Jacqui had to do something. Rob Thomas was scheduled to serenade the happy couple any minute now. A jazz trio was quietly playing standards in the patio as guests trickled inside.

She spotted Eliza walking through the front door on Jeremy's arm. The two of them were giggling, and Eliza was glowing. There was a visible new tenderness between them. Jeremy was wearing a linen suit, and Eliza looked gorgeous in a long white linen dress with a slit up to her knee.

Jacqui greeted the two of them warmly.

Eliza hugged her friend close. Her eyes shone. Part of her wanted to tell Jacqui everything. How Jeremy had surprised her with a reservation at the Bentley Hotel and how they had spent the night in the best room in the house when the hotel staff found out "Eliza Thompson" was staying there. Jeremy had learned there were some benefits to being a princess. And then how Jeremy had taken off her clothes so slowly and with such delicacy, she had almost died from anticipation. She hadn't even needed to wear the lingerie set. Everything had been perfect, and she hadn't planned a single thing. She restrained herself from spilling the beans. What had happened the night before was a beautiful secret that she wanted to keep to herself for the time being. The girl who used to suffer from TMI now realized why people didn't want to kiss and tell.

"You guys, you have to help me," Jacqui said, skipping the usual pleasantries.

Eliza immediately noted the urgent tone in Jacqui's voice. "What's wrong? What do you need?"

"Anna isn't here."

"Where is she?"

"I don't know. I checked her ATM card and tracked it down. She got on the flight, and she took a car from the airport, and she should have been here by now, but no one's seen her. I don't know what to do."

"Calm down," Jeremy said reassuringly. "She lives here. She's got to come home at some point."

"I know, but Rob Thomas—"

"Rob Thomas!" Eliza cackled.

Jeremy raised a questioning eyebrow. "Rob Thomas?"

"Is going to be on that stage in five minutes to serenade the 'happy couple.' Kevin is already on his way; he's going to be here any minute. I don't even want to think about what's going to happen if he finds this party and no Anna."

"Okay, let's figure it out. Where does Anna usually spend most of her time? Maybe she went there," Eliza said helpfully.

Jacqui furrowed her brow. Anna . . . where did Anna spend her time. . . . The beauty salon . . . shopping on Main Street . . . but lately, she was always next door, at the Reynolds castle, participating in some drinking game. Jacqui took a quick look around the assembled guests and noticed that the web site guys weren't at the party yet, which was odd, since they had promised to be there.

"I think I know where she is," Jacqui said ominously. Duffy thought Anna was an MILF. She wouldn't put it past him to make a move on an older, married woman. Duffy would probably think of it as just another adventure. Anna probably liked all the attention too. Maybe she shouldn't have let Anna tag along with her to all those clubs that summer or have introduced her to the web site guys. If Anna had hooked up with some guy half her age, it wouldn't bode well for a reunion. . . .

The door to the Reynolds castle was unlocked. Jacqui led her friends into the game room, where the Beirut Ping-Pong table was housed. Alas, no one was flicking Ping-Pong balls into the paper cups of beer.

"Ben? Duffy? Grant? Where are you guys?" she called.

For a long moment, there was no sound. The house was empty. *Damn.* Her cell phone rang—it was Georgina, wondering where the Perrys were. Rob was setting up and was ready to sing their song.

"Let's go; she's not here," Jacqui said despondently, kicking at a beach ball with the web site's logo.

"In here!" a voice called from the kitchen.

They trooped in to find Anna Perry leaning on the kitchen counter, hanging out with the three guys. "Oh, hey, Jacqui," Anna said. "Eliza, haven't seen you in a while. And is that Jeremy, who used to work for us?" she called happily, waving them over.

The three guys were all wearing beachy formal wear—Duffy in a tan linen suit, Grant in seersucker, and Ben in a festive guayabera shirt.

"These guys say I'm throwing some big party at our house this evening, but they're just pulling my leg." Anna smiled. Her luggage was on the floor, and she looked tan, rested, and happy after her week at the spa. Jacqui was relieved to note Anna wasn't drinking. The perennial party girl cup of beer was absent from her hands.

"This place is such a mess!" Anna said, spritzing the counter with lemon cleaner and wiping it off energetically. "I thought I'd give them a hand getting it back in shape."

"Uh, that's really nice, Anna, but I think Kevin has a surprise for you," Jacqui said. "You really need to come home now."

"A surprise?" Anna asked skeptically. "What kind of surprise?"

Just then, the sounds of the first chords of "Lonely No More" wafted from across the way.

"A nice surprise." Eliza grinned.

the perrys are lonely
no more

WHEN THEY RETURNED TO THE PERRYS' BACKYARD, ROB Thomas was onstage with a guitar.

"What's going on?" Anna asked, mystified, but she had the presence of mind to bid hello to all of her society friends. "Why are Kevin's parents here?" She stopped when she saw her bald husband walk through the crowd.

"There's no gazebo!" he kept saying to anyone who would listen. "What's going on?" he asked, turning to Madison, who had yet to explain why there was a full-scale event complete with ten-foot-high chocolate fountains in their backyard.

He stopped when he saw Anna.

The two of them stared at each other.

But before they could say anything to each other, Rob Thomas was leaning into the microphone. "I'd like to dedicate this song to a really special couple, who I'm told are celebrating their fifth wedding anniversary tomorrow. Here's to Anna and Kevin Perry! In this day and age, it's so great to see a couple who can stick together!"

"But how—?" Kevin asked, sputtering.

"Oh, Kevin!" Anna said softly as Rob started singing the song. "Remember when we . . . ?"

Kevin still looked upset. Who were all these people? Why were there three fifty-foot tents set up on his lawn? But when he saw the look on Anna's face, his features relaxed. "You got my e-mails?"

Anna nodded. "Are you serious? You really don't want to go through with it?"

After Shannon had stopped sending them the fake love note e-mails, it turned out that Anna and Kevin had struck up a correspondence after the disastrous lunch at Babette's anyway. Seeing how jealous Kevin had acted had made Anna feel beautiful again, and she had reached out to Kevin with a barrage of flirtatious and tender e-mails that he had actually responded to. Would wonders never cease.

Jacqui, who had been watching with bated breath, exhaled.

"Happy anniversary," Kevin said softly. "I'm glad we're able to celebrate."

"I've missed you," Anna said, putting her hands around his chubby neck.

"I missed you too, babe," Kevin admitted.

The crowd cheered and lifted their glasses in a toast. The Perry kids surrounded their parents (well, their dad and their stepmom) and hugged them happily. Ryan punched his dad on the shoulder and congratulated him on his fifth anniversary. Kevin kissed Anna on the cheek and ruffled the girls' hair and chucked the boys under the chin. Madison and Zoë beamed, while William and Cody ran around them, hooting loudly.

"And I have a surprise of my own," Anna said. "I'm pregnant!"

"You are?" Kevin yelped.

"Three months. That's why I've been so cranky. Hormones. Mood swings. The whole thing. I just found out at the spa." Anna smiled. "And I promise I'll tear up the credit cards."

"I promise I won't work weekends anymore," Kevin replied.

"So you're not getting divorced?" Madison asked.

"Nope, not a chance," Kevin promised.

As they awkwardly slow-danced to the Matchbox Twenty song, Jacqui left them alone and found a stone bench to sit on. She gripped the edge in triumph. She'd done it. The Perrys were going to be together. They would need her to au-pair, and she would be able to complete her fifth year. Her future was safe for the time being. There was still no guarantee she would get accepted into NYU, but she was willing to try again. She would ace those math and science requirements. Jacqui was nothing but determined.

Nothing motivated a girl to succeed like the fear of having to help the spoiled trophy wives of Brazilian billionaires stuff themselves into Gaultier corsets for the rest of her life.

sting was right after all

AS ANNA AND KEVIN PERRY GROSSED OUT THE YOUNGER guests with their suddenly overly passionate reunited-and-it-feels-so-good make-out session in front of the stage, Mara and Ryan were sitting quietly in the hammock in front of the au pair cottage. Mara had come back to the boat late last night, still angry, and had slept in one of the guest berths. The two of them were still technically not speaking to each other, but Mara had promised she would attend the surprise party, and once Ryan had found out what the girls were up to, he'd decided to attend as well. After all, it was his dad they were talking about.

Ryan had pulled her away from the throng, and they had sat down uneasily in the hammock. It was the site of their first kiss—something that couldn't have escaped their notice.

"Look, Mara," he said, sighing deeply. "I did make a call, but it's not what you think. I was going to try and help things along, but you had already gotten in. The only thing I had the admissions office do is hold a place in the dorm next to my fraternity. That was what I meant about us being together. You got in on your own. My dad had nothing to do with it."

"Why didn't you tell me that last night?"

Ryan gripped the hammock cords in frustration. "You were so ready to believe the worst about me. It pissed me off."

"Oh my God, Ryan, I'm so sorry," Mara said. She felt terrible. She'd been so ready to assume that just because he was rich and privileged, he wouldn't be able to resist using his connections to help him get whatever he wanted.

"No, don't be," he replied. "There's no need."

"I think I'm going to go to Columbia," Mara said softly. "I think it's a better fit for me."

"I know," Ryan said glumly, softly kicking back on the grass so that the hammock swayed gently in the evening breeze.

"I'm sorry," Mara said helplessly.

"I would never hold you back, you know. All you had to say was that you didn't want to be at Dartmouth, and I would have understood. I just thought you did, so I made all those plans—I wish you'd believe that I only want the best for you," he said softly.

"I know that now. Oh, Ryan, I messed up so many things," Mara cried. It broke her heart to know how much she'd doubted him all summer, thinking that he wasn't supportive of her ambitions and that he felt resentful of her career, when all along, he'd had the best intentions at heart.

"So what happens now?" Ryan ventured. "With the two of us?"

"We break up," Mara said bravely. She'd given it a lot of thought, lying alone in the V-berth by herself the night before.

She'd started out the summer so nervous about her writing skills, intimidated by her boss and her subjects, but now she was confident she could make it as a journalist. At the very least, she wanted to try. Plus, she truly doubted whether she and Ryan really belonged together. Maybe he would be better off with a girl who could share his love of the ocean, not one who wanted to spend the evening in front of a keyboard. She very much hoped she was the girl for him, but she also didn't want to make him miserable, the two of them trying to bend so far back to accommodate each other that they lost sight of who they really were.

Ryan exhaled. "Is that what you want?"

Mara sighed. If you loved somebody, you had to set them free. If they were meant to be together, they would be together, no matter where they ended up. Maybe it would be a year or two years or maybe even after they graduated from college. Someday, she hoped they would find their way back to each other. But she had to take that chance, she had to risk it, for both of their sakes.

"Yeah. I think we need to grow up a little. Both of us."

"I love you," Ryan said, squeezing her hand tightly. "I'll always love you."

"I love you too," Mara said back.

They kissed, and it was a heavenly, soul-searching kiss. It was just like their first kiss on the hammock, but so much deeper, because it was bittersweet.

They went back to the boat to have one last great night together as a couple. And the next day, they would leave as individuals.

a door is closed, but a new window opens

THE TWO LONG BEEPS OUTSIDE THE DRIVEWAY SIGNALED that Eliza had arrived. Jacqui quickly packed up her bags in the au pair cottage. The boys had offered her a ride to the city on the Black Hawk, but she'd declined, wanting to spend a few more hours with her friends. She felt a little wistful that none of the boys had worked out as a boyfriend, but she was eager to go back to New York and everything it offered. In a city of eight million people—there had to be *one* boy who was right for her. She was certain of it.

Shannon was zipping up her carryall, stuffed with the clothes she'd bought on numerous shopping trips with the older girls.

"Thanks for all the help this summer," Jacqui said, offering her a hand.

Shannon shook it. "No problem. It was fun," she said with a wicked smile. "Is it always like this in the Hamptons?"

Jacqui laughed and thought about it. "Pretty much."

"So, I'll see you in the city? And don't worry about me staying with you. Madison said I could stay at their town house when I come to visit. No offense, but I heard their place has a lap pool in the basement."

That girl was too much, Jacqui thought, smiling.

Eliza was in the driver's seat, leaning on the horn. She had her hair in a high ponytail, and she was wearing Jeremy's work jacket. It made her feel close to him. The two of them had spent the night at his apartment, and he was planning to come visit her in the city before she had to go off to college. Since he had his own company now, he would come up whenever he could, and she'd promised to come down every month. They were going to make it work. He was her one true love, and she wouldn't let go of him.

She had broken the news to her parents the night before. She was going to defer a year at Princeton and apply to Parsons instead. She was serious about becoming a fashion designer, and she wanted to see where this path would take her. All her life she had lived up to someone else's expectations, but she wanted to see what would happen when she tried to live up to her own. Her parents had not taken the news lightly, and they still hoped she would come around—hence the compromise of deferring a year.

Mara was sitting in the shotgun seat, leafing through the final issue of *Hamptons* magazine. Her column had been a huge success, and for its last installment, Sam had approved a six-page exclusive on the designer whose name was on everyone's fall shopping list— Eliza Thompson. The magazine had a double scoop as well—after the dismal failure of his fall fashion show, Sydney Minx was out of business, and the designer had announced he was going to retire to his French villa. As for Paige McGinley, Eliza had heard that the former high-handed assistant had been reduced to working the counter at Saks, where she could use her skills at flattery to sell women expensive clothing they didn't need.

Mara was going back home to Sturbridge to pack. She and Ryan had said a tearful good-bye that morning, and her eyes were still red from crying. She had to be brave, but already she was wondering if they had acted too quickly. In any case, he wasn't going anywhere. Mara knew exactly where he would be, and Dartmouth wasn't too far away. But they had agreed on no strings. They were free. Free to return to each other as well.

She tried not to feel too sad. After all, there was so much to look forward to. Already, Sam Davis had asked her if she would think about interning at *Metropolitan Circus* during the school year. The general-interest magazine famous for plastering nude pregnant celebrities on its cover had hired her as editor in chief, and Sam Davis was going to back to the New York media world as fast as you could say "private town car."

Jacqui finally emerged from the front door. She stuffed her bags in the trunk and slid into the backseat.

"Ready?" She smiled at them.

Eliza gunned the engine, and Mara put down the magazine. She plugged her iPod into the auxiliary connection, and the car's stereo reverberated with Gwen Stefani's sultry voice singing, "Your lovin' is better than gold. . . ."

It had been another hectic, arduous summer. The Hamptons had been a wonderful host to their adventures, and they would miss its rocky beaches, its shingled cottages, its rustic yet elegant charm. Perhaps they would come back again, older, wiser, less likely to end up dancing on tables at Cain. Or not.

Whatever happened, they knew they would have each other to turn to for support, advice, love, and friendship. The Hamptons had brought the three of them together, and they would always be grateful for that gift.

And now, New York City beckoned. . . .

acknowledgments

This book would not have been possible without some high-octane girl power! Shout-outs to my homegirls Siobhan Vivian and Sara Shandler at Alloy Entertainment; the supadupafly chicks over at S&S: Emily Meehan, Jennifer Zatorski, Elizabeth Law, and Tracy van Straaten; and the chic ICM gals: Josie Freedman, Karen Kenyon, and Kate Lee. And where would I be without the boys: mad props to Richard Abate and James Gregorio at ICM; Ben Schrank, Josh Bank, and Les Morgenstein at Alloy Entertainment; and Rick Richter at S&S.

Very special thanks and love to all my family: Mommy-Papa-Chito-Aina-Steve-Nico-and-the-one-on-the-way, Mom-J-Dad-J-John-Anji-Alex-Tim-Rob-Jenn-Val-and-Lily, and all of my insanely wonderful friends—you know who you are (see the back pages of all my other books!)—especially MaryClare Williams, the coolest surfer chick in Malibu; the fabulous Jennie Kim, my MySpace webmistress; and the awesome Arisa Chen, who keeps my home page looking good.

As always, thanks and love to Mike "My Husband" Johnston,

who for a long time was known as Mike "My Boyfriend" Johnston because I could never say his name without giving him his full title. Thanks for living on takeout for the last two months. We can eat real food now.

about the author

MELISSA DE LA CRUZ is the author of many books for teens and adults, including *Blue Bloods*, *The Au Pairs*, and its sequel, *Skinny-dipping*. *The Au Pairs* has been published in ten countries. She is also the author of the novels *Cat's Meow* and *Fresh Off the Boat* and co-authored the tongue-in-chic handbooks *The Fashionista Files: Adventures in Four-Inch Heels and Faux Pas* and *How to Become Famous in Two Weeks or Less* (which was sold to Universal/Reveille as a reality television program and to Walt Disney Studios as a full-length motion picture).

Melissa has appeared as an expert on style, trends, and fame for CNN, FOX News, and E! Entertainment Network and has written for *Glamour*, *Marie Claire*, *Harper's Bazaar*, *Allure*, *Teen Vogue*, *Cosmopolitan*, *CosmoGirl!*, *Seventeen*, and the *New York Times*. She is a graduate of Columbia University, where she majored in art history and English and minored in New York nightclubs and shopping. She has many fond memories of writing for *Hamptons* magazine, where her wonderful editors were nothing at all like the one portrayed in this book. Melissa currently divides her time between New York City and Los Angeles, where she lives with her husband.

Check out Melissa's web site, www.melissa-delacruz.com, for her shopping diary and for more information on forthcoming books. She loves to hear from readers, so send her an e-mail at melissa@melissa-delacruz.com.